HIDDEN

Rapunzel's Story

Destined Series, Book 2

KAYLIN LEE

HIDDEN: RAPUNZEL'S STORY

First Edition

For information contact:
Kaylin Lee
http://www.kaylinleewrites.com

Editing by Kathrese McKee of Word Marker Edits
Cover design by Victoria Cooper Designs

ISBN-13: 978-1977538444

CONTENTS

Part I 1
Chapter 1 1
Chapter 2 11
Chapter 3 17
Chapter 4 34
Chapter 5 39
Chapter 6 54
Chapter 7 67
Chapter 8 80
Chapter 9 86
Chapter 10 91
Part II 98
Chapter 11 99
Chapter 12 111
Chapter 13 115
Chapter 14 130
Chapter 15 135
Part III 138
Chapter 16 139
Chapter 17 150
Chapter 18 160
Chapter 19 180
Chapter 20 191
Chapter 21 199
Chapter 22 213
Chapter 23 216
Chapter 24 224
Chapter 25 229

The *Destined* Series

Prequel Novelette – *Torn*

Book 1 – *Fated: Cinderella's Story*

Book 2 – *Hidden: Rapunzel's Story*

Book 3 – *Twisted: Belle's Story* – Release date TBA

For my fellow military spouses, and for anyone else whose happily ever after is taking its sweet time.

The impediment to action advances action. What stands in the way becomes the way.

Marcus Aurelius

PART I

Chapter 1

It's been three weeks since my last outing.

Three weeks since I last stole a life. A clan leader's life—a guilty life—but still, a life that wasn't mine to take.

Sixteen days since the last time the Wasp Queen's servant brought a basket of food. Five days since I finished everything but the hunks of dried meat and the rock-hard bread rolls. I'm only grateful I don't depend on her for water.

Has the Wasp Queen forgotten about me at last? Or has she finally lost control of her clan?

There's no one to ask. My sole visitors to the tower are foolish birds from the garden outside, and they only twitter senselessly, more interested in worms and twigs than politics.

Would it be better to die of hunger if it means I'll never be forced to leave this tower again?

"Rapunzel," hissed a sharp, feminine voice from below my window.

I jolted in my cozy chair, knocking my journal and pencil to the floor. The Wasp Queen. She hadn't abandoned me after all.

"Rapunzel, let down your ladder."

I held my breath.

"And Rapunzel … do no harm."

My shoulders sagged, and I sighed. Too bad she never

forgot the second command.

I rose from my chair by the crowded bookshelf, scooped my journal and pencil from the floor, and tucked them behind a row of books. The merciless power of my True Name cinched around me like a leash. Before I drew my next breath, her will controlled me completely.

My feet carried me obediently to the window. I let down the fine, golden ladder and then waited with my hands folded, several polite steps from the window. The warm night air whispered against my skin, sending shivers up my arms. I inhaled the scent of early summer growth from the lush garden and woods around my tower, trying to keep my mind off the fresh nightmares tonight's outing would bring.

The Wasp Queen swept over the windowsill with haughty grace, managing to look elegant even with her pointy, heeled boots in the air. Her sparkling, mage-craft red skirts swirled around her ankles like pools of wine as she landed on the floor and tossed her long, black hair over one shoulder. She was petite and dark-skinned, with pretty, delicate features at odds with her sharp voice and perpetual frown.

She wasn't truly called the Wasp Queen. I called her so in my head because I had no notion of her formal title or name. That way, if another clan caught me, I could never reveal her identity. I only knew my parents had sold me to the Wasp clan when I was six, after a starving street dog had roamed into our slum and discovered that the scrawny girl with golden hair was the worst possible choice for dinner.

My parents had been delirious with joy. Their own daughter, an absorbent mage? Even better, I was a mage with the Touch, capable of draining a life in the blink of an eye.

My parents had never exhibited powers themselves. They'd never dreamed of having a child with powers who might earn them a boon from a Dracian clan. They'd rejoiced in their good fortune and promptly traded me to the Wasps for a basket of fresh vegetables and a small pouch of gold marks. They'd learned too late not to do trade with the Wasps. I'd lived in my narrow, dusty tower ever since, controlled by the Wasp Queen.

The Wasp pursed her impossibly red lips and looked me up and down. "We'll have to get started immediately. You look like a street urchin. I don't know why I keep you in such fine accommodations when you can't be bothered to take care of yourself."

Perhaps if she fed me more, I might take better care of myself. She starved me before each outing, as though hunger might make me a more willing killer.

A sniffling noise came from the window, and then a trembling young woman struggled over the windowsill. Another new appearance mage. What did the Wasp do to her mages? The last girl hadn't survived two months.

"Work quickly, Helis. We've no time for your sloth tonight." The Wasp narrowed her eyes at the shaking girl, who stumbled across the stone floor to my dusty wooden wardrobe.

Helis removed a sparse black shift from the wardrobe and held it out to me, her hand shaking like a leaf.

I stepped forward and swiped it from the girl's hand without touching her, but my quick movement caused her to cringe back. If only the Wasp herself were half so frightened of me. With mechanical motions, I put on the dress, ignoring the two women who'd invaded my dark, quiet tower. My smudged wardrobe mirror reflected a gaunt, pale girl with a long, blonde braid fidgeting in a plain black dress. I'd lost weight since my last outing and the dress was far too loose, hanging away from my ribs by a hand's breadth at least.

Helis hung back. If only I could startle her out of her fear. If she couldn't get a handle on herself soon, the Wasp would be done with her. Now that she knew who I was and where I was kept, I doubted she'd leave the Wasp clan alive.

"Helis …" The Wasp's voice was ice-cold. The appearance mage wouldn't last beyond tonight if she didn't get moving.

Cringing, Helis lurched forward to stand behind me. We faced the mirror, and she waved a slim hand over my shoulder. The thin black shift transformed instantly into a sparkling gold dress. She wiggled her fingers, and the fabric bunched into straps over my back and shoulders, sucking in to hug my too-thin torso. This dress was practically indecent. Just where was the Wasp sending me tonight?

Helis flourished both hands near my head, and my mussed braid unraveled in the air as if she'd given it a life of its own. I fought to keep my shoulders relaxed as my hair lifted into the air, the tangled tendrils smoothing down on their own and then twisting into a high knot at the top of my head.

Once my hair was complete, the mage leaned closer, holding her breath as though afraid to inhale the same air as a killer like me. She waved one thin hand across my face and then leapt several steps back.

A warm wave of magic covered my skin, washing my face in smooth, golden light and highlighting my cheekbones with a rosy color that made me look more alive than dead for the first time in weeks. A nice illusion. My eyes were lined with dark kohl, and my lips were coated with a stark gold paint that matched the dress exactly.

I blinked. So much for a quiet night at home, and so much for being forgotten.

The Wasp strode to the mirror and paused, looking me up and down with a critical eye. "You'll do." And then she went to the window. "Rapunzel, come with me. And Rapunzel, speak to no one."

My throat dried up at her command. The Wasp disappeared over the windowsill, and I followed woodenly on the high-heeled sandals Helis tossed at me before she huddled against the far wall. Her job was done. Now it was my turn to get to work.

I climbed down the ladder in the ridiculous gold dress, nearly losing a sandal with each precarious step. Even when

I missed a rung and terror flooded my veins, I didn't make a peep. Thanks to the Wasp's command, my throat was as dry and silent as a pile of bones.

Thick trees surrounded my tower. The narrow, uneven path was difficult to navigate in the moonless night, but my feet propelled me forward under her command anyway. I had no choice but to stay close and follow her.

We broke through the trees and exited through an iron gate at the edge of the Wasp compound. A sleek, black fomecoach waited on the cobblestone street, lurking like a hungry wolf from the desolate Badlands outside the city.

A guard jumped out of the fomecoach and opened the door to help the Wasp inside. I followed at her heels, too compelled by her command to keep a reasonable distance. The guard hissed and yanked his hand back as I slid past him and onto the velvet seat beside the Wasp.

I busied myself spreading the flimsy gold skirt over my bony knees. The guard huddled against the far window of the fomecoach, his hands clasped between his knees to hide the tremors. I smiled to show I wasn't a threat, but he flinched. My smile faded. With the strange gold paint on my lips, I probably looked more frightening than usual.

The fomecoach sped through the city streets, swinging wildly this way and that around gaping potholes and tight corners. Draicia was dark these days, even darker than when I was a starving, miserable child in the slums. The luminous streetlamps had all broken or died by now, and there was no one left from the city government to fix them. A hazy cloud of wood smoke covered the city, making it impossible to see the stars or the moon. Perhaps they no longer bothered to shine over Draicia at all.

When I curled up in my cozy chair in the tower, I read stories of smiling families and chubby, giggling toddlers in cities like Lerenia and Asylia, where mages grew vegetables with their powers and provided magical fuel so no one needed to burn wood to cook. The silly stories fueled my daydreams, but I knew they were too fantastic to be true.

Draician mages only served the clans, and their magic had but two purposes—pleasure and power.

We sped past flimsy shacks interspersed among grand mage-craft villas that belonged to clansmen. Children begged on the street corners for coins from the rich, dangerous clan youths who roamed at night.

I'd hated living in Draicia as a child, never knowing what danger lurked in the shadows or where my next meal would come from. Now, I lived in an even darker shadow—now, I was the shadow myself.

I fingered the gold dress and pressed my lips together, careful not to smudge the gold paint. This was no kind of life. Impossible or not, I had to escape tonight. At least, I had to try.

~

We reached the far side of the city before the fomecoach slowed to a stop. From the armed, black-clad guards lurking on every corner, I surmised that we were in Wolf clan territory. My old tutor, Master Oliver, had taught me about the clans in my tower, and I'd learned whatever I could on my outings with the Wasp.

The Wasp Queen leaned close, her lips near my ear. "Rapunzel," she whispered, so softly I could barely hear her. "Obey the manager of the staff in everything. You may speak only when necessary for the success of this outing. I will find you inside and give you further instruction."

Her command washed over me, and I relished the relaxation of my throat muscles as her previous command faded. When I opened my eyes, the coach door was open, and she was glaring at me.

I climbed out, and the fomecoach sped off before the door was even fully shut. I wobbled on my high heels across the cobblestones. The alley ran along the side of a grand, fenced-off estate packed with massive stone villas—the Wolf compound.

A door in the fence swung open, and a frazzled looking man beckoned to me. "Quickly," he hissed. "Get in here. You're late."

This must be the manager of the staff. My feet propelled me through the gate, and I entered the villa through the servants' entrance.

He looked over his shoulder at me, and his expression soured even more. "You're far too thin. It will be a miracle if you pass as one of them."

I kept quiet. What could I say to that?

The portly manager guided me through a dim maze of hallways and staircases. At last, we reached a large, crowded anteroom with a set of tall, closed doors at one end. The room was full of women in gold shifts like mine. No one spared me a glance.

"Another one for you, Magda. She was late. I'll dock her pay, of course."

The tall, olive-skinned woman named Magda looked me up and down and curled her lip. "We're so desperate to save funds, we must dress up urchins now? She's lucky the crowd is so thick tonight. We need every pair of hands. Even the skinny ones."

The sharp-tongued woman gestured over to the far wall, where a line of gold-clad girls balanced trays piled with overfilled wine goblets and small, piping-hot meat pies. The pies looked deliciously greasy, and my stomach ached at the sight. "Over there, girl. If you can't carry your trays, then you're back on the streets without pay. We only need girls who can do the work tonight."

"Yes, ma'am." I dipped my head in acknowledgement before scooping up two trays from the serving table and joining the line of gold girls. The trays were heavy, but my arms were stronger than they appeared. I hadn't missed a day of old Master Oliver's training exercises in years, even when food was scarce and my strength was waning.

The room buzzed with conversation until the manager let out a piercing whistle. The other servants fell silent as we all faced the tall, double doors.

One of the doors opened, and a tired-looking girl in a gold shift slipped into the anteroom with two empty trays. "There are more guests every minute," she said to Magda, wiping sweat from her forehead. "Best send the fresh ones out, rather than wait."

Magda tapped the first girl in line, and after an awkward pause, the girl tottered toward the door. "Keep your eyes open," Magda said as we filed through the door. "No serving one clan over another. No denying any of the guests."

I crossed the threshold into a cacophony of noises, sights, and smells in the crowded ballroom. Wine splashed over one glass's rim, and I nearly laughed aloud. No one would notice a bit of spilled wine in a mess like this.

Hundreds of guests filled the Wolf clan ballroom. Luminous chandeliers dripped haphazardly from the ceiling, looking like they'd fall down at any moment. Guests laughed and swayed, some dancing, some fighting, and all drinking heartily.

I kept one eye out for the Wasp Queen as I offered drinks and pies and fended off the occasional swipe at my rear.

The biggest Draician clans had gathered here tonight. I recognized the Wolf clan brothers, the hosts, by their slick, dark hair and barbaric necklaces. Draician legend held that the Wolf clan ancestors had ventured out into the Badlands to hunt during lean times and returned with the teeth of the wolves they'd killed. The clansmen still wore the teeth on straps around their necks, the frightening necklaces at odds with their crisp, black suits, handsome builds, and impeccable grooming.

Wasp clan members in their signature, deep-red garments circulated in twos and threes, but the Wasp Queen was not among them. Members of the Snake clan, with their bronze serpent necklaces, mingled tentatively with the Hawk clan members, easily identified by the feather-covered jewelry they draped on their necks, wrists, and ears. All the dominant families in Draicia were represented except the Tiger clan. Perhaps the Wolves were attempting a show of unity.

No wonder the staff manager worried about showing too much favor to one clan over the other. It was a miracle the clans were all gathered together without bloodshed.

Of course, I corrected myself, my presence ensured the evening would end in murder. Just not yet. I didn't even know my target, but the Wasp's command to do no harm kept everyone safe for now.

I served meat pies to a group of boisterous young Hawk clan women. Their warm bodies and perfume made my head ache, and they pressed against me from all sides, jostling against me to snag pies and wine from my trays. I'd been ensconced in my tower for three weeks, lonely and untouched. Now, the crowd was simultaneously too much and not enough. My absorbent power stretched as though waking from a long sleep. I couldn't help but be aware of the life pulsing around me, the invisible magic that rushed through every living form, putting breath in their lungs and pumping their hearts.

My conscience knew these lives were not mine to take. But my magic? It wanted to absorb every last bit of life it could find.

A man slid his hand around my gold-clad waist. I gritted my teeth but managed to ask, "Would you like some wine, my lord?"

He was a young Wolf, and clearly, he was already quite drunk. One heavy strand of black hair fell into his eyes. He leered down at me as his grip tightened on my waist. "I'd like a little something else," he mumbled.

My magic pulsed. His life flowed against my skin. If only he knew who he was touching. But I would do him no harm. I couldn't, thanks to the Wasp's command. Even if I could, I didn't want to. I couldn't resist the Wasp Queen's control, but at least I still had a conscience. Perhaps a bit of food to absorb the drink in his stomach wouldn't be a bad idea.

I sidled out of his grip and gave him a meat pie instead. "Have something to eat, my lord." Then, I made my escape.

The Wasp Queen stepped into my line of sight. She raised one eyebrow at me, and I made my way over, my feet moving of their own accord across the crowded ballroom floor. I held out a glass of wine.

She took it and leaned in close. "Rapunzel, he's the one. There, with the gold-topped cane. Kill the one I speak to."

She flitted through the crowd and approached a man with a cane, waving her hand in greeting.

He was an elderly Wolf with salt-and-pepper hair slicked back from his forehead, and his belly was soft and paunchy under his crisply pressed, white shirt. He rubbed his thumb on the top of his cane—a carved, wolf's head made of gold—as the Wasp Queen approached him.

He bowed over her hand and kissed it. They exchanged words, and she walked away, hips swaying as though she hadn't a care in the world.

I could only gawk as the pieces fell into place. My target was no lackey. He was the head of the Wolf clan, the host of this gathering. She'd just ordered me to start a clan war.

Chapter 2

The command to do no harm lifted, and the new order squeezed around me like a hungry, powerful snake.

When I had no resistance left, I moved numbly across the floor and approached the man with the gold-topped cane.

I kept my face blank. The last thing I needed was to be caught on an outing with the Wasp Queen. I'd be tortured until I gave up my clan, and then I'd be put to work in the same fashion for a new clan. I hated the Wasp Queen, but life would be no better with a new clan. Quite possibly, it would be worse.

Nausea rocked my stomach as I crossed the ballroom. I hated this part—the feeling that my body wasn't my own, the horror of destroying a man's life. The clansmen were far from innocent, and the Wolves were more violent than most. But still, a life was a life.

He was three steps away. Two steps. I offered him a meat pie. "Hungry, my lord?"

He raised an eyebrow but then shrugged. "Why not?" He took the pie, and his fingers grazed mine.

And that was all I needed. My magic inhaled like a starving creature, and a heartbeat later, his life was mine.

I turned on my heel and strode away as quickly as I

could. Behind me, his body thumped to the ground. I focused on the double doors, balanced my tray, and dodged guests in my flight. The chaotic ballroom masked his collapse for a few moments, but as I neared the doors, a voice cried out for a healer.

Immediately, I added my voice to the tumult. "Healer! Get a healer!" I rushed forward as though on a mission to find a healer, but I knew better than anyone it was far too late for that. He was gone.

A man by the double doors caught my eye as I neared him. He watched me with an odd expression on his face. Tall and well-built, the stranger had wild, brown hair, ruddy cheeks, and several days' beard growth on his jaw. His fine clothing held no trace of a clan marking. Who was he? A foreigner? And why was he staring at me?

I had no time to worry about such things. I exited through the double doors and shouted at Magda, "Healer!"

She gaped at me, and I repeated, "Healer, they need a healer."

The staff manager who'd smuggled me in met my eyes as Magda left the room. He jerked his head back in a nearly imperceptible motion, and I walked to the end of the room and slipped through the door where we'd entered. He didn't follow. I was on my own from here.

The Wasp's first order, to do no harm, had been lifted automatically by her kill order, since my True Name could never accept contradictory commands. The second always canceled the first. And my kill command had already been completed.

For the moment, I was under no one's control. These were the moments I lived for.

I wove through the dim maze of hallways, wobbling in the impractical gold sandals until I finally stumbled out of the doorway and into the back courtyard. The evening wind whipped through the thin fabric of my dress and made my teeth chatter.

There was the same small door in the gate I'd entered

through. I could leave the compound through it, assuming it was still unlocked, but the Wasp's fomecoach and guards would be waiting to pick me up. What if I could find another exit? I could escape before she had the chance to issue a new command.

I raced through the courtyard and skittered to a halt in front of another gate on the far side of the compound. I yanked at the handle, but it was firmly locked. I grabbed the upper bar of the fence and pulled with all my might until I was high enough to reach a toe up to the bar. I levered my body to the top of the gate. The iron spikes at the top pressed into my stomach. I winced but kept moving. Pain I could take if it meant I could be free.

A spike ripped through my dress, and a sharp, hot feeling told me it had pierced my skin as well. I ignored the pain and scrambled over the fence, landing in the street with a bruising crash, a pile of limbs and shredded gold fabric.

I tore off the worthless sandals and chucked them beneath a bush before racing along the street. My bare feet ached. I saw movement from the shadows by the Wolf compound fence and dove to the left instinctively, pelting down a narrow alley. I couldn't risk meeting a witness.

The alley was dark and filled with puddles, broken cobblestones, and mud. My heart pounded wildly, and my chest heaved. I had never come so close to escaping. I'd never made it so far on my own. This could be it! This could be the time that I finally—

A bone-crushing weight hit me in the back and sent me sprawling, planting my face in a foul puddle of what I hoped was mud. I struggled under the pressure, straining to move my head to get my nose and mouth out of the muck, but the heavy force wouldn't let me move.

My lungs cried out for air, but I inhaled mud instead. The pressure was unbearable. I would suffocate. I would die here. The Wasp had finally tired of my escape attempts.

Just before I succumbed to the darkness, she let me up. I staggered to my feet and turned around, gasping heavily.

The Wasp Queen smirked and pointed at the fomecoach waiting behind her. "Rapunzel, get inside. And don't touch anyone."

I obeyed stiffly, gasping for air, my whole body bruised. For the thousandth time, I cursed my fate. The Wasp Queen wasn't just a human clan leader. She was a powerful expellant mage—a mover mage. And no matter how fast I ran, she always found me.

~

I huddled against the side of the fomecoach in my torn, muddy dress, trying not to cry. The Wasp kept looking over at me with a smug, superior smile, and I'd never wanted to use my power against her so badly in my life. The fact that I was restrained only by the order not to touch anyone made the car ride even more maddening. She loved to keep me close without a true "do no harm" command, as though she enjoyed showing me how little she feared me, reminding me I could never truly hope to escape her.

Why did I keep trying? Why did I do this to myself again and again, nearly dying at her hands each time? I should have given up long ago. What was wrong with me?

The fomecoach bounced and rattled as it swung around each corner at top speed. I held my body as still as I could. My bones ached with each movement of the coach. I longed to be home in my tower, to lie down in my little bed and huddle beneath the covers, to pretend this night never happened. To forget the Wolf man's shocked eyes as I took his life. To forget the feeling of mud filling my nose and mouth. To forget everything.

But I could never let myself forget.

Five years ago, my childhood tutor Master Oliver had come to say good-bye to me. "You're ready," he'd said gruffly. "Nothing more to teach you. You're on your own now."

I'd hoped he would be pleased with my progress the way

the Wasp Queen was, but he'd grown surlier as our training progressed.

"Thank you, sir," I'd said hesitantly.

He only scowled. "Don't thank me. Not ever." He ran a callused hand through his gray hair and let out a huff. "A piece of advice, girl. She's got your will. There's no changing that. But you've got your own mind and your own heart." He glanced over his shoulder at the window as though expecting the Wasp to come through at any moment. "Just don't forget that. Got it? And don't shut things out. The things you'll do … the things you'll see … you'll want to shut them out, forget they ever happened. Don't do it. Those things will teach you. They'll make you stronger. They'll separate you from her. And that's the most you can ask for." His eyes glistened. "Mourn them, girl. She can't stop you from mourning or remembering them."

At that, he'd left and never returned.

I'd been utterly confused. Mourn whom? Remember whom? I didn't want to mourn anyone. I wanted to survive and make the Wasp Queen proud enough to let me out of my tower.

Not long afterward, I'd learned what he meant. There was no point in trying to please the Wasp. I was too dangerous and too valuable. She would never free me from the tower, but she couldn't stop me from mourning and remembering the victims. My victims. And sometimes, those memories were all that kept me from going mad.

I closed my eyes in the dim fomecarriage and shut out the scent of the Wasp Queen's heavy goldblossom perfume. I pictured the Wolf man's face in my mind's eye, imagining his raised eyebrow and the bemused way he took the meat pie from my hand. The Wolf clan was full of ruthless killers. Everyone in Draicia knew that. But he'd been someone—a brother, a friend to someone. And I'd taken him away.

I'm sorry. I imagined whispering the words to him in my head. *It's not enough. But it's all I can give you.*

The garden was chilly so late at night, even in summer.

Cold wind ran down my back as I stood at the bottom of my golden ladder and faced the Wasp. I was nearly doubled over from pain where the spikes on the Wolf compound gate had stabbed me in the side. Blood oozed from the wound, soaking the thin dress and dripping down my leg.

The Wasp stood before me, wrapped in a black cloak over her red evening gown, and tapped her chin. My head ached from exhaustion, but she looked positively energized.

"Rapunzel, Rapunzel," she said softly. "What do I do with you? You're the most disobedient pet in the city, and yet, you're just so … useful." She tapped her chin again. "Rapunzel, put yourself back in your tower and stay there. Oh, and Rapunzel—you may touch whomever you like." She gave a tinkling laugh at her little joke, and my bruised, blood-soaked body dragged itself obediently up the gold ladder, pain shooting through me with every rung.

Chapter 3

I awoke to the sound of someone coughing outside my window. I sat up in bed, body aching, and checked my side. The bandage I'd attempted last night before collapsing was dark red.

My side stabbed with pain as I rolled out of bed and went to the window, shoving my wild, blonde hair away from my eyes. Helis again. The Wasp Queen's new appearance mage stood beneath the window, a canvas bag over her shoulder.

What exactly would Helis have done if her hesitant cough hadn't woken me? I huffed out an annoyed breath, but I was too glad to see the canvas bag to tarry. I lowered the gold ladder down as fast as I could, and my stomach growled hungrily as she climbed it.

To avoid frightening her, I waited several steps away from the window. After an eternity, she finally flung the bag up and over the windowsill without even daring to climb high enough to peek her head through the window. The bag landed with a satisfying thump on the floor.

Fine with me. It wasn't as though I wanted to see her anyway.

I rushed to open the bag, my hands fumbling with the tie at the top, and I pulled out a honeybread loaf wrapped in cloth. Finally! I shoved it in my mouth, accidentally taking a bite of cloth with it. I spat out the cloth and continued to scarf the bread down. Sweet relief. The taste of real, fresh food distracted me from the pain in my side. I sat on the floor like the street urchin I was, enjoying every bite of that rich, filling honeybread.

The last mouthful disappeared far too quickly. I scooted back a few feet and rested my back against the rumpled edge of the bed to inspect my side. I needed a clean bandage, and soon. Perhaps … I pawed through the canvas bag and nearly crowed aloud when I found it. Mage-craft healing salve.

I stripped off the blood-soaked bandage and spread the salve on my side before I relaxed back against my bed, enjoying the cooling, numbing effect. It must have been high quality because moments later, my wound healed over completely. I sighed. The Wasp definitely didn't want to lose me. The thought brought no satisfaction. As long as she was determined to keep me, she would never allow me to escape—not even to escape through death.

When the gash in my side had faded to a thin red line, I rose from the floor. I sank into the soft, worn chair by the bookshelf, curled my legs beneath me, and pulled out my journal and pencil.

How many times have I tried to escape and failed? Twenty? Thirty? I've lost count. Is it truly worth the pain?

After all, it's not actually me killing these poor souls. It's her. I'm not the one in control. She is. Maybe I should just give up and stop trying. Just do what she says. Stop making things so difficult, so painful. Why do I torture myself like this?

I shook my head even as I wrote the words. Maybe I would never be able to escape, but for the sake of my victims, I had to know I'd done everything I could. That meant trying to escape whenever I had a chance and paying the price for failure.

I know why. I echoed Master Oliver's parting words to myself, words I'd written in the journal so many times, I could have scribbled them with my eyes shut. *She has my will, but she'll never have my heart and my mind. I'll never give up. That's the one thing she'll never take from me.*

~

I changed into my training clothes with a renewed sense of purpose. I knew what I had to do now. Get faster. One day, I'd run so fast she couldn't catch me. I'd run straight out of this forsaken city, and I'd never look back.

My daily warm-up sent me moving back and forth across the round tower room I called my home. My bones and muscles ached from the night before, but I was newly energized by the honeybread and by my plan to improve my speed.

The early summer air was warm but still breezy, and the wind sent welcome drafts through the windows of the tower as I worked. The midday sun shifted out from behind the clouds, brightening the tower so I had no need of the luminous lamps to light the room.

After a few minutes of aching movements, I stopped and dragged the furnishings to the walls. I'd need more space than usual if I were to improve my speed. Then I got back into my warm-up routine, jumping into the twists, turns, rolls, and flips Master Oliver had taught me during the years of training when I'd learned to be a more efficient monster.

I stretched my arms high above my head. I could do this. I had to do this. First thing, I'd work on my—

A thump came from the window behind me. I whirled around. A tall man climbed right through it and into my tower. He leapt to the ground and stood before me, his face flushed, his chest heaving.

"Your ladder." His voice was a hoarse whisper. "You left it down. Pull it up, or they'll find me."

I gasped. I'd forgotten to pull it up when Helis left! What had I been thinking?

"Haul it up. Please! Do it quickly, before they arrive." He strode toward me, and I took a quick step back. "I'd do it, but they might see me in the window. Better for them to see you."

I moved to pull up the ladder and had it halfway up the tower before I realized he hadn't used my True Name to command me. Even if he'd heard the Wasp speak my True Name, he wouldn't be able to use it to control me. My True Name had to be given for it to work, and the only person I'd ever given it to was the Wasp, in exchange for sparing my parents' lives. She hadn't kept her end of the bargain.

I finished yanking the golden ladder up out of habit. There was no one below me, although the garden had gone strangely silent. When the ladder was up, I stepped to the side to spy on the group of guards in the Wasp clan's colors who raced into the clearing. They searched the empty clearing and left, ignoring me and my tower completely.

I looked back at the man who stood near the tower wall, watching me with a slight smile on his face. He was broad shouldered, with heavily-muscled arms, unruly brown hair, and a rough beard on his cheeks and chin. He wore plain black clothing and boots, with no markings or clan signs of any kind. This was the same man I had noticed at the Wolf compound by the double doors.

His size and beard made him seem mature, but the humor glinting in his eyes spoke of youthful fearlessness. Perhaps he was not much older than me. Did he not know who I was?

I advanced on him and held out my hand, letting him see my bare skin as I stretched it toward him. "Who are you? And what do you want from me?"

"You have nothing to fear from me," he said, holding his hands up and stepping backward as I advanced toward him.

"Oh, is that so?" How much trouble could I get in for harboring an enemy of the Wasps? And yet, who would ever find him? Her lackeys would never dare search my tower. "You appear to be here in my tower without the permission of …" I trailed off. I'd nearly called her the Wasp Queen.

"Of my mistress. And I'm to believe that you mean me no harm?"

He held out a hand as though he could stop my approach. "Forgive my intrusion, but it appeared to me that you were no friend of that Wasp lady either. I thought I might find temporary refuge. The enemy of my enemy is my friend, as they say."

I snorted. "That must be a foreign proverb. Here in Draicia, we don't know the meaning of friend."

He folded his thick, muscular arms across his chest. "I saw you," he said. "I saw you at the Wolf compound, I saw what you did. I followed you."

A witness? Not good. Then I shook my head. Idiot. Why had he told me? "You should have kept that knowledge to yourself, and taken it back to … well, wherever you came from. The Wasps will never allow you to live now."

He leaned against the wall, apparently unconcerned. "I also saw you try to escape," he said, his voice even and steady. "And I saw what she did to you."

I flushed. "So?"

"I can help you. I was sent here from Asylia to investigate the balance of power between the Draician clans and to find out how the Wasp clan is so small, yet so influential."

In other words, he'd come to find out about me. I fiddled with the end of my braid. It was one thing when only the Wasp Queen and I knew the depths of my crimes. But to have someone else know? An outsider, at that? My stomach roiled.

"Don't worry," he said. "You don't have to be scared. Just come with me. I can get you to safety. The King of Asylia is not a … well, not a kind man, but he's just. Mostly. You'd be far better off as an Asylian mage than a Draician one."

I snorted. So that was his plan. "You've got it all solved. I'll just go be a slave for your king instead of my mistress, murdering whoever stands in his way."

He frowned. "I'm offering to help you. Get you to freedom. Or do you like being cooped up in this ridiculous tower every day?"

I spread out my arms. "You know what they say. A girl's home is her castle."

His smile finally faded. "I take it there has been some sort of command placed on you so that you may not leave your tower."

I huffed out a sigh. "Correct."

He rubbed a hand through his hair and wrinkled his brow. "Well, can I at least hide out here for a while?"

I looked him over slowly, and his mouth turned up a bit at the corners. Why was he smiling this time?

"I…" I found myself torn. I spent the weeks between outings longing for human contact, but the last thing I wanted was to share my tiny space with a strange man. Even worse—a man who knew what I had done last night.

He took a step forward, away from the wall. His face was earnest and pleading. "You can trust me," he said. "What's your name?"

I crossed my arms. "You may call me Zel."

"Zel."

No one had spoken my name since Master Oliver had left me. It sounded strange and foreign on his lips, but for some reason, I liked it.

"You can trust me, Zel. I promise." His lips slid into a real smile, his eyes crinkling at the corners. "My name is Darien Mattas." He gave a little bow, and it looked almost comical with his tall, broad figure and wild, scruffy hair. "It's a pleasure to meet you."

~

Over the course of the next hour, it became clear to me that he took up far too much space.

After poking around my circular tower room and the small closet-sized bathroom at the edge, he settled his long form into the chair by my bookshelf—*my* chair—and busied himself picking through my books.

We hadn't spoken since he introduced himself. The silence in my tower had never bothered me before. If I wanted to fill it, I talked or hummed or sang, or I threw myself into my exercises and forgot about it. But now, the silence was all I could think about.

That, and the fact that he was a witness to my greatest shame and humiliation.

What did he think of me? I ached to know, yet my cheeks burned with heat at the thought of initiating more conversation with him.

I perched primly on my bed, facing the window, my back angled toward him. I couldn't look at him. Could he read my shame on my face? Could he tell, from the set of my shoulders, how much I hated his presence?

How I regretted letting him stay. I should kick him out. I should send him from my window this very moment. After all, I was under no command save the one to stay in my tower. He would be unable to stop me if I decided to end his refuge here.

But after all the lives I had taken, now I had the chance to save one. Could I live with myself if I cast him out and the Wasps caught him? Surely, I could endure a bit of embarrassment if—

"Oh, this is too much!" He chortled behind me, and I spun around on the bed.

He was shaking with laughter in my chair, holding a book in his hands. He reached up and wiped a tear from his eye.

"Um … what, exactly?"

"This book! It's— It's too— Oh, I can't take it!" He shook his head as the laughter overtook him again.

"What book?"

He held up the book he was reading, and at the sight of the rosedrop bouquet on the cover, I leapt to my feet.

"And just what is so funny?" I screeched.

"Here, let me read it to you. 'Rosedrop, Goldblossom, and Butterflower loved to wear beautiful dresses and braid their long, dark hair.' Those names! And that's only the first sentence. Can you believe this silly novel?"

I clenched my fists. How dare he?

He kept reading. "Here's the next part. 'One sunny day, Rosedrop decided to go on an adventure.' And then her adventure consists of picking berries in the park and getting caught in a bit of rain. Hah! Why on earth do you have this?"

I scowled and strode forward to yank the book from his callused hands, then hid it behind my back.

His smile faded slightly. "What are you doing?"

"This book is mine. Don't touch it. Or any of the other ones."

"That's fine," he said slowly. "I won't touch them. Just satisfy my curiosity, will you? Where'd you get that book?"

I clutched it tighter behind my back. "Why does it matter?"

He cocked his head. "Just want to know."

I stalked to the bookshelf and shoved the book into place, feeling odd when I realized his face was only a few inches away. Even seated, his head nearly reached mine, though I knew I was tall for a girl—far taller than the Wasp Queen.

I stepped back, away from the bookshelf and away from him. "A servant brought them when I was a child. Another servant didn't want them anymore, and the … my mistress thought I might be more biddable if I had something to occupy my mind between training sessions." I twisted the pleats on my loose pants. "They're excellent books," I ground out. "And they're mine."

"They're not quite excellent," he said slowly.

My cheeks burned. What was his problem? Here I was, doing him a favor, and he had the nerve to critique my library? "Well, if you're not happy with your accommodations," I spat out, gesturing to the tower around us, "why don't you just get out?"

He didn't move.

I'd been torn about whether to let him stay, and now I knew it had been a mistake. A terrible mistake. What had I been thinking? This was a disaster. I held my hand out to him threateningly. "I said get out! Now!"

He stood slowly, his hands up, but instead of picking up his pack and leaving, he stepped closer to me. "Zel …"

"What are you doing? I said you're done here. Just get out. I don't want you here. The guards who were looking for you have gone, so just go."

"Let me stay a little while longer." His eyes creased. "I won't be a nuisance. I promise. I'll do whatever you say. Just let me stay until I have a better chance of getting away unseen. Please?"

He ran his hand through his hair again. For all his height and strength, his face held a hint of vulnerability too. He needed shelter. But could I trust him?

I bit my lip. What was the point of trust? A monster like me had no need of it. If he turned on me, I'd just kill him. "Fine. You can stay. For now."

~

When my stomach growled a few hours later, I went to the larder to search out food from my fresh stash. I pulled out a hunk of cheese, a dull, rusted knife, and a linen pouch filled with savory, oily herb rolls.

I hovered at the larder with the food clutched in my nervous hands for far too long. Should I offer some to him? Rosedrop was always offering cakes and rolls to Butterflower and Goldblossom when they came to visit her seaside villa on the hills of Lerenia. But he'd laughed at the book, so perhaps that wasn't a widespread custom.

Besides, it wasn't as though I had a lot of food to spare. What if they didn't feed me again for another three weeks? I would regret wasting precious food on some strange man.

In the end, my hand made the decision for me, for when

I went to reach my plate, I grabbed two. My chest tightened. I'd share, just this once. That was it. After this, he was on his own. Perhaps he had brought food in his pack.

I sat on my bed and set the two plates out before me to portion out the rolls. Normally, I would only eat one each day, to make them last. But I didn't want him to think me stingy. Ugh, what was wrong with me? What did I care what he thought of—

"Ah, time for the midday meal, is it?" He got up from the chair, where he'd been cleaning some sort of bow contraption, which he set on his pack. "What's this? Where do you get your food?"

I gestured to the rolls. "My mistress's maid dropped off a bag of food this morning. They usually feed me more, after … an outing. It's … um … some kind of herb rolls. And some cheese. You're welcome to share it, if you're—"

My bed sagged as he sat down beside me, and I had to restrain myself from leaping off and rushing to the other side of the room.

"I'd love some. I'm famished. Thank you," he said, his eyes glinting with an odd humor.

"You're … um … welcome." I focused on the food. I unwrapped the cheese, then took the dull knife and sawed through it to cut a few slices.

"May I?"

"I suppose." I couldn't help flinching when I realized he was holding a sharp, dangerous-looking knife.

He sliced several paper-thin slices for himself, then twice the amount for me. Then he wrapped the cheese back up in the paper. "Is that enough for you?"

Was he holding back on his portion because he'd guessed I didn't want to share? I shrugged. Not my problem. "It's fine."

I scarfed down the food, sensing his eyes on me the whole time. Why was he watching me eat? I didn't like it one bit. Perhaps I'd have to add that to the rule about my books.

When I finished, his plate was already clear. He took my

plate, then went to the little sink in the bathroom and rinsed them off. "Thank you for sharing your food," he said over his shoulder.

I only grunted in response. Hopefully, it sounded something like "You're welcome," though I still wasn't sure I'd made the right decision.

When the plates were clean, he set them on the narrow wooden shelf by the larder, then went to stand in the center of the room. "I just realized your furniture has all been pushed to the walls. Were you in the middle of doing something when I arrived?"

I stood, rolled my shoulders, and dodged his gaze. "I was just doing my training," I mumbled.

"Your training?" He came closer and bent comically so he could look into my face. "That sounds interesting. What kind of training, exactly?"

I sighed and shuffled backward, rubbing my hands along my arms. I wasn't sure I preferred this to our awkward silence from earlier in the day. "My training. You know, so I don't get caught when I'm out. And, well, you saw what happened last night. If I'm ever to truly escape, I've got to be faster than she is. And right now, I'm just not."

"I see." Darien glanced around the room with a thoughtful, appraising expression. "Not much space."

I couldn't help but scowl. "I do what I can with what I have. Wouldn't expect you to understand."

He smiled, and it was almost a smirk. "But I do."

"What do you mean, you do? How could you understand?" My chest tightened again. How I wished I had never let him stay this morning. I hated having him here. I hated opening my life to him, giving him the opportunity to judge and criticize my pathetic existence. Perhaps I simply hated him.

Darien stretched his arms over his head and clasped them behind his neck. His gaze never left mine. "I'm from Asylia. You've heard of it?"

I nodded slowly and flicked a glance at the bookshelf.

"Of course. Your books." He had the good sense not to chuckle, though I could see the humor in his eyes again. "I've trained most of my life to be a Sentinel. Last year, I finally became one. And they sent me here to find out about you." He paused as though waiting for a reaction.

I raised one eyebrow. "Yes? A … Sentinel, you say?"

"You've never heard of us, have you?" He rubbed a hand over his face.

"Can't say that I have."

"Well, it's just that … the Sentinels, you see, we're the best …" He trailed off and laughed under his breath. Then he shook his head. "Doesn't matter. The point is, I've been training for years, and now that I'm a Sentinel, I train every day."

"Good for you." I bit my lip when the words came out more sarcastic than I'd meant them, but he only smiled.

"Would you like to know what the Sentinels specialize in?"

"Specialize?" I'd gathered they were Asylian soldiers or guards of some kind. What need had they to specialize?

"We train to fight mages. Powerful mages. And we do it without any magic of our own."

I snorted. "Fight mages? Without magic? Impossible. And do Asylian mages dare to fight against humans?"

He shook his head. "They're all controlled by their True Name, same as you. But not every mage on the continent is controlled by humans. Like your mistress, for example. And not every city is friendly with Asylia. Our king recognized the need for such a defense, and the Sentinels were born."

I turned away. Uncontrolled mages? Humans, training to fight mages without the use of magic? Madness. It was too much for my exhausted brain to comprehend.

I felt a warm presence behind me and whirled around. Darien had moved closer while my back was turned. I tensed. Did he tell me that because he intended to fight against me? Did he not realize that I needed only the slightest brush of skin to end him completely?

He held up his hands and didn't come any closer. "I've told you this," he said softly, "because I want you to know there is hope. Not everyone lives under the thumb of your mistress. And because I can train you, if you want. I can help you get faster, help you escape."

I was silent for several long moments, unable to look away from his kind face and crinkling green eyes. Could he possibly be sincere? What if he was only waiting for me to let my guard down, so he could slit my throat with that sharp knife and put an end to the Wasp Queen's influence?

Besides, why would anyone want to help me escape? I was a nightmare, a creature of the shadows. I'd taken countless lives. Anyone with sense would want me to stay here in my tower, safe and secure, under control. What kind of madman would want me to be free?

I searched his face again, hoping for some key to the mystery as I wrestled with my thoughts. "Why?" I finally asked, my voice hoarse. "Why would you help me?"

His hand crept up to the back of his neck again and an unreadable expression came onto his face. "I don't like to see anyone trapped. Not ever. And I know you don't want this. You wouldn't have risked what you did last night, knowing the punishment you'd get, if you were willing to stay here. I'd rather see you free than imprisoned. That's just who I am. Can that be enough?"

What could I say to that? I could barely make sense of the whirlwind of thoughts and emotions swirling within me. "I suppose so," I heard my own voice say.

He nodded and stepped back. "Good." He cleared his throat. "We've got today, at least. Show me what you do to train. I'll see what you can do, and then I'll know how I might help."

"Fine. Um … step back, then."

He walked backward until he hit the curved tower wall and leaned there with his arms crossed over his chest. "Go ahead," he said, nodding at me.

I fought a flutter of nervous energy that rose up in my

stomach. I hadn't done my exercises with an audience since Master Oliver left me. But the promise of getting faster was worth a bit more humiliation, wasn't it?

I repeated my warm-up from earlier. I rushed from one side of the room to the other with sprints, tumbles, and leaps. When my body had heated up sufficiently, I stopped to stretch my arms out. Darien still leaned against the wall with his arms folded. "That was what I do to get my body warm. Now, I'll do the training."

Darien only nodded, so I continued.

I tried not to think about how silly I must look, dancing around, feinting left and right, leaping up, and throwing myself down. Master Oliver had taught me to be quick in my movements, to dart around to evade capture or to get near a target who was already on guard against me. It was hard to practice without another person to spar with, but I did my best.

After nearly an hour of practice, I finally stopped and stood panting in the center of the room. "That's—" I gasped for breath. I put my hands on my knees and bent over, doing my best to restore my breathing to normal, feeling like the city's biggest fool.

Darien watched me quietly from the wall.

When my breathing finally calmed, I straightened. "That's my training. But I've been trying to add more sprinting. I'm quick, when it comes to getting close to targets." I clenched my fists. "But I'm just not fast enough to get away from her. Not when it comes to running longer distances. And if she's close enough to use her power as a mover, or to use my True Name and command me to stop, I don't stand a chance."

Darien nodded once and then shifted his weight off of the wall. "You're quick. That's good. It's likely kept you alive this long. But you lack the two things you'll need to escape: speed at longer distances, as you know, and strength."

"Strength?" I crossed my arms. "I'm quite strong—"

He walked toward me, shaking his head. "You're strong.

I've no doubt. But not strong enough. It's too easy for her to overpower you."

Ridiculous. "She's an expellant mage." Didn't he understand? "A mover. A powerful one. It would be impossible to overpower her magic."

"No." He stopped walking and removed his outer jacket. "I could resist her."

Now that was just arrogance. "You? You don't even have magic. And how would you know, anyway?"

The corner of his mouth pulled up on one side, forming a cocky smile that was far too handsome and made my chest flutter strangely. "I've done it. Not with her, but with other mages. Other movers. They work by propelling their own stored-up magic and pushing it against their target. But there's only so much magic they can push out. If you were stronger, you could resist her power."

Resist her? The wild fluttering in my chest got stronger. Could it truly be possible?

"The second thing you need is to improve your speed." He chewed his lip and spun in a slow circle, taking in the whole room. "There's not much space, but we can work with it. Can we move your bed?"

I nodded. "That's fine. I would have moved it myself, but …" It was too heavy. But now that he'd spent so much time dissecting my lack of strength, I didn't feel like admitting that.

"Good." He strode to the bed and put a hand on each side, then dragged it, with a bone-chilling screech until it was pressed tightly along the wall. "There we go." He clapped his hands. "I think I've got it. Are you ready?"

No. Not in the slightest. But I was ready to be free. I just had to keep that in the forefront of my mind. "Y-yes."

He showed me a series of exercises meant for strengthening my arms, legs, and back. I copied his movements self-consciously, avoiding eye contact as he evaluated my form and made suggestions about how to increase the weight as my strength grew.

When my arms and legs were visibly shaking from the exertion, he clapped his hands again. "Time to work on speed."

He strode to the far end of the room and grabbed two books from the bookshelf. Then he placed one on the ground by his feet, jogged in a straight line to the opposite side of the tower, and dropped the other one. "Watch me."

Darien bent his knees and placed one foot ahead of the other, then shot me a meltingly handsome smile that sent warmth spiking through my stomach. Then he launched himself forward and sprinted across the tower in several leaping steps, where he skittered to a halt beside the other book and swept it up in one hand. Then he turned on his heel and sprinted back to the other book, dropped the first, scooped up the second, and raced back.

Four laps later, he jogged to a stop in front of me. My head spun from his rapid movements. "Can you do that?" He was barely out of breath.

"I believe so."

As it turned out, I couldn't. Not quite. I made it two rounds in before my legs seized up and I tripped, landing hard on my knees mid-sprint. I forgot myself and cried out from the pain. How humiliating!

He reached down and pulled me to my feet. "You're tired," he said. He didn't let go of my hand. "You're bruised, and your muscles are sore. You pushed yourself hard last night and again today, and then I went and pushed you even further on top of it all. I wasn't thinking. I'm sorry, Zel."

The feel of his skin on mine had my ears buzzing, and I could barely follow the words of his apology. Why would he touch me?

I stared down at my hand clasped in his, my legs shaking and my breath still coming in gasps—not from the exertion, but from his nearness.

He moved his thumb on the back of my hand in a small circle, a strange, tender gesture that made me want to weep. Then he dropped my hand and patted me once on the shoulder, shoving me toward the small bathroom at the edge of the tower. "Take a bath," he said, his voice gruff. "Your muscles will feel better with the hot water. I'll show you some more speed exercises to do later."

I practically ran to the bathroom, shutting the door with a thud and leaning against it. I stared down at my hand, holding it out in front of me like it had been covered with a deadly poison. Why would he do that? The questions echoed in my head, whirling and pummeling me until I thought I might be sick.

The gentle stroke of his thumb on my hand wouldn't leave my mind. I could still feel it on the back of my hand. My heart fluttered like a caged bird in my chest, skipping beats here and there, irregular and confused.

I had to put him from my mind. It felt impossible when he was taking up far too much space in my narrow tower, waiting on the other side of this thin door, but I couldn't just stand here like a lovesick girl. "Wake up. You're not a girl," I hissed under my breath. "You're a killer."

Chapter 4

Darien was right. The bath helped. I collapsed into the hot tub and couldn't help groaning aloud as I sank deep into the steamy water. Leaning back against the end of the tub and shutting my eyes, I willed the memory of his hand on mine to go away.

A series of footsteps thumped around next to the bathroom door, and I jumped, tensing in the tub. When they stepped away, I relaxed.

I couldn't get used to the idea that Darien was on the other side of the door. I had to send him away soon—as soon as it was safe. I couldn't live like this, so nervous and jumpy, so uncomfortable in my tower. The tower was my only refuge. I couldn't lose it for the sake of a strange man, no matter how handsome he might be.

Had he forgotten who I was when he held my hand? Or had he done it knowingly? And why did I so desperately want to know the answer to that question?

I slid down in the water as a breeze slipped through the small open window beside the bath, sending goosebumps over my arms and shoulders. Bright sunlight filtered through the window and reflected off the white surfaces in the little bathroom. I focused on the water dripping from the bath faucet, the rustling leaves in the garden outside, and the noisy chirping of the birds in the trees.

I knew why I'd reacted so strongly to his touch. I just didn't want to admit it. But what was the point of cowardice? If I could face myself in the mirror each day, I could face the truth.

I desperately wanted someone to touch.

If only I could know the kiss of a husband, the embrace of a sister, or even a casual pat on the back from a friend upon meeting at the market. Anything—I'd take anything. But touches like that would never be a part of my life. Not for someone like me.

I sighed and sat up in the water, grabbing the thin sliver of spiceberry soap from the shelf to wash myself off, massaging my sore muscles as I went.

For a few moments, I allowed myself to indulge in my old daydreams, the ones that had formed years earlier while poring over the novels that Darien had found so silly. What would it be like to live in my own seaside villa in Lerenia? Or perhaps a brightly lit apartment in Asylia? I imagined going to bed beside a loving husband who would stroke my back until I slept and bouncing a rosy-cheeked baby on my hip the next morning. I dreamed of safety, of abundance—fresh fruits, hearty meat stews, beautiful frosted cakes—luxuries I'd only glimpsed on outings with the Wasp.

But when the water cooled and the soap was rinsed from my skin, I put the dreams away, pressing them back down into the dark, dusty box in my mind to wait for the next time.

If I ever escaped, there could be no chance of a peaceful life for me. At best, I would find an empty patch of earth in the Badlands and eke out a solitary existence away from the control of the Dracian clans or anyone else. I'd never have love, peace, or comfort.

My fantasies were useful. They kept me moving, day after day, no matter how hard things got. Even so, the dreams had to be kept in their place.

~

"Your food. This is it?" Darien stood before me in the center of the room, holding the canvas bag of food Helis had brought that morning.

I hovered just outside the bathroom door, my hair hanging in wet ropes down my back, soaking my clean blue dress. "Yes."

Darien grimaced. "And how often do they bring you more food?"

"It depends." I cocked my head, thinking back over the past few months. "Usually right after an outing. So, it could be anywhere from a few days to a few weeks. I try to make it last. But some of the foods must be eaten quickly, or they'll spoil." I'd learned that one the hard way.

His frown deepened. "Weeks?" He shook his head and tossed the bag back to the shadowy corner where I normally stored it. "This isn't enough." He ran a hand through his hair. "Zel. You can't—" He broke off and made a frustrated sound under his breath. "This isn't—"

I stepped closer. "What? It isn't what?"

He crossed his arms. "This is a problem, Zel. You can't demand that kind of training from your body without fueling it properly."

My cheeks flushed. "Well, it's not as though I have any choice in the—"

He huffed and cut me off. "I know, I know. It's not up to you. But this isn't going to work. You can't increase your strength and your speed when all you eat is a small bag of greasy, nearly-spoiled foods every couple of weeks. You need consistent, nutritious food."

I'd agonized over sharing my food with him for the noon meal, and he had the nerve to complain about its quality? Just what did this man want from me? "You're a fine one to criticize. You know, I didn't have to let you—"

He laughed, cutting me off mid-sentence again. I bared my teeth at him, but he didn't step back. In fact, he stepped closer, and then put two overly-warm, strong hands on my shoulders.

My heart nearly stopped beating.

"I know. It's amazing, what you've managed to do. To survive this long. To become this strong. I mean no disrespect." He dipped his head to peer into my face. "I admire you, Zel. I only want to help. Can you please trust me? Believe me?"

I didn't speak. I couldn't look away from his warm, green eyes. His touch and sincerity shook me. I wasn't sure if I hated the feeling or loved it. All I knew was that I didn't want to say or do anything that might cause him to remove his warm hands from my shoulders.

After a moment of silence, he released me.

Restraining a groan of frustration, I said, "Fine. I believe you. But I don't see how you expect me to find more food when I'm trapped in here for weeks on end."

He stared down at me with an indecipherable look. Heat from his body warmed my cool skin, and I leaned toward him unconsciously. He did the same.

What was I thinking? What was he thinking, for that matter? And yet, I couldn't pull away. I wouldn't. I wanted to be close to him.

When his eyes dipped down to my lips, my heart skipped a beat. I leaned closer, and he bent his head. Was he …? Could he possibly …? He wouldn't, would he?

"Rapunzel. Your ladder. Let it down this instant. And Rapunzel, do no harm."

I yelped and leaped away from Darien at the harsh sound of the Wasp Queen's voice coming from the garden below my tower. What would she do if she discovered him here?

Darien's shoulders tensed and his fists clenched, as though he was preparing for a fight. Would he fight her? Could he? No! I couldn't let that happen. She'd order me to kill him, and then she'd destroy me—what was left of me, anyway.

My feet moved toward the window of their own accord,

so I spun to face Darien, walking backward. "The bathroom," I hissed. "Don't make a sound. Promise me." I spat the words out with as much force as I could inject into a whisper.

He remained in that tense posture, watching me with a guarded expression. I glared at him. He had better not reveal himself, or all would be lost. Then a new thought struck. I swallowed back the bile that filled my throat and flicked a glance over my shoulder to the window. I was nearly there.

"While I'm out," I whispered loudly, praying the Wasp couldn't hear my words, "The ladder will be down, and the tower will be unobserved. It would be the best time to escape."

His face remained shuttered, giving no indication that he'd heard or agreed. My back hit the stone wall by the window, and I turned away from Darien, my hands rushing to put the ladder down in response to the Wasp's urgent command. I could only hope that Darien would do as I said. I didn't want to have his death on my conscience too.

A useless tear leaked out of one eye, and I dashed it away. The ladder hit the ground, and the Wasp Queen scaled it more rapidly than ever before. I stepped away from the window, not daring to look behind me to see if Darien remained.

Not his death, I whispered in my head. I could mourn the others. I could apologize for the others. But not this one. *Please, not this one.*

Chapter 5

"Helis, is that the best you can do?" The Wasp Queen's voice was acid and sharp today. She stood behind me, facing the mirror, her shoulders tense and slightly hunched. Was the Wasp nervous?

I strained to hear every sound around me. There'd been no noise from the bathroom since the Wasp and Helis had arrived in the tower, but I couldn't let my guard down. I could only hope that, if the worst happened and he was discovered, he'd have time to escape before the Wasp's kill order sank into my will. Perhaps I could create a distraction, give him time to—

A hot wave of magic hit my head, and I flinched, unprepared for the burning heat. What was that fool Helis doing now?

"My lady, her hair was too wet from washing to style properly. I've done my best to heat it and dry it, but I'm not a mover or creator mage."

I put a hand up to the damp bun coiled at the back of my neck. It was still wet, but significantly drier after her attempt to burn me. It had to be good enough for the Wasp. I didn't relish the thought of another burning session.

"Fine." The Wasp Queen crossed her arms. Her dark hair hung loose and wavy around her face, and her lips shone with deep red gloss. But her dress was odd. Today, she wore a thick, structured gown of pale gray instead of her typical garb of thin, body-hugging red mage-craft fabric. It dipped low in the chest and hugged her waist tightly, but otherwise, it flowed normally to the ground.

Perhaps this was how the Wasp dressed in the daylight hours when she wasn't plotting the murder of an ally. Of course, her appearance at my tower in the middle of the day suggested otherwise.

What had happened in the streets and villas of Draicia since I'd killed the Wolf clan's leader last night? To my knowledge, the Wolf clan was one of the most powerful in the city. Had there been reprisals yet? Did his brothers know the Wasp had killed him? And just where was she taking me?

Helis waved her hand in front of my face, and a warm wave of magic dusted a light pink color on my face that brought life to my cheeks. I wore a modest black gown with a bright white collar at my neck, and my thick blonde hair was pulled into an austere bun at the nape of my neck.

It was odd to see myself with a mage-craft appearance in the light of day. The gray light from outside cast unflattering shadows on my thin face, making the bones appear to jut out more than usual. The Wasp typically ordered her maids to beautify me before an outing, especially in these past few years as I'd grown into a woman. Today, she'd made me look plain and dull. An unassuming maidservant, then, meant to escape notice. That must be it. But whose servant was I supposed to be?

I slipped my feet into the black boots on the floor in front of me and faced the Wasp.

She huffed out a breath. "Let's get moving, girl." She glared at Helis who stepped away from me reflexively. "Rapunzel, follow me. Remain at my side, no matter what. If anyone tries to harm me, kill them. And do not speak a word to anyone."

She spun on her heel and strode to the window.

Helis huddled against the tower wall as my feet carried

me along, following the Wasp. If only I could insist that Helis leave the tower now. What if Darien didn't realize she was still here, and he came out of the bathroom? What if she took it upon herself to explore the tower? There was nothing I could do now. I couldn't even speak, much less force her to leave.

My True Name carried me the rest of the way to the window and forced me over the edge. I hurried down the ladder to keep up with the Wasp's command not to leave her side.

The wind rustled the leaves in the trees as I followed closely behind her through the wood around the tower. The sky was a smooth whitish-gray, and I squinted against the pale light that shone down through gaps in the tree canopy.

If I had the chance to escape, would I? Fleeing without the cover of darkness did not seem ideal. What if someone else caught me—someone worse than her? Besides, I needed to practice my strength and speed like Darien had said. If I escaped today, I'd only be caught, punished, and locked away again.

I shook my head as I hurried along the root-strewn path through the wood. I wouldn't escape today, not even if I had a clear chance. It had nothing to do with the dangers of being caught, and everything to do with the kind, wild-haired man hiding in my tower.

When had I become such a fool?

~

"I don't care what she told you. The guards stay outside. That's the rule." The stone-faced Tiger clan guard stood between us and the massive Tiger compound, crossing his tanned, heavily-muscled arms over his chest.

The Wasp Queen's face flickered, but then a calm smile graced her lips. "I understand completely. Thank you, sir." She reached out and patted the guard's arm, then waved at the five hulking Wasp clan guards that hovered behind us.

"You heard the man. Wait in the coach." She gestured toward me. "Surely my maidservant will be permitted to accompany me? For the sake of decency!" She smiled, softening her sharp words.

"Fine," he said gruffly. "Inside, then, and don't tarry. They're waiting for you."

The Wasp's smile grew brittle, but she only nodded politely and slipped past him into the compound. I followed at her heels. Could the guard see the guilt on my face? I supposed not, or he would never have let me in.

We strode through the Tiger courtyard, weaving between groups of guards performing synchronized training exercises. Did they always have so many guards at their compound? I'd never been to the Tiger villas before. All I knew was what Master Oliver had taught me—the Tiger clan was one of the most powerful clans in Draicia, second only to the Wolves, and in constant rivalry with all the other clans, especially the Wolves. What was the Wasp Queen doing, waltzing into the Tiger compound on her own with no protection except for me?

We passed through the arched entryway of the largest villa and entered a large room filled with the scent of wood smoke and male voices. Uniformed guards packed the room. I could barely see through the crowd to the grand spiral staircase, high windows, and ornate, mage-craft decorations that covered the walls. My throat itched to cough at the scent of so much wood smoke, sweat, and leather inside the stifling villa, but I didn't want to draw any more attention. The guards closest to the entrance noticed us and grew quiet, watching us warily. I kept my hands tense and ready at my sides.

A male servant in a simple black suit waved to get our attention, then turned and marched up the staircase. We followed in silence. The light at the top of the stairs was dim, and I couldn't shake the feeling that we were walking straight in to the mouth of a large, hungry beast.

At the top of the stairs, we followed the servant around

corners, passing through rooms with polished, wooden floors, arched windows, and luxurious leather and wood furnishings. The wood smoke followed us, at odds with the elegant décor. Finally, we halted in a dim hallway outside a set of carved, wooden doors. The servant knocked once, then opened the doors. The Wasp Queen marched inside, and I followed. She paused, just inside the door, and I barely avoided hitting her. She sank into a deep curtsy, and I copied her as best I could, hoping that was the right thing for a maidservant to do.

"Rise," said a soft, papery voice from across the room.

Behind us, the door shut with an ominous thud.

From the corner of my eye, I saw the Wasp rise from her curtsy, and I did the same. I squinted in the bright, white light gleaming through the windows facing us. Between us and the windows stood a long, rough-hewn wooden table and five dark shapes seated in tall chairs, their backs to the windows. Then, my eyes adjusted.

Three men and two women, clad in close-fitting black armor, watched us with narrowed eyes. Their faces were painted with black, white, and orange markings—the infamous Tiger clan war paint. They were ready for battle.

After a painfully long moment of silence, during which the sound of my own breathing echoed in my ears, the woman seated at the center of the table spoke. "You've got nerve to demand an audience on such a day." Her quiet, thin voice was at odds with her fierce face paint and sharp-edged armor.

I darted a glance at the Wasp. She'd demanded an audience with the Tigers just after murdering the leader of their greatest rival? Just what was she planning? An alliance, I fervently hoped. Not a betrayal. Not a massacre.

"Not nerve, dear friends." The Wasp's back was iron-stiff, but her voice was sweet as honey. "Faith. In your leadership. And shared concern for our city."

A male voice from the far side of the table gave a hoarse scoffing noise, and the Wasp's shoulders tensed almost imperceptibly.

The woman at the center spoke again. "And what is your concern?"

The Wasp Queen took a small, mincing step toward the table. That step was the wrong choice if she meant to convey peace. Even I could see the Tiger leaders tense at her movement. Too bad they were worried about the wrong woman.

"Concern for the safety of our clans and our leaders, of course. Last night, poor Rodolfo was murdered in the middle of a crowded ballroom, in his own home, in cold blood." She took another small step forward, then held out her hands in a pacifying, pleading pose that contradicted her tense muscles. "If even the Wolves can't protect their own patriarch, should the other clans be concerned as well?" Another small step. "And what of the culprit? Has any clan come forward to claim his murder?"

The man on the far right leaned forward. "No one yet." He smiled thinly, his lips stretching in a hungry mockery of a true smile. "The safety of the Wolf clan should be the least of your concerns. Rest assured, all will be set right in your beloved city soon."

I shivered at the obvious threat in his tone. They were ready for war—ready to absorb the Wolf clan into their own, if I had to guess. They'd be unstoppable, by far the most powerful clan in the city. There'd be nothing to stop them taking over the Wasps next.

The Wasp Queen stopped moving forward at the man's words, and stood still for a long, strange moment. Then her shoulders relaxed, as though she'd just released a long breath. "I thought as much. Rapunzel," she said, her voice ringing out in the silent room. "Kill them all. Now."

The command washed over me, giving me the courage that had deserted me the moment we walked into the Tiger compound. Then I bounded forward and dove across the table.

Within moments, three Tigers were gone, and I faced the

remaining two—a man and a woman. Their eyes were wide, set in the dull orange paint across their faces. They backed up, sharp swords at the ready, as I advanced. I wanted to be as far from the swords as possible, but the Wasp's command allowed me no outlet for the sake of my own safety. I'd get close enough to kill them or die trying.

I stepped closer. I hated this magic. I hated this Touch. Why had I been given this horrible curse?

The man struck out wildly with his sword. I dodged to the side, only to take the woman's sword in the shoulder. I darted away, wishing I could howl at the pain, but the Wasp's command silenced me. Hot tears slid down my cheeks, but still, I advanced.

"Rapunzel! Rapunzel! Cease this instant!" The woman who'd struck me spoke, her voice shaking.

I didn't respond. Her command meant nothing, even though she'd heard the Wasp speak my True Name and was now trying to use it against me. A True Name could only be given, not taken. No doubt the woman was too frightened to think clearly at this point.

Their backs hit the red brick wall by the windows, and the man charged me with a scream, his face contorting as he rushed toward me with his sword raised. My body responded by continuing to advance as though the sword wasn't even there.

I darted forward just as he reached me and put my hands around his neck since the rest of his body was protected by armor. He swung the sword toward my back, striking sharply, but I held on. The wound on my back burned, and he lifted his sword to strike again. Before he could swing, he crumpled to the floor.

The remaining Tiger woman pressed her back against the wall and thrust her sword out between us. "You're a monster," she said. "A thing of evil, pure evil." Spittle flew from her mouth as she spoke, and her orange face paint dripped down her cheeks along with rivulets of sweat.

I could neither agree nor disagree, my voice dry and

forbidden from use. I only advanced.

She lifted her sword to strike, and I used the opportunity to dart forward, close to her body. My hand shot up to her neck. I held on as she brought the sword down onto my shoulder once, twice, three times. I was too close for a deep cut, but even the shallow cuts burned painfully. Hot blood soaked my dress. I dropped my hand as she crumpled to the ground.

The Wasp came to stand beside me, her form oddly blurry. Why was the room swaying so violently?

"Time to go. Rapunzel, follow me." She threw out her arm in a quick motion, and the window beside me shattered outward in an explosion of glass shards, pummeled by her magic. Then she ran and leapt through the window, and I followed, my sluggish, dazed body helpless to disobey.

~

The drop injured my ankle. The Wasp had used her powers to cushion her own fall, but she must have forgotten about me because I slammed to the ground like a pile of bricks. The Wasp raced through the compound. The True Name command forced me to press on, limping along on the twisted ankle that refused to fully bear my weight.

Miraculously, we reached a side entrance before the alarm sounded. We sped away in her armored fomecoach, packed in amongst the waiting guards, as alarm bells clanged.

I leaned my head against the side of the coach as blood gushed from the wounds on my shoulder and back. The inside of the coach turned fuzzy, and nausea rocked my stomach as we bumped along the pothole-ridden streets. A nervous noise came from one of the guards, and I peered at him from the corner of my eye, too tired to lift my head.

"My lady, will they not attack us next?" A handsome guard sitting beside the Wasp Queen wiped sweat from his upper lip.

Instead of punishing his impudence, she smiled indulgently, her eyes bright with a strange energy, a smile gracing her lips.

The coach darkened, its inhabitants turning into deep, wavy shadows. I blinked. Was I losing consciousness? I strained to stay awake to hear her answer.

"Not to worry, Lars. There are so many factions in the Tiger clan, they will rip themselves apart before they ever—"

The blackness that had been threatening my vision took over, and I heard nothing more.

~

My bed was soft and luxurious against my wounded back. Too comfortable. Where was the pain?

I tried to sit up, but my muscles didn't obey. Was this it—the end? Merciful freedom from pain as I finally departed from this nightmare life?

A pair of crinkling green eyes hovered in my mind's eye. I wasn't ready. Oh, I wasn't ready at all. I wanted more time! Why must I die now, having only just met Darien?

Then I relaxed. Perhaps that was just it. I'd met him. I'd known his kindness and the softness of his caring touch. It was enough. I could die now that I'd felt the heaven of a gentle hand on mine. I pressed the memory of that touch into my mind. I'd cling to it in my final moments, and it would be enough. It had to be.

But the end didn't come. I floated on a cool, tingling cloud for hours. Why did my back and shoulder feel so good?

Then a new pain entered my awareness, a dull throbbing at my ankle. Why? Wasn't I supposed to lose consciousness of pain as my life faded away? My body was not cooperating. The pain grew worse by the moment. I tried to go back to the sleepy, tingly cloud, but it only retreated further and further away.

Then something sharp came into my mind, coiling tightly around me like a stiff wire. I jolted into a sitting position and then cringed against the bright light in the tower. I had to tend my wounds. Where was the salve? I had to do it now. I'd wasted too much time already.

I rolled out of bed and landed on my injured ankle. I gave a cry of pain, and a pair of strong hands went to my sides, lifting me off my feet.

"Back in bed," said a terse male voice. Darien. He'd stayed.

I forced my eyes to focus on him, and gradually, his image became visible. Then I pulled back and put my weight on my good foot. "I must tend my wounds. Now."

"I already—"

Why was he still talking? I tried to shove him out of my way, but he didn't budge. I dove around him and hobbled across the room to the canvas bag of food where I'd left the healing salve. I dug through it, tossing food to the floor in the process, but found no tin of salve.

I lurched toward Darien. "What have you done with it? Give me the salve. Now!"

He held up one placating hand, then drew a small tin from his pocket. There. Finally. I yanked it from his hand, stripped down to my slip, and searched my back for the sword wounds. Nothing. No pain. Not even raised skin. "What … what happened? I don't understand."

My wounds were completely healed. My ankle was bound in a crude splint. The urgency of the command finally left me, and I relaxed at last. I'd never gone so long without obeying a command from the Wasp before. Who knew how long I'd been unconscious?

She'd slapped me awake in the fomecoach when we arrived at the Wasp compound, and then she commanded me to follow her to my tower and to tend my own wounds when I got inside. But I'd collapsed immediately upon reaching the windowsill. Darien had no doubt saved my life.

I looked for Darien and realized he'd turned his back to

me. He was standing with stiff shoulders, his fists clenched at his sides. "As I've been trying to tell you, I already tended your wounds."

Humiliation burned its way across my face. I threw my dress back on over my slip, hobbled past him to my bed, and drew the covers over my body. "Thank you," I whispered. *You saved my life*, I wanted to say, but the lump in my throat was too large for me to speak.

Hot tears streamed out of my eyes and pooled on my pillow. I'd just stripped my dress off in front of Darien as though he wasn't even there. I'd been helpless to resist a command that wasn't even necessary. What did he think of me?

Then again, why did I care? I wasn't a woman. I was nothing but a monster, a weapon. I'd murdered five Tiger clansmen, and nearly killed myself in the process, all in obedience to the Wasp's commands. The Tiger woman was right. I was a thing of pure evil. Perhaps Darien had been wrong to save my life.

I forced myself through the apologies. The woman with the papery voice. The man who'd charged me. The woman with the dripping face paint who'd told me I was a monster. "I'm sorry," I whispered to each one, mouthing the words so Darien wouldn't hear. "I'm so sorry. It's not enough. It will never be enough. But I am."

The ritual brought me no peace. Not that it ever did. Eventually the tears slowed, and I used the blanket to wipe my face.

My bed sagged as Darien's heavy weight sank into it. I tensed. A tentative hand grazed my shoulder and then rested lightly on my arm.

"Zel, what happened?"

I couldn't help it. Monster though I was, I wanted his comfort. I leaned back slightly, pressing into his hand, and he shocked me by edging closer behind me on top of the blanket. His body pressed against the length of my back and legs, his hand gently gripping my arm. His breath tickled the back of my neck. "Tell me."

"She …" My voice was thick and hoarse, and the word was barely audible. "She made a move against the Tiger clan."

I rubbed my fingers against the wrinkled, light-gray coverlet by my face. If I told him what I'd done, would he pull away? Was this the last gentle touch I'd ever experience? I let out a breath. If so, I'd face it head on, just like I faced my victims.

"I killed five of their leaders in a private meeting room. We escaped by jumping out of the window. That's how I hurt my ankle. My mistress believes that there are so many factions within the Tiger clan, they will destroy themselves with infighting rather than take revenge against the Wasps."

Instead of pulling away at the revelation, he drew closer, pulling me in to his body with the hand that remained on my arm. "And your wounds?"

His voice was soft, close to my ear. I drew in a shaky breath and then closed the gap between us so that my head was pressed against his shoulder where it rested on the bed. His rough beard rasped against my cheek.

"What happened?" he asked when I didn't answer.

"The Tiger leaders were armed with swords. They struck me as I approached them, but the Wasp's command did not allow me to take refuge for my own protection. I fainted from blood loss in the fomecoach on the way back to the tower." I shuddered at the memory, and he pulled me in tighter. "You saved my life. Thank you. I'm so glad you stayed. I don't know what would have happened if you hadn't."

I kept my eyes shut as I spoke, my entire body tingling with awareness of his close embrace, the warmth of his hand burning my arm through the blanket that separated us.

Finally, I couldn't take it anymore. I opened my eyes and twisted to face him, leaning back slightly so I could look into his somber green eyes.

He held his head up with one elbow, his face betraying

no emotion or response to what I'd said.

"I have to—" I bit my lip. Was it my imagination, or did he lean closer? Why did he look so serious? "I have to ask why. Why did you stay? Why didn't you—"

Before I could finish my question, his lips closed over mine. I froze. His kiss was warm, gentle, and persuasive. A thousand thoughts whirled in my head at once. My first kiss? Never had I dreamed anyone would ever want to—

I pushed him to his back, meeting his gentle kiss with my own urgent one. He made a strangled noise, rolled away, and stood, taking a step back away from the bed.

Oh, no. I sat up, gathering the covers around me, watching him as I waited for my breathing to slow. What had I been thinking? No doubt he just wanted to comfort me, and I'd practically assaulted him.

"Zel." He took another step back from the bed.

I scowled, torn between shame and frustration. He was brave enough to touch a monster, and yet he feared to kiss me?

He ran a hand through his hair. "Zel," he said again, his voice harsh. "Don't look at me like that. I just— I wanted to show you why I stayed. I told you before … I don't like to see anyone trapped. Well, it's true. But that's not the whole reason. I suppose I'm a selfish man because I hate to see *you* trapped most of all. You're beautiful and strong and kind. You shouldn't be here. You don't belong here. And I stayed because I want to help you get out of here. More than that, I want … you." His cheeks burned red as he spoke.

Was he embarrassed to be speaking so plainly? I smiled at the thought, but then a niggling doubt chased my smile away. "If you want me, then why did you …?" I gestured to where he stood, several steps from the bed.

He broke into that same smile I'd found so aggravating earlier in the day—arrogant, cocky, and far too handsome. "I have my reasons."

I waited for him to explain, but he didn't continue. "Fine."

"Oh!" He went to the corner where he kept his pack and rummaged through it. "I almost forgot. I went out while you were gone and picked up some supplies. Nothing much, a little something to help out with your food." He came toward me with a bowl, a thermos, and a dented tin canister.

I didn't respond. I was still reeling over his words. He'd already escaped in broad daylight, and then he'd come back for me? I'd thought I was generously providing shelter to keep him safe. Perhaps he didn't need me as much as I'd thought. Was he truly staying because of some sort of affection for me? The thought was absurdly tantalizing.

He sat beside me on the bed again and shoved a bowl filled with thick, gray paste into my hands.

I fingered the spoon and used it to carve a path through the paste. Provisions. Interesting. "What is this … substance?"

He laughed. "It's called victus. Creator mages in Asylia make it for the poor and give it away for free so no one in the city has to starve when times are lean. It doesn't taste like much, but it has all the elements your body needs for nourishment and none of the ones it doesn't. Unlike that nasty bag of old food they've given you." He jutted his chin over to the food that was still on the floor beside the canvas sack, his lip curled.

"Well … the food isn't nasty, exactly …" The food from the canvas bag tasted quite delicious, especially when I'd gone several days or longer without fresh food.

He smiled, and it occurred to me that I very much liked the shape of his lips. My thoughts must have been betrayed on my face because he stood and backed away, shoving his hands in his pockets.

But his smile widened. "Cheese slices and herb rolls taste better than victus, I'll give you that. But you need consistent nourishment—three bowls a day—morning, noon, and night. And extra to refuel when your body has been treated harshly on an … outing." His smile faded, replaced with a look of concern. "It will take time to build your strength so that you can resist your mistress's power. Without proper fuel, it will never happen. But if you feed your body well, you have a chance."

A chance. Better than anything I'd had in a long time. I shoved the first bite of victus into my mouth and choked it down. The victus was not exactly delicious, but as it sank down into my stomach and settled, I felt nearly full already without the greasy queasiness that normally accompanied the feeling of satiety. I shoveled down another bite and a third as Darien grinned. "Oh," I said, wiping my mouth with my hand. "Um … thank you. For this."

He bowed gallantly. "You're quite welcome."

I laughed, and the sound tickled my ears with its strangeness. Here I was, sharing laughter, kisses, and food with a handsome man in my tower. I barely recognized my own life. What would I do once he left?

We spent the rest of the daylight hours talking, and I ate another thick bowl of victus before bed. He spread his bedroll on the floor beside the bathroom, his pack hidden inside the bathroom just in case he had to hide his presence quickly. Hopefully, the Wasp would not deign to visit me tonight.

I turned down the luminous dial beside my bed and snuggled under the covers, sinking into the memory of his body pressed into mine. "Good night, Darien," I whispered.

"Good night," came his reply. It sounded as though he was smiling.

I was nearly asleep when the throbbing of my ankle reminded me of the one thing I hadn't dared mention that afternoon. Unless my ankle healed, I'd never be able to escape the Wasp.

Chapter 6

I'd been awake only long enough to bathe and devour another bowl of victus when the Wasp's commands reached me through the window.

I dragged my feet as I crossed the tower to let the ladder down, glancing anxiously over my shoulder to make sure Darien was well hidden in the bathroom and no trace of his pack remained. He gave me a wink before shutting himself in the room, and even with the command settling around me, I still felt the butterflies in my stomach at his smile.

I shook my head, hoping to clear it. I couldn't be thinking of Darien, not when I had yet another outing with the Wasp. I had to focus on survival.

The Wasp made Helis dress me as a lady's maid again, and when she saw me limping to follow her toward the window, she stopped and smiled widely. "I could have your ankle healed, you know."

I tensed and tried not to let the hope show on my face, but she saw right through me.

"You'd like that, wouldn't you? I have some of the best healer mages in the city at my disposal." She paused and cocked her head to the side as though considering it. "But I do enjoy the sight of my dear pet limping along so slowly. I have a feeling it will cut down on your obnoxious escape attempts." Her smile faded, and her eyes took on a strange gleam. "And I need you, little pet, now more than ever. Now, come along, Rapunzel, and follow me."

~

The sound of something thumping against the tower wall jolted me awake. I'd been in that tingly cloud again, floating and relaxed. Another thump. I tried to sit up, but my body wouldn't move. I cracked open my eyes. The bright, white light filtering in from my tower window blinded me, but gradually, my eyes adjusted.

There was another thump, and the sound of a gruff, masculine voice uttering a string of curses.

What was happening? Was Darien in danger? Was he fighting the Wasp?

I flicked my eyes wildly around the room and finally convinced my head to move along with them, increasing my field of vision. I found him standing with his back to my bed, his shoulders heaving, his fists clenched, a pile of books on the floor by the wall.

I tried to open my mouth, but no words came out. How long had I been asleep this time? And just what was he doing to my books?

He grabbed another book from the bookcase, reached back, and flung it to the ground with such force I thought it might bust open the spine. Another curse. Then he ran his hand through his unruly hair, standing it up on end.

"Darien?" My voice worked, but his name was only a hoarse whisper.

He whipped around and rushed to kneel beside the bed. "Zel? You're awake."

I'd never seen him so wild-eyed and frustrated. What had happened? I tried to nod, but my head only jerked awkwardly. "I'm awake," I whispered. "How long was it this time?"

The last several days, we'd developed a sad, bloody

ritual. I'd return from an outing with the Wasp, half-dead from her machinations in the ongoing clan wars, and he would tend to my wounds with the mage-craft salve, saving my life each time. I would sleep forever. Then she would return, and we would start all over again. And somehow, he still hadn't given up and left me.

He reached for my hand and pulled it to him, pressing his forehead against the back. "A day," he said, his voice hoarse. "A full day. If she follows her pattern, she'll be here—" His voice cracked, and he pressed his forehead harder against my hand. "She'll be here any moment for another outing." He spoke the last word like it was a curse.

I brushed my fingers against his face, and he shut his eyes. "Darien, I—"

"Rapunzel." The Wasp had arrived. Her voice held that strange, excited energy I'd seen in her so much in the past few days. "Let down your ladder. And Rapunzel, do no harm."

I sat up and leaned away from Darien, but he pulled me closer and buried his face against my shoulder. "I'll kill her this time," he mumbled against my skin.

I shook my head and shoved him away as her command tightened around me. He stood, and so did I.

Was he serious? He couldn't be. "Darien … you can't. If she finds you, she'll command me to kill you. I know she will."

He clenched his fists without answering, his face a study in pure torment and frustration.

"Promise me." I walked backward as my feet carried me to the window. "Promise me!"

He let out a breath, and his shoulders deflated. He didn't promise, but I took that as a yes. I let down the ladder as the bathroom door clicked shut.

Helis followed the Wasp Queen over the window, still shifty and fearful as she hovered against the wall of the tower. How had she lasted so long?

This time, she dressed me in the skin-tight, dark green

uniform of a Snake clan servant girl. I glanced in the mirror and despised the costume immediately. My skin was covered from neck to toe, but the tight, glimmering magecraft dress left little of my figure to the imagination, and a long slit up the side of the skirt revealed the rest. Whatever the Wasp had planned for today, it wouldn't be good. I just hoped I made it back to the tower afterward.

Helis wound my golden hair into a twist up the back of my head and lined my eyes with a wave of her hand, spreading black kohl around them until my face was completely overshadowed by my eyes.

"Helis, are you finished or not?"

Helis stepped back and nodded hesitantly, and the Wasp beckoned to me.

"Rapunzel, follow me. And Rapunzel, try not to limp so. You look foolish, and you'll attract too much notice."

The command forced my spine straight, and a shooting pain darted up my leg from my foot as I spread my weight evenly between my hurt ankle and my good one. I kept my face blank to deny her the satisfaction of knowing how much pain I was in. How I hated this woman.

I followed her out of the window, turning back to see Helis still huddled by the mirror and, behind her, a slight crack in the bathroom door. Darien had better not make his presence known.

There was nothing I could do now. I struggled down the ladder, followed the Wasp across the garden, and entered her waiting fomecoach, sharp pain stabbing at my ankle with every step.

After an eternity in the coach, we reached the Snake compound. The Snake clan was on high alert with dozens of armed guards standing at the main entrance, but the bored guard at the servant's entrance only nodded me through. I sighed inwardly, keeping my face blank. How long would the Wasp be able to get away with these tricks?

The Snake compound was lush and fragrant, overflowing with trees, shrubs, and flowering plants in thick patches and courtyards, filling nearly every open space between the villas. As the Wasp had commanded, I entered the largest villa, picked up a tray from the kitchen, and joined a stream of green-clad servant girls carrying food to what I assumed would be a dining room.

After twisting and turning through narrow, dimly-lit hallways that reeked of incense, we reached a massive dining hall. Loud voices echoed from the wooden rafters as Snake clansmen and women laughed and argued with each other. I served the middle of the long trench table, setting out dishes of pickled fish, cabbage, and spongy-looking loaves of bread. The Snake clan diet wasn't any more appetizing than my bag of greasy, week-old food back in the tower, but it looked a bit healthier.

What was the Wasp Queen planning to do? I knew my orders—wait until she created a distraction before I took out the clan leader and her second-in-command at the head of the table. But why? Why did she keep striking down the clan leaders? What purpose did it serve? The other clans were still stronger than hers, and if they ever discovered who was behind all of the murders, the clans would unite and overpower the Wasps in a heartbeat. What was I missing?

When I was done serving, I joined the other girls against the wall. Their made-up faces looked eerie in the flickering light of deteriorating luminous sconces, and their tight dresses made them look truly snakelike. I avoided looking down at my own dress. The sooner I could get this over with and get out of this sorry excuse for a dress, the better.

I watched the head table. The Snake clan leader was young and energetic, seated with her legs sprawled out beside the table. She laughed uproariously with the other leaders at her table every few moments, tossing back huge gulps of whatever was in her goblet. Did she even know she was in a clan war?

My power pulsed toward her, the Wasp Queen's control cinching around my will as I waited, on edge, for the Wasp's signal. I tapped my fingers against my thigh and tried to keep my mind off the pain in my ankle as my weight bore down upon it.

"Attack on the compound! Guards, to defense positions!" A man's shout tore through the dining hall, and chaos erupted.

At the head table, the Snake leader leapt into a defense position, her sword at the ready, her muscles tense and eyes alert.

My stomach sank. Her casual demeanor had been an act. The others seated at her table circled around the Snake leader and her second, forming a protective circle, and I groaned.

They must have known I was coming. Would I survive this one? How long would Darien wait for me, if I never came back to the tower? I hoped he would escape safely and not waste precious time trying to find me.

The many guards in the dining hall rushed from the room, and the remaining clansmen drew their swords and followed. Soon the room was empty save for cowering servant girls streaming to the side door where we'd entered. The circle of leaders remained at the head table, swords at the ready.

I took one step toward the head table and then another. My ankle throbbed. When would they notice that I was the only green-clad servant girl not running away? I counted their number. Four armed guards plus the two leaders at their center. I'd never taken on so many at once, and I had certainly not approached a group so well guarded against me.

Had the Wasp known she would be ordering me to my death today? A pitiful voice in the back of my head cried out in frustration. Didn't she call me her pet? Didn't she say she needed me now more than ever? Why was she so quick to throw me away?

Five more steps, and then one of the guards cried out, "You! Halt!" He pointed his sword at me, and the others followed suit.

I kept walking, wishing the Wasp had provided me with a defensive weapon of some kind. A shield. A sturdy piece of wood. I'd take anything. I scooped a chair from beside the table as I drew closer. It would have to do.

The guard stepped forward, glaring at me. "I said, halt! Who are you? And who is your master?"

I didn't answer. As usual, I couldn't speak. I hoisted the chair higher as I walked closer. One girl and a wooden chair against six swords. And Darien waited back at the tower. Would he be able to patch me up again? Would I die in his arms, too far gone for the healing salve? Or would I meet my end here, alone, bleeding out on the stone floor while Snakes hacked at me?

Three more steps.

The guards raised their swords higher, and the Snake leader bared her teeth.

A tear escaped my eye and rolled down my cheek, no doubt taking some of the obnoxious black eye paint with it.

Two more steps.

One.

And then the first guard swung at me.

~

A callused hand caressed my cheek and was replaced by warm lips and a scratchy beard.

I groaned and leaned into Darien's face. "I'm alive," I whispered.

He nodded against my cheek, lying down on the bed beside me without speaking. I rolled toward him and pressed my face into his shoulder. Every bone in my body ached at the movement. I pried my eyes open. The tower was dark except for the soft glow of the luminous by the bookshelf. I shut my eyes again. "How long?"

He pulled me closer in a gentle embrace. "Two days." His voice was rough. "The Wasp came to the tower but couldn't rouse you to put the ladder down. She left. No doubt she'll try again tomorrow."

"You saved my life again," I said into his shoulder, my words muffled by the fabric of his shirt. "What is that, ten times now?"

He laughed softly, and I felt the vibrations through his chest. "At least." He stroked my arm with his hand. "You should sleep. Rest more. For tomorrow. Then eat when you next wake."

At the suggestion, a dark, heavy cloud pulled at me. I wanted to sleep, but I didn't want to leave him.

The question bubbled to the surface of my slow-moving thoughts, and I asked before thinking better of it. "Why don't you fear me? I'm a …" I didn't bother finishing. He knew what I was.

Darien pressed me closer, and I relished the movement of his breaths coming in and out of his chest. They were slow. Steady. Unafraid. "I know your will," he said softly. "I knew from the moment I saw you in that ballroom at the Wolf compound—you don't want to do this. I trust your will."

"My will?"

"You've never used your power accidentally, have you? Not even when you were younger?" His voice was gentle, and he rubbed my arm as he spoke.

"No. Never. But what does that matter? I have no will of my own."

"A mage's power is driven by will. Your power doesn't rule you, Zel. Your will does. And your mistress's will is only a temporary shroud over you. It doesn't change who you are or what you want. And you, at your core…you don't want to take lives. I know you don't. I trust you."

I love you, spoke my dazed, tired mind in response. "I trust you, too," I whispered instead.

He was still and silent for a moment.

Had I accidentally spoken the first words aloud?

"I … You should sleep. I'll wake you when it's light so you have time to eat before she comes."

I must not have spoken out of turn.

Then he pulled himself up from my bed, and I curled into the warm covers he'd vacated. I loved him. When had it happened? How? What was wrong with me? Why did I persist in dreaming of things I'd never have?

~

I'd just finished scarfing down a gritty bowl of victus when distant screams reached us.

"What's that?"

The screams drew closer. I rushed to the window and hovered just beside it, peeking around the edge to see what was happening. The morning clouds were gray and hazy, as usual, hanging low over the city. I could see nothing beyond the thick grove of trees and bushes of the garden around my tower. The screams came from the Wasp villas within the compound on the other side of the garden.

The Wasp Queen was under attack at last.

"Gather your things," Darien said. He had appeared beside me holding the empty canvas food bag. "This is it."

"What?" I stared at him blankly. What was he talking about?

"Your mistress hasn't come for you yet. If she is killed in the attack, your command will be lifted. We can flee before anyone else comes for you."

"I…" This? Now? I didn't… I wasn't… "How do you know she won't come for me?"

Darien put his hands on my shoulders and gripped me tightly. "I don't. But if she's under attack, she no doubt needs your assistance. And she hasn't come, which means she can't get here. We might finally have our chance."

My confidence grew under the comforting touch of his hands on my shoulders. Now? This might be my chance.

My thoughts couldn't catch up. One moment, I'd been eating victus and preparing myself to face death again today. The next moment, I was staring freedom in the face instead.

"Yes. I'll do it. I'll… I'll pack my things now."

I shrugged off his hands in a daze and took the bag from him and then looked around the room. What did one need for freedom?

"Spare clothes. Spare shoes. Anything you can't bear to leave behind in the tower." Darien answered my unspoken question.

I laughed under my breath. I didn't want to bring anything with me. No reminders of the past. No belongings. I wanted to leave it all behind and start again. Start fresh!

I limped to the wardrobe, the thrill of possibility finally energizing my steps. I swiped my loose black training shirt and pants from the wardrobe and stuffed them into the bag, and then, after a moment's hesitation, I grabbed my worn journal from its hiding place behind the books on my shelf and added it to the bag. I didn't look at Darien to see if he'd noticed. Perhaps I did want a reminder after all, if only so I'd never forget what she'd done to me.

I slipped on my boots and laced them tight, wincing as the laces aggravated my sore ankle. I'd endured worse pain. We'd escape, and for the first time in years, she wouldn't find me.

No one else knew my True Name. I didn't know whether to weep or laugh with joy at the thought. Once she died, there'd be no one else who knew my True Name. I'd be truly free for the first time since I was six years old.

I picked up the canvas bag and went to the window to stand by Darien. His pack and bedroll were already on his back. He'd been ready. Perhaps he'd been waiting all along for a moment like this one.

My stomach twisted, and my hands shook. I gripped the strap of the canvas bag and slung it over my shoulder, keeping my focus on the garden outside the window. The sky was too smoky to see beyond the nearest trees in the garden, but we could still hear the screams. What was happening out there?

I focused on the feel of the Wasp's final command to

stay in my tower. There was not the slightest hint of give. Wherever she was, she was still fully alive. The bright, smoky white of the sky outside hurt my eyes and made my head pound. I took a deep breath and tried to calm my nerves, but only succeeded in beginning a string of too-fast breaths.

It was too much. It was just too much. I turned away from the window as my lungs sought more air.

"Zel." Darien's voice came from a distance, as though he spoke from far above me.

I shook my head. What was I denying? "I'm fine, I'm fine," I whispered. I gripped the strap of the bag tighter and focused on the command. How would it change when she died? Would it weaken slowly, or would it suddenly disappear?

I was dimly aware of Darien placing his hands on my shoulders again. "Breathe," he said. Why did he feel so far away?

"Where are you?" I heard myself ask.

"I'm right here." He gripped me tighter. "You need to breathe." He shoved my shoulders down, and I yelped, then sat hard on the bed behind me. How had I gotten here? Darien pushed my back down so that my head was between my legs, and then he rubbed his hand on my back. "Breathe," he kept saying.

"Stop it," I wanted to say. But the room was going dark and hazy. I had to stay awake. I had to escape. This was my chance. Why was it all too much for me?

Darien knelt on the ground before me and pressed his forehead against mine, his hands on either side of my face. "Breathe. Breathe with me. Follow me."

I tried to copy him, but there was barely any air in my lungs. I gasped inward and puffed out breath as he did. Then I managed to do it again and again—I didn't know for how long. Eventually, my breathing slowed down. Nausea continued to roil my stomach, but the room was no longer dark and hazy. I was back.

"I'm fine," I said as I straightened.

Darien didn't let me go. He pulled me closer, and then his lips met mine in a gentle kiss. "Zel," he whispered against my lips, "we're going together. I'm going to take you to my home in Asylia. You'll be safe there. I promise you."

"But what about you?" I kissed him back, pressing my lips against his a little too hard. Could he sense my desperation? I leaned away from him, but he held on.

"What about me?"

"Where will you be?" My voice broke mid-sentence, and I forced the rest of the words out with a hoarse whisper. "Will I be alone again in your city?"

Instead of answering, he kissed me again. "You will never be alone again," he said between kisses. "Not while I have breath in my body. I will be with you, and I will not leave you. I promise."

Cool air from his sudden absence made me open my eyes. He stood several feet away, his chest heaving, his expression fierce. I stood hesitantly, keeping my gaze locked on his. What was he doing?

He put his fist over his heart, and a rush of anticipation flooded my body. "What …?" I knew what this meant. Hadn't I read the stories a thousand times? Hadn't I fallen asleep dreaming that a husband's love like Butterflower's and Goldblossom's would one day come to me? Hadn't I known it was a foolish, childish fantasy? And yet—

"My heart is yours," he said, and he thumped his chest once with his fist in the traditional movement. "I am yours." His voice was hoarse as he spoke the old words of the promise ritual, and his eyes never once left mine. "Will you be my wife?"

Wild thoughts whirled in my head, pelting me with questions and doubts.

I opened my mouth to speak, and then an ear-splitting cracking sound came from outside the window. I turned to the window in time to see a bright white wave rushing toward us over the trees, crackling and sizzling at it drew closer.

"Get down!" Darien screamed. "The bed!" We dove to the other side of the bed, and he shoved it up on its side as a barrier between us and the window just as the crackling white cloud swept into the tower.

My hair lifted from my shoulders, floating around me like a wild, golden cloud. Then my skin burned for one searing moment, as though it had been lit on fire, and everything went black.

Chapter 7

I was awake for several long, uncomfortable moments before I realized what was different. I was lying on the floor, not my bed. The stones were cold and hard, and a heavy, warm weight was preventing me from moving.

Darien and I lay in a heap beside the bed, his body partially covering mine. The room was coated in a fine white powder. Dust? Ash?

I flicked my fingers toward Darien and managed to move my hand to his chest. His eyes were shut, his face slack and strangely red, but his chest was moving. He was alive.

I searched my will for the Wasp's last command. Had I any possibility of escape now? Had that strange white blast killed her?

No. The command was as tight as ever.

She would never give me freedom. I would never escape this miserable place. Never.

I pressed my hand against Darien's chest and took comfort in its rise and fall and the gentle rhythm of his heartbeat. Could I marry this man if I wasn't free? Could I bind myself to him in love, trapping him in this lifelong prison with me?

The Wasp came. I heard her rustling steps through the eerily quiet woods before she issued her first command, so

I shook Darien awake. "Get to the bathroom. Go now!"

His eyes were unfocused, but he did as I said, dragging his large body along the floor with his arms. It took all my strength to shove his pack in the room after him. I tossed the blanket from my bed in front of the bathroom to cover the trail we'd left in the dust on the floor. I could only hope she wouldn't look too closely.

The bathroom door shut just as her commands cinched around me. I let the ladder down and stood obediently beside the window, waiting for the Wasp Queen to ascend it.

For once, Helis didn't follow her inside.

An unnatural energy illuminated the Wasp's face. Not a single bruise or cut marred its smooth and glowing surface. The gleeful expression on her face was at odds with the dried blood that clumped in her hair and stained her rumpled, dusty dress. "You're alive, I see," said the Wasp.

What was I supposed to say to that? I nodded silently.

"Good. You've no need of a disguise today, dear pet. I think the city has seen enough from me." She smiled widely, and my stomach roiled at the glassy, hungry look in her eyes. "Rapunzel, follow me. If anyone tries to harm me, kill them."

I trailed after her through the woods. A thin, white powder coated the entire thicket. I peered through the trees as we walked, but the haze obscured my view. It was as though the smoky sky that normally hung over Draicia had fallen to the ground.

Near the compound fence, bodies littered the ground. Guards lay limp on the ground, coated in the white dust, their faces red and flushed, their chests unmoving. We drew closer. Bodies in red Wasp clan uniforms intermingled with bodies in Wolf and Tiger uniforms.

I gagged as we left through the small side door in the fence. The same scene awaited us on the street. Bodies, utterly silent, covered in dust.

"They know me now, pet". She smiled proudly. "They

know I won't hesitate to make the sacrifices required. Everyone knows me now."

My mind reeled. She'd caused the white storm, and she'd killed her own people to repel the attack on the compound. I swallowed back bile and tried to keep my face blank.

We entered the waiting fomecoach. Someone had hastily brushed most of the dust from its black shell.

I peered out the smudged, powdered windows as we drove. The soundless footpaths near the Wasp compound held nothing but corpses. Fomecoaches huddled at odd angles in the street. The haze diminished as we left the Wasp clan's territory. Red-faced, tired-looking people watched the fomecoach warily as we passed.

No mage had magic like this—no expellant mover or creator mage, not the strongest absorbent mage. No one. My own absorbent power was the most lethal mage power ever documented, according to Master Oliver. What magic had she used to do this? How had she survived? How could she have sacrificed her own clansmen, killing them along with her enemies?

Monster. She is the true monster.

But I was still her creature. I hunched my shoulders and sank back into the fomecoach's seat as we drove.

We pulled up to the last place I expected, the front gates of the Wolf compound. I had started the clan war for the Wasp here by murdering the Wolf leader, Rodolfo. And Darien had seen me commit the crime.

The compound scraped the sky, bleak and formidable in the gray light of day. A light dusting of the white powder covered every stone.

We exited the coach and approached the front gate. A small group of guards watched us in silence. The Wasp smiled. They bowed their heads and opened the gate.

I shuddered. Just what was she doing now?

We passed through the solid, wide doors of the largest villa in the compound. No one greeted us in the quiet entryway. The inside of the villa held dark wooden rafters, rough stone floors, and bulky leather furniture. Long, thick, black curtains covered the windows, and the luminous lamps shone dimly. The villa smelled of wood shavings and smoke.

Someone cleared his throat behind us, and we turned around. Five men stood before us. They all wore crisp, black suits with slicked-back hair in the traditional Fenra style. Each one wore a collection of sharp wolves' teeth on a leather strap around his neck.

The oldest stepped forward. He was about the Wasp's age with a handsome, golden-brown face and muscular arms that strained his black suit jacket. The Wasp's shoulders tensed, and her command for protection forced me to move forward so that I stood between her and the Wolf leader.

He growled. "She's the one, then?"

The Wasp laughed lightly. "She's the one. And I'll have your tribute now, Wolves, unless you'd like to meet her personally. Each one of you."

After an agonizing pause, the Wolf leader sank into a kneeling position and bowed his head, and one by one, the rest of them followed suit and knelt beside him. My feet finally allowed me to move back, and I retreated to the Wasp's side.

She stared down at their bowed heads. I glanced at her. The look on her face wasn't quite satisfaction. It wasn't regret, either. She simply looked tired, as though she had completed a difficult task, and now it was on to the next one.

"I receive your tribute, Wolves. You may keep your lives and your clan."

She strode to the door, and I followed, glancing back once. The Wolf leader raised his head and sent me a gaze filled with sheer hatred. His eyes burned into my back as I left.

On the way back, my thoughts wouldn't stop spinning. The Wasp wasn't taking over the other clans. Was she showing her dominance over them? Completing some kind of test?

She'd demanded no money or trade from the Wolves, or at least, none that had been mentioned. She'd only wanted the Wolves' act of submission. Their tribute, as she'd called it.

"They know I won't hesitate to make the sacrifices required," she'd said as we'd stood in the middle of the Wasp territory, bodies in the white dust at our feet. They. Who were *they*? The Wolves? The other clans? And the sacrifices required for what?

I closed my eyes to shut out the horrific scene as we neared the Wasp compound. I didn't know what magic the Wasp had used to cause such destruction, and I couldn't fathom her reason for wanting to show her dominance over the clans of Draicia.

I only knew one thing. She was getting more powerful and things would get worse for me. Not even an attack from the other clans had stopped her, so my chances of escape had dwindled to nothing. Allowing Darien to stay with me in this nightmare and letting him bind himself to me as my husband would be an act of selfish cruelty.

He was a good man. I was a monster. There was no world in which we belonged together. I might be bound for destruction here, but at least I wouldn't take him down with me.

Perhaps that would be my only act of good in this life. Better than nothing.

~

"Victus?" Darien held a bowl out to me.

I took it without meeting his eyes. "Thank you." The victus felt gritty and dry on my tongue, and it settled uncomfortably in my stomach. I forced myself to finish, though the lump in my throat made it hard for me to swallow.

It had been three days since the Wasp had nearly killed

us with her strange, dusty magic. For the first time in a fortnight, I had returned to the tower without injury only to find Darien unconscious in the bathroom where I'd left him.

I'd cared for him as best I could, and he'd finally awakened later that night. The magic had seared his skin, burning it red and making his body shaky and weak, but now, he'd finally regained much of his strength. He'd taken the brunt of the magical, white storm by shielding me with his body, and the guilty knowledge pained me.

Darien nudged my shoulder. "How's your ankle?"

I edged away. "Fine."

"Fine?" The smile in his voice was undeniable. I couldn't help it. I checked his face. I'd meant it to be just a quick glance, but then I couldn't look away. I'd avoided closeness with him since my return. I'd also avoided mentioning his words of promise.

But my heart longed for him, and I wanted nothing more than to be near him every moment of the day.

I leaned further back but couldn't bring myself to break eye contact. Why was he so kind and good-natured when I had done everything in my power to push him away? Why did I keep falling further and further in love? "My ankle still hurts, of course. And it's still a bit swollen. But I try to keep my boot laced tight during outings, and it acts as a sort of splint."

He lost the easy smile. "Swollen? Can I take a look?"

No. Terrible idea. "Yes." I stuck my foot out and lifted my skirt, curling my lip at the sight of the swollen, bruised ankle. The injury looked no better than it had after that wild leap from the Tiger villa.

Darien sank to his knee and pressed gently on my ankle.

I flinched. "Ouch! What are you doing?"

"Sorry." He prodded it a few more times, but then he moved his hands up to my calf and stroked my leg gently as though he could sooth the pain away.

I should have moved away, but I was too weak. I

couldn't stay away any longer.

"I know what you're doing," he said. "What you're trying to do. And it's not going to work." His hands stilled on my calf as he met my eyes. "I love you. That's not going to change, no matter what happens and no matter what your mistress does."

What did he mean by that? I had treated him poorly. I had pulled away from his touch many times in the past three days.

"How can you possibly still love me?" I blurted out the words without thinking, and heat spread across my cheeks.

He sat beside me on the bed and took my hands in his. "What can I even say to that question? How can I not love you?" His voice was hard, despite the sweet words. "I told you, my heart is yours. That doesn't change when things in this city get worse. I won't leave you in this nightmare alone. I won't. That's not who I am. If you love me too, and I think you do, then you should know that about me."

I looked down at our clasped hands and then back at his face. He'd lost the good humor. He looked strong, serious, and perhaps a bit intimidating, but the way he held my hand was achingly gentle.

If I loved him, I should know that. Know what? That he wasn't the kind of man who would leave me alone here? My heart pounded wildly. Was he saying he would be here, no matter what—and he truly meant it?

For the first time, it struck me that the words of promise he'd spoken before the magic storm weren't simply pretty words on the pages of a book, offered by a handsome man with his hand on his heart. They'd been a pledge, a lifelong promise—one he would act on, and one he might die to keep.

I studied the hands caressing mine. They were strong and broad, roughened from constant training but gentle and loving at the same time. He'd bound my wounds and applied the healing salve to save my life countless times. He'd mixed bowls of victus for me and washed our dishes in the little bathroom sink. He'd descended the ladder and squandered his best chance for escape finding more food for me to eat.

I stroked his right palm with my thumb and then ran my hand up his forearm, marveling at the cords of strength. He sucked in his breath.

I leaned toward him. For three days, I'd dreamed of his lips, of this moment. I'd thought I'd never experience his love again. And yet, here I was, ready to take him at his word.

Did it make me evil, that I was willing to let him into my nightmare once again, as my husband?

I leaned closer and licked my bottom lip.

He held completely still, as though he feared to startle me.

For so long, I'd survived on my own. I'd held onto my sanity and feigned peace by myself. And now I wouldn't be alone any longer. He would never leave me alone. I let the truth of those words sink deep into my heart and accepted them, received them for the truth they held, with no more doubts and no more resistance.

Then I pressed my lips against his, igniting a fire between us.

When the kiss grew too intense, he sat back, chest heaving. "Is that a yes? Will you be my wife? I can't do this—can't kiss you and go back and forth. I just can't. I've given you my heart. Do I have yours?"

The tower seemed to hold its breath. Could I welcome him into my nightmare? Could I entrust myself to him? If I had to be trapped in this prison, there was no one else I'd rather be with. Perhaps in him, I'd found my freedom.

I gave him a shy, hesitant smile. "Yes."

~

We wrote our vows on scraps of paper torn from my journal, scratched with my dull pencil—words of love, promise, and sacrifice. He fashioned me a bridal necklace from leather torn from his gear, and I folded him a paper flower in lieu of the traditional garland of promise.

The early evening air smelled of wood smoke and spiceberry soap as we stood in the center of the tower to exchange our vows. When we pressed our hands together, my heart pounded so fast I thought I might faint. I wore my old, blue dress and braided my hair down my back. He wore his black Sentinel uniform. And there, in the hazy, pale twilight of the cloud that still lingered after the attack, we pledged our hearts and our lives.

Later that night, we talked until the sky brightened, lying side by side in my little bed that was both too small and too big. I told him of my dreams, the silly ones, the ones I kept locked away in that dusty cabinet in my mind. He told me of his life in Asylia—his beloved mother and his sisters, the father who'd shown them nothing but cruelty before he left their family and never looked back. He'd smiled as he spoke of the men in the Sentinels who'd become like brothers to him.

Finally, when I couldn't stay awake any longer, he curved his body protectively behind me as I drifted toward sleep.

I was nearly asleep when he spoke the words that changed everything.

"You won't be able to escape until that ankle heals, Zel," he whispered. "And I'm too weak from that magical storm to take on your mistress myself. If we're going to escape to Asylia, to safety, we're going to need help."

~

Late the next morning, I awoke, curled up in Darien's arms. I pressed my face into his chest, relishing the feel of his warm body holding mine. Safety. Comfort. This was perfect, and I never wanted it to change.

He kissed my cheek. "I don't want to go. Believe me, that's the last thing I want."

"I know," I said. "I know. It's the right thing. And all the people she's killed. Even her own clan. It's only going to get worse. We have to stop her." And yet …

"It will only be for a few weeks, if that. I just need to get back to Asylia. When I tell King Anton what's happening here, he'll agree. The safest thing for all of Theros would be to stop her from taking over Draicia. The balance of power among the clans of Draicia keeps the city stable and stops Draicia from attacking the other cities. That's why he sent me here, after all. He'll listen. They'll send a team. And we will get you home."

I snuggled closer, unable to speak.

He ran his fingers through my tangled hair. "I will get you home. I promise I will. And you're going to love it there."

I nodded. "I know." I kept saying that, didn't I? What else could I say? It was the right thing. It just felt so … wrong.

I couldn't stay here. *We* couldn't stay here. Something had to change. And if the Asylian Sentinels could defeat the Wasp Queen, didn't I owe it to Draicia, to the whole land of Theros, to do whatever I could to help stop her?

We shared a bowl of victus while cuddling beneath the blankets. I found the gritty, dry porridge more difficult to eat than usual. I tried to keep a smile on my face, and I tried to meet his eyes as he continued to search my face while we ate. What was he looking for? I didn't know. Assurance? Hope? I had none of either.

I'd only dreamed of escaping the Wasp's control in order to be alone so that I wouldn't be forced to harm anyone else. But now I had yoked myself to Darien, and everything had changed.

It wouldn't be enough for Darien and me to escape by ourselves and simply scrape by in the Badlands. After all, he was a Sentinel. A soldier. He'd been sent here to find out how the Wasp was becoming so powerful, and now he knew that she was in the process of accomplishing something far more evil and destructive than anyone had ever imagined. He had to take action to stop her. It was his job, wasn't it?

Besides, I'd never escape while the Wasp still lived. It was that simple. If my ankle healed and I had months to strengthen my own muscles and to grow faster, perhaps I could escape before she could use my True Name. But my ankle was growing worse with each passing day, chaining me to this tower. To her.

No. Something had to change. I understood that. I did.

I just didn't like being the one to pay for that change.

I'd managed to fake a smile when I caught sight of Darien washing our breakfast bowls in the bathroom sink. The bowls were laughably small in his large hands, and his tall form bent low over the sink as he washed them.

Air whooshed out of my lungs in a violent sob. I couldn't do it. I couldn't say good-bye. Not so soon! I buried my head on my knees, and soon, Darien's arms came around me. I tried to calm down, but I couldn't stop sobbing.

I didn't want to do this. He'd promised he wouldn't leave me alone, and now, my husband, my love, the one I'd entrusted myself to, was leaving me? How could I possibly do this? How could he ask this of me?

"Zel. Zel. Listen to me."

"No!" I cried between sobs.

I tried to shove him away, but he held me closer. He pulled me toward him so that my face, wet with tears, was buried in the crook of his neck. The warmth of his skin brought some comfort, but I rejected the sensation. I didn't want comfort. I wanted him to stay.

"Please. Please stay. I'm begging you. Please stay. Don't leave me. Please! You're my husband." The words poured out of my mouth like an out-of-control river, and I hated myself for saying them. What did I know about husbands? What was I thinking, begging him so? I'd been married for all of one night. But I couldn't say good-bye now. I just couldn't.

"Please." I said again, my voice pitiful.

He held me without speaking, rubbing my back. He offered no reassurances. No promises. No empty words.

Finally, my tears dried up. I had nothing left to say. I was done. He would go. "Just promise me you'll come back," I whispered.

"I promise."

I pulled away.

Regret etched lines on Darien's face. "I'd stay if I could," he said.

"I know."

"We have to get you to safety. You can't stay here. Not anymore. We should get you to Asylia. You'll see. I'll come back. We will defeat your mistress. And you'll be free—completely free. We'll go to Asylia, and we'll be together, and I'll never leave you again. I promise. No matter what happens, I will come back for you." His voice shook as he ground the words out, and I wondered if he was as frustrated as I was.

I shook my head. I was tired of words. We'd said the same ones too many times. I pressed my hands on his chest and kissed him hard, and our lips mingled with the salt from my tears. He kissed me back, and I felt the same frustration in the pressure of his lips. Don't leave, I wanted to say again.

"Zel," he said, his voice thick. "I—"

Then a voice spoke from the garden. "Rapunzel. Let down your ladder. And do no harm."

Darien pulled away. "I will come back for you," he whispered. "I promise."

I nodded. It was all I could do. He got up, took his pack, and went to the bathroom.

I stood beside the bed and shot one last glance at the door as it clicked shut. We'd already decided he would escape while the ladder was down during my next outing. This was it.

Another sob coursed through me, and it took all my strength to make it a silent one so the Wasp wouldn't hear as she scaled the ladder. I forced my face into a neutral expression and shoved my wild sorrow down as far as it would go. I had to survive while he was gone so I would be here when he returned. With the Wasp's violent outings, surviving would demand all my focus.

The Wasp Queen lifted her lithe body through the tower window and strode toward me, a smile on her lips. "Time to go, pet."

I nodded and started for the window, but she stopped me. "What's that on your face? Have you been … crying?"

I swallowed. What did she care? She already controlled everything about me. Surely, she didn't suspect—

"Hmm. Not my concern," she said. She strode to the window. "Rapunzel, follow me."

And I did.

Chapter 8

Days turned into weeks, and weeks turned into months. My stomach was constantly twisted in knots, and the nervous fear had me retching every morning. A strange lethargy took over my body, so that I slept all the time when I wasn't on an outing with the Wasp.

My thoughts revolved around Darien. So, this was what heartache felt like. I hated it, and yet … I loved it. I loved him.

Wasn't it a beautiful thing to love someone so worthy of love? A good thing? How could I regret loving someone so brave and honorable, so faithful? I knew he would come back. One day.

As time passed, my lethargy grew worse. I should have been doing the strengthening exercises he'd taught me, preparing for his return. I could have at least done the exercises that didn't use my sore ankle. My ankle ached and throbbed every day, but it neither healed nor worsened. I was simply too tired to move any more than I had to.

The Wasp's outings grew less frequent but more vicious. One by one, beginning with the Wolves, each clan offered tribute to her. Even the small clans that ruled the slums were required to offer tribute, as were the powerless holdovers from the old government. The white-haired professors at the old, crumbling college. The lonely, bespectacled docent of the ransacked historical museum. Each one paid her tribute, under threat of death by my touch. Those who refused to bow the knee met an immediate end at the Wasp's command.

Then I would go back to my tower and sleep the days away.

I had no desire to write in my journal anymore nor to read any of my old novels. How could I read and dream of imaginary love when I had known real love? How could I read of kisses when I had felt his? How could I read of hope when I was wracked by heartache?

The canister of victus grew lighter. The Wasp Queen sent the occasional bag of food, but I ate it sparingly. Her provisions usually spoiled before I had finished them.

One thought pierced my fatigue and distracted me from dreams of Darien. Just what would the Wasp do when she had subdued all the other clans? What was the point of all this killing? She was only one woman. Her clan members were few now, thanks to her magic, yet she was determined to receive tribute from all the other clans. Why?

I only hoped Darien and his Sentinels would come and stop her before I had a chance to find out.

~

Helis was back. And, as usual, the Wasp was not happy with her work. "Can't you make it tighter? And shinier? You've used far too much fabric for a Tiger servant girl."

The sparkling, black dress tightened around me and clung to my figure. I strained to keep my face blank.

"Like this?" Helis' voice was soft and shaky. How had she survived this long? It was beyond me.

"I suppose." The Wasp's sour voice bespoke her foul mood tonight. The fact that I needed a disguise again for the first time in months was not a good sign. It had to mean that she felt she had to rely on her old methods again, that confronting the Tigers head on wouldn't work. No wonder the Wasp couldn't be pleased.

Her dominance over Draicia's clans must be surface level at best. Was that good for me, or was that bad?

Another wave of warm magic washed over me before Helis stepped back. The black, Tiger clan dress hugged my body suggestively, sparkling with imbued magic. The dress's low neckline showed off my assets a little too well. I narrowed my eyes. Surely, my bust had never been quite so … healthy. Perhaps the dress was cut to enhance that area? I shook my head. How strange.

"What's the matter, pet? You don't like the dress? Not fancy enough for you?" The Wasp's sharp voice cut through my distraction.

"It's fine." I coughed. "I mean, it's lovely."

The Wasp gave me a hard look, as though searching my face for signs of insubordination. Then she tossed her hair back and smirked. "Rapunzel, follow me."

I followed her out the window and down the ladder into the moonlit garden. The cool autumn air brushed against my face like an icy hand, smelling of smoke from the evening sky and the rotting leaves that lay thick on the path through the wood. Late autumn already? I'd expected Darien to return with his Sentinels by the end of the summer at the latest.

Didn't matter. I would wait as long as it took. He'd promised to come back for me, and I knew he would.

"Wait!"

The Wasp paused, and we both turned back to the tower. Helis looked down at us from the window. "Wait," Helis said again, breathless. She hurried down the ladder with rapid steps, slipping here and there, with something clutched in one hand. When she reached the ground, she rushed to the Wasp and whispered something in her ear.

The Wasp held out her hand, and the girl put a thin sheet of paper in it. Helis backed up and glanced at me, venom in her eyes.

What was that about?

"Thank you, Helis," said the Wasp. "You're dismissed."

"But—"

"Sophohelis, you're dismissed."

The power of Helis's True Name made the air tingle with magic. Her face fell, and she left us in the forest, going the opposite way from the fence.

The Wasp resumed walking. I followed close behind her, and then I sat across from her in the fomecoach that waited in the street outside the Wasp compound.

The Wasp tapped the piece of paper on her knee, unfolded it, and read it. The rough paper was torn on one edge, ripped from my journal. Why would Helis take a page from my journal? Why not take the whole thing? Unless—

"Rapunzel, you've been hiding something. Tell me what it is."

Nerves twisted my stomach in knots. How could I answer such a broad command?

"Rapunzel, you've been hiding something about a man. Who is he, and what have you done? Tell me now."

Nausea threatened to overwhelm me as the fomecoach bumped through the city streets. The vows. Our wedding vows. Why had I kept them? I'd stuffed them into the space between my mattress and my bed, certain that no one would ever find them. Helis must have gone searching for something to give to the Wasp.

Fierce anger coursed through me, but when the command finally found its mark, I had no choice but to answer. "His name is Darien." I hated the sound of the words as they exited my lips of their own accord. "He's a soldier from Asylia. And he's my husband."

The Wasp was silent for several long, uncomfortable moments before she finally spoke. "Your husband, you say? So, he's real? And not in your imagination?"

Heat flashed across my cheeks. "He's real," I spat out. Did she think I was a foolish child?

"And have you lain together? As husband and wife?"

The heavy weight of dread sank deeper into my stomach. "Yes," I whispered. "I told you, he's my husband."

The Wasp flared her nostrils, but then she smoothed her expression into one of indifference. "You may live long enough for me to find out whether you are carrying his child. If you do carry a child, the child will be mine. Either way, your service to me is at an end."

Chills racked my body. Me, carrying a child? Darien's child?

"And if you carry no child, I'll kill you. I have no need for a pet who dares to betray me." She shook her head, and her face contorted into a strangely sad mask. "After all I've done for you—taking you in from the streets when your own parents would trade you for a bit of gold, teaching you everything you know, giving you a place of honor in my own clan. And this is how you repay me? A secret affair? A secret marriage, even?" She tapped the fingers of one hand on her knee. "No. I have no use for pets like you. And besides, I already have what I want."

Fear pummeled my stomach until I thought I would retch right there on the floor of the coach. Not once had it occurred to me that I might be pregnant. My monthly cycles had been irregular my whole life. How could I know if it was true? I placed my hand protectively on my stomach.

The Wasp laughed as she followed my gaze to the placement of my hand. "You belong to me, pet. As does your child, if you carry one. And if that child holds even one drop of your power, it will be useful to me. If not?" She shrugged and made a flicking motion with her finger.

Icy chills came over me.

"You may complete this outing. Then you will stay in your tower until I know if you carry a child."

How could she do this? Surely, she still needed me. She was sending me into the Tiger clan in secret, wasn't she? How could she say that she didn't need me anymore? My breathing came in gasps, and the shaking grew worse.

"Rapunzel. Snap out of it. And listen to me." Her razor-sharp command cut through the air between us like a knife.

A wave of numb, cool calm washed over me, and the whirlwind of fear evaporated completely. All that mattered was the Wasp, and her will. Nothing else.

Chapter 9

The Wasp gave me my instructions—a new crop of rebellious Tiger clan leaders to be eliminated. "Now go."

I opened the door and got out. My injured ankle shook and stabbed with pain. I entered through the small servants' gate, ignoring the guards as they ignored me. A girl in a matching sparkly black dress met me and led me through the compound.

I walked as though in a trance, the numbness from the Wasp's command at odds with the chaos of my thoughts. This couldn't be happening. I touched my stomach. Was I truly carrying a child? Could I feel it?

I was a monster. A selfish, thoughtless monster. I had agonized about tying myself to Darien, but I had never considered the possibility of bringing an innocent child into my horrible life. What had I done?

The thought of our child growing up in that tower, controlled by the Wasp, was too much. It was just too much. I couldn't allow it. I had to escape.

I cursed my weak, soft body and the lethargy that had overtaken me since Darien had left. Then I cursed the worthless ankle that refused to heal. I'd never been in worse shape for an escape attempt. I could only hope desperation would provide the fuel I needed to get away.

A child. A child. I followed the servant girl into the largest Tiger villa as the words echoed in my mind. Darien's child—my child—sheltered in this body of death? Impossible. Perfect. Amazing, yet terrifying.

I had to get away. Whatever the cost, I had to get away.

~

The job was done quickly in a haze of nervous energy. The servant girl waited outside the Tiger clan leaders' private chamber to guide me back, but my series of commands had been completed. I was free.

Before I left the counsel room, I stopped to yank two curtain ties from the long windows. My guide didn't even notice because she was too intent on getting away unseen. We hurried through the hallways toward the small side door where we'd entered. Now was my chance. This time, I couldn't fail.

"Wait," I said.

The girl stopped walking and raised her eyebrows. "What are you doing?"

My hand trembled as I stretched it toward her. "Sit down. Or I'll ..." I didn't bother finishing the sentence.

She stilled and widened her eyes. "What? What are you—"

"I said, sit down." I made my voice as harsh as I could to cover the sound of its nervous shaking.

She sank into a slow crouch and then sat on the floor in the narrow, dark hallway. I held up the curtain ties to tie her hands to her ankles and gag her mouth. She shuddered every time my skin brushed hers.

"I'm sorry," I whispered. She looked away from me.

I stood and stepped back. The hour was late, and the hallway was deserted. I turned back to the main part of the villa. This time, I'd go out the front entrance.

Dim luminous lamps lit the hallways. Would anyone find the leaders' bodies before morning? They'd be more likely to find the servant girl first. Hopefully, I'd be long gone by then.

Quickening my pace, I reached the grand entryway, a vast room marked by tall, dramatic windows, lush carpets, and ornate furniture. My legs shook as I strode toward the doors. The lethargy that had consumed me for the past few months was gone completely. It was all I could do not to sprint.

Miraculously, I didn't encounter anyone. The black-clad porter snoozed on a chair beside the door, his body slouched against the wall. I held my breath and slipped past him.

The chilly, moonless night wrapped around me. Hazy skies hung low over the city, and the heavy wood smoke made my eyes water.

I had to get away. I placed a hand on my belly again. I needed strength, but I had none. All I could do was be faster than I'd ever been for this baby—if there was one—and for Darien.

The guards at the entrance to the Tiger compound took no notice of me. I supposed they weren't worried about servants leaving, and I'd already been able to get in. They'd be called to task for their negligence soon enough.

When I was beyond their line of sight, I ran, kicking off my shoes as I went. Before I'd made it to the end of the street, I was gasping with exertion. I regretted losing my shoes as my weak ankle buckled beneath me, but what could I do? The flimsy slippers would have provided little support anyway. My fear-fueled sprint slowed to a limping jog, but I kept going. I couldn't let myself stop.

I turned down a narrow alley and realized I had no idea where to go next. In my flurry of nervous urgency, I had lost my bearings completely. I hadn't been near the city walls since I was a child.

"Just pick a direction," I whispered under my breath. Eventually, I'd hit a wall, wouldn't I? Beyond the wall would be the Badlands and freedom.

I tore down the alley, crossed a deserted street, and fled down the next alley. There was no sign of the Wasp. Was I finally free?

Then a fomecoach pulled up at the end of the alley. It had to be her. The door opened as I spun away and ran back in the direction I'd come. A force hit me from behind and knocked me to the ground. I curled around my belly as I lay on the hard, stone street. Please, not this time. Not this time!

I struggled to my feet, but the force shoved me to my knees. I strained against it the way Darien had taught me. I managed to move away from the Wasp's magic, but I had nowhere near enough strength to escape it completely.

Then, inexplicably, the force disappeared. I struggled to my feet and searched the shadows for the Wasp. Her fomecoach loomed at the end of the alley. The body of her guard lay still on the ground. But two bodies were locked in a struggle on the cobblestones nearby.

I limped toward the fray. A man gripped the Wasp from behind with one arm around her face, blocking her mouth. She must have been attacking him with her power, because they shook and swayed together. The man was tall and bearded. I squinted into the darkness.

"Darien?" My voice was painfully soft in the silence of the dark alley.

He grappled with the Wasp and faced me, his expression tortured. "No, Zel! Run! Get away. You have to go, now!"

I didn't move. "You came back." My thoughts moved in slow motion.

"Don't wait for me." Her magic pummeled him, and she strained against him. "Go. I couldn't get help, and I … Just run. Promise me. And don't come back."

I stood there, torn with indecision. I couldn't leave him. And yet … What if there truly was a baby? What if she commanded me to kill Darien? I couldn't stay, but how could I leave?

"Run!" He screamed. The desperation in his voice hacked at my indecision like a knife, and I finally turned away.

I pushed my legs into a limping run, looking back several times. I was out of their line of sight, almost all the way down the next alley, when the Wasp screamed, "Rapunzel!"

I was too far away to hear the command that came next. I kept running.

Then a man's gut-wrenching scream echoed through the streets, followed by nothing but silence. I doubled over in the middle of the street. Darien? What had she done to him?

The Wasp shouted again, but I couldn't hear distinctly. Her shout echoed off the empty streets. My breath came in gasps. It sounded like she'd screamed a promise, "I'll always find you!"

Tears streamed down my face, but I resumed my flight, my ankle stabbing with pain at each halting step. I didn't stop until I left the city walls.

Chapter 10

The Badlands stretched before me in a cloudy, dark landscape of stony outcroppings, narrow washes, scraggly trees, and shifting shadows. Behind me, Draicia's walls soared high into the smoky, midnight sky, looking for all the world like a smoldering chimney. I forced myself to move south, away from the city gates.

What if the Wasp made good her threat to find me? She had always found me before, but I'd never made it more than a few blocks away from her. Now I was finally outside the city. But would that stop her? I, better than anyone, knew how relentless and heartless my mistress could be.

Former mistress. She was done with me, after my betrayal with Darien. She'd told me herself. Now, she wouldn't be satisfied until I was dead like he was. I nearly sobbed aloud at the thought, but kept silent, forcing myself to move away from the city even as my lungs were crushed with grief.

My ankle throbbed and threatened to give out entirely as I stumbled along the rough ground of the Badlands, dragging myself further away from the city walls. I didn't even have a change of clothes. No water. No food. The Wasp would get her wish. I had escaped the city, but I was surely going to die in the Badlands.

How could I ever have dreamed of reaching Asylia? Darien was my only hope. He knew how to survive in the wilderness. Was there any chance he lived?

No. I'd heard that horrifying scream. The Wasp must have destroyed him with her magic. I clenched my fists. He had saved me, but at what cost?

A dry river bed led me through high, jagged rock walls that blocked the city walls from view. I followed it for hours, until a weak, gray dawn eased into the sky overhead and my tongue stuck to the parched, dry roof of my mouth.

For the third time in the past hour, my ankle collapsed under me. I crashed to my knees with a low groan, then struggled to my feet. But I couldn't make myself move forward. Why bother to go on? Death was inevitable. Either the Wasp would find me, or the Badlands would kill me.

But if I gave up, the child would die with me. I had to move forward, didn't I? I couldn't allow Darien's sacrifice to be wasted.

My bare feet were stone-bruised already, but I managed to climb a short rise beside the wash to sit atop a boulder and get my bearings. My gaze sharpened on a puff of grey smoke in the distance ahead of me. It was just after dawn, so it had to be a cook fire. That meant people. The distant campfire beckoned me. If I could only reach it, maybe I'd survive.

I scrambled from my perch and found a stick to use as a staff. The terrain was rough, and two hours later, I was ready to drop. Had the smoke been a mirage?

I'd come too far to go back, and I was certainly lost. All the stories about the Badlands were true. This barren place was impassible for a person who didn't have the proper skills. Even experienced travelers died on the rough journey between cities. I didn't know anything. I had nothing. I would never make it.

But when I rounded the next bend, I spotted the small collection of tents ahead. It was real. The countryside opened up, and the riverbed continued straight ahead. I left the dry wash and ventured across a flat plain toward the weak column of smoke that rose near the tents, waving my stick above my head as though I could attract attention from whoever tended the fire.

Something like panic drove me forward, energizing my weak, exhausted limbs. What if I couldn't reach it? What if I collapsed in the scrub brush, just a few hundred feet away, and nobody found me until I was a pile of bones?

I tried to shout, but all that came out was a croak. I hobbled forward at a painfully slow pace, my bare feet stabbing with pain at each step, my ankle buckling beneath me. Somehow, I got closer. I couldn't stop. I had to make it.

The sky had brightened to a pale gray by the time I made it to the edge of the camp. A group of thin, ragged Badlanders with wild hair watched me warily from the other side of the fire, and then a man with deep, tan wrinkles and thinning gray hair stepped forward, coming between me and the camp. He brandished a stick at waist height like a club, but even in my desperate state, I could tell his hand shook.

"No trouble. Please, mage, we don't want any trouble." His voice was raw. "Why have you come here? Please, don't touch us."

My heart sank. *Don't touch us.* How did he already know what I was? "Water," I rasped. "No trouble … won't touch … I promise." Weakness swept over me, and I landed hard on my knees.

The man edged closer and prodded my shoulder with his stick, but I couldn't even work up the strength to lift a threatening hand. I rolled from my knees to my back. The pale sky seemed to be falling down upon me, and I closed my eyes against the sky's dizzying descent. *Darien, I'm sorry. So sorry.*

~

The dry leaves of autumn had dropped from the trees

not long after I'd arrived, and the harsh Badlands had turned soon after from dry and cool to frigid, icy, and miserable. For three months, I shivered in the small settlement of Badlanders who sheltered me while I waited for Darien.

They'd shown me mercy when I most desperately needed it, and thanks to the stubborn kindness of their leader Belen, had cared for me when I was helpless in their midst. Some were still terrified me, but I hadn't been able to bring myself to leave, hoping against hope that Darien would make it out of Draicia and find me.

My tent was small and cramped, and my back ached from stooping over whenever I stood inside it. But I slept beneath a pile of furs and stayed warm enough each night. I stretched and shoved the furs off my bed, then shivered in the frosty morning air. My breath puffed out in a warm, visible cloud. The dim winter light filtering in through the tattered canvas tent told me it was just past dawn. Time to rise, and to see what I could do to help the Badlanders today. I didn't have much to offer in the way of survival skills, but the occasional hunting party found a use for me. I had a feeling they were eating more meat now than before I arrived.

I left my small tent, straightening gratefully as I stepped out into the wintry morning air. Bare patches of old, dirty snow dotted the rocky hills around the camp, but the camp itself was clear of snow.

Belen met me at the main campfire and handed me a small, chipped mug of hot porridge as I sat beside him. I matched his forward-leaning posture to soak in heat from the fire, and steam from the porridge added extra warmth to my face as I shoveled the food down in silence.

"Hala says it won't be long now," Belen muttered around a mouthful of food.

I glanced over. "What?"

He gestured at my belly, then returned his attention to the porridge.

"Oh. Really? I suppose …" My belly had grown in the

past three months, it was true. There was no denying it now. Darien had left me with a baby. But surely, I still had time—

"You can't stay here much longer, Zel. The Badlands are no place for a child, much less a newborn. And the longer you wait, the more difficult it will be to travel."

I swallowed down a hot bite of porridge, wincing as it burned my throat. "I … I know, I know. I can't. I just …"

"You wanted to go to Asylia, was it?"

I nodded slowly. Belen was from there. He'd been the man who knew me—knew I had the Touch—when I stumbled upon their camp after my flight from Draicia. He was a tracker, he'd told me later after I'd recovered. A weak, absorbent mage the Asylian government had trained to use his power to police other mages. But he'd been cast out, and eventually, he had found himself leading the small group of Badlanders who'd sheltered me and helped to heal my ankle.

Belen gulped down the last bite of porridge, then set his mug on the ground and leaned back against a weathered stump, folding his hands over the back of his head. "You won't make it there. Take my word for it. You'd be better off back in Draicia."

I scowled. "I'm not going back. I'm going to Asylia. No matter what." Even if Darien was dead, he'd meant Asylia to be our home. I had to make it there.

"Thought you'd say that." He shook his head but kept his gaze on the fire before us. "It's full of trackers like me, you know. Better trackers than me. They'll recognize you in an instant. And the Asylian king is mad. Paranoid, cruel, and mean as a rabid wolf. He'll find you and make you his, and you'll be as much a slave in Asylia as you were in Draicia." He shot me a worried glance, the wrinkles around his eyes deepening in obvious concern. "You understand?"

Perhaps that was why Darien hadn't been able to secure help to rescue me. I shoved the thought away. Memories of Darien still threatened to undo me completely, and I couldn't stand to begin another day with tears. As the months passed, I had finally admitted the truth to myself—

Darien was dead. I'd known it from the sound of his horrible scream and the Wasp's triumphant promise to find me. Darien wasn't coming out of Draicia.

I rubbed my hands on my upper arms, cold despite the warmth of the fire on my face. "The king won't find me, and neither will the trackers. I'll stay hidden. I'll … I'll make a way."

Belen was silent as the tents around the campfire began to rustle. The other members of the camp would be up soon. He sighed and leaned forward, resting his forearms on his knees, and stared into the fire. When he spoke, his words were almost too quiet to hear. "Master Eric Stone. The Golden Loaf Bakery in Asylia's Merchant Quarter."

My heart leapt. "Who is that? Will he help me?"

"He offers temporary shelter to cast-off mages, when they've been deemed too weak for service and have no home outside the Mage Division. I've never heard of him turning anyone away." Belen glanced up at me with a raised eyebrow. "But last I heard, he had a wife and young daughter, so you might be the first."

I hunched over and bundled my arms around my knees. The fire was too hot now, but I didn't dare move. "I'll take that chance."

Belen nodded curtly. "I'll give you directions, but you must leave soon. The spring rains often flood the Badlands, and you'll be in no condition to survive them if you wait much longer."

The Golden Loaf Bakery. Even the name made the place sound like a treasure. Hope unfurled in my chest, a fervent longing that took the edge off the relentless pain of Darien's death.

I'd found a way.

~

The next morning, I said good-bye to Belen and his camp. After several days of walking southeast through a wasteland of melting snow and muddy dirt, I finally made it within sight of Asylia.

Then I lost my nerve.

Asylia's walls stood taller and smoother than Draicia's. What did it mean that even the city walls were more intimidating than anything I'd seen before? The ancient stones looked clean and had clearly been repaired in several spots. Asylia still had a functioning government. That had to be an advantage. But it was also a disadvantage.

What if their trackers caught me? I'd be forced into captivity as a weapon for yet another mad ruler, and I'd be ensuring that my baby would be born into captivity as well.

I rubbed the underside of my swollen belly to ease the ache that plagued me when I walked too great a distance, as I'd done today.

If only Darien had survived his fight with the Wasp. If only he were by my side, as he'd promised he would be. He could have helped me decide what to do, helped me navigate the unfamiliar streets and politics of a new city.

What was the point of wishing? Darien wasn't here. He'd promised to be with me, and now he was gone forever. I was alone.

The thought crushed my chest. Tears rushed down my cold, windburned cheeks in heavy torrents, and I clutched at my belly, suddenly unable to breathe. Then the baby gave a tiny, subtle kick, and I jumped. The reminder of the life within me replenished my courage and my will. I straightened and drew in a long breath.

It was up to me to ensure our baby survived so Darien would not have given his life for us in vain. I dashed the tears from my eyes with my dirty, ragged sleeve. If that meant sneaking into this wealthy, foreign city and throwing myself on the mercy of Master Stone, whoever he was, I would do so.

Failure was not an option and neither was captivity—not this time, and never again.

PART II

Chapter 11

I basked on the warm pallet beside the oven, luxuriating in the feel of the soft bedding and delicious warmth that still emanated from the oven after yesterday's baking. Outside, the city was cool and wet, the chilly rain of a spring storm constantly tapping on the kitchen window. Inside, the kitchen was a warm, cozy oasis.

The bakery's kitchen smelled of yeast and cinderslick. I loved it. The scent of cinderslick—the strange, magical cooking fuel they used in Asylia—was truly glorious. Sweet, dark, and slightly singed, the aroma was nothing like the acrid wood smoke that hung over Draicia like a shroud.

I cracked open my eyes. It was dark, but I didn't mind. The bakery was perfect. I'd snuck into Asylia three months earlier, and against all odds, I'd found my new home. The baby kicked and somersaulted violently inside me, and I grunted aloud at the discomfort.

"Hello, there, sweet one," I whispered when the pressure faded. I couldn't help but smile. The bakery was the perfect home, but it wasn't just my home—it was *our* home.

I pushed aside the book I'd been reading when I fell asleep, rolled to my other side, and stretched. Master Stone was a kind and gentle man, a talented baker, and a thoughtful scholar. His bakery was full of Western books with fascinating titles like *Through Ice and Fire: Journeys to Theros* or *Encyclopedia of The Lost Cities of Theros*, and my current favorite, *A Scientific Exploration of Therosian Mage Powers*.

The Western authors of the last book posited all kinds of strange theories about the nature of absorbent and expellant mages, which apparently were only found in Theros, including fascinating theories on how Asylian trackers worked. I read everything I could, storing up the knowledge to distract myself from thinking of Darien.

I got up slowly, rubbing my sore back with one hand, and then I put away my bedding, folding it into a small bundle and setting it on the bottom shelf beside the oven. I dressed for the day's work in a loose house dress that had belonged to Master Stone's late wife. It was far too nice for working in the kitchen, but then again, everything they owned was nice. Besides, the waist tie made it easier to adjust around my belly.

I covered the fine dress with an apron and got to work punching down the dough we'd left to rise the night before.

"Zel!" A pair of strong, childish arms folded around my middle as Ella buried her face in my back.

I laughed and tried to turn around, but she wouldn't let go. "Ella-bella! Why are you awake so early, hmm? It's still dark out."

"Daddy doesn't feel well," she said, finally letting go of my back and coming around beside me. "He told me to come down and help you."

No doubt he'd hoped to get her out of his hair so he could rest. "Well, lucky me. I'd love some help, sweet girl." My hands were sticky with dough and coated in flour, so I rubbed her tousled, dark hair with my elbow. She giggled.

Master Stone's daughter, Ella, was only five years old, but she was exceedingly bright and energetic. She'd taken to me immediately, for some reason, a little bundle of intelligence and warmth, always ready to help in the bakery, and constantly overflowing with affectionate sweetness. Perhaps I could have done without her incessant, curious questions, but after years of silence alone in my tower, they weren't entirely unwelcome.

In the classic Fenra mold, she had bronze skin and dark hair, but her pale green, Kireth eyes lit her face, a contrast that gave her face a stunning, unforgettable beauty. She'd be dangerous when she got older, that was for sure. I almost felt sorry for the little boys on the lane who teased her about her green eyes. One day, they'd feel quite foolish.

We put in the morning's baking, and then I made us a small breakfast of boiled eggs, buttered bread, and fresh brambleberries. A small breakfast. Ha! After months of nothing but bowls of victus followed by the meager, scavenged fare in the Badlanders' camp, a small, Asylian breakfast was an extravagant treat.

Every bite lingered on my tongue. The golden egg yolks were rich and fatty. The airy, flavorful bread was soft on the inside and surrounded by a deliciously chewy, floury crust, with each slice drenched in creamy butter. The tanginess of the fresh brambleberries capped it all off perfectly. It was a meal fit for kings and queens, and here we were, enjoying it in the little bakery kitchen. I loved Asylia.

When we finished our breakfast, I carried a small plate to the top of the stairs, along with a folded copy of the *Asylian Herald* Ella had fetched from the corner stand. I knocked on the door to the family's living quarters. "Master Stone? Some breakfast?"

An odd-sounding cough greeted my knock. "Thank you." His voice was barely audible. He coughed again, and I put my hand on the knob. Just how sick was he? "You'd best leave it there, and I'll come get it. Don't want you and Ella getting sick too."

"Yes, Master Stone. I'll leave it here." I set the plate and the newspaper gingerly on the floor. "Do you need anything else?"

I waited as he went through another coughing fit. "Keep

Ella downstairs with you, please. Just…just in case. Thank you."

"I will." What was he worried about? The Asylian government had armies of healer mages in their public hospitals, not to mention fancy healing salves stocked in every home. Master Stone had used some on my blisters when I'd arrived.

Surely, there was no sickness the powerful, Asylian mages couldn't heal. Was there?

~

I stood just inside the room, holding a pitcher of water and trying not to cry. Master Stone was dying.

Two days after he first took sick, Ella's father lost his healthy, golden-brown skin tone. Now, his sagging skin was a dark grayish color, as though his life was seeping out. The morning he took sick, the *Herald* brought news that a plague had entered Asylia's walls via a contaminated shipment of imports from distant Western lands. Too late, the government learned that the Western cities had been utterly decimated by the same disease.

The plague had already wreaked havoc on the merchant families living in our lane. Our neighbor Gregor's wife had passed away the very first day, and that night, the king called for all imported goods to be burned in bonfires in the street. We'd dutifully thrown Master Stone's prized Western books and Ella's imported toys into the fire. We had also burned the Lerenian wheat and flavorings the bakery depended on for operation.

But it was too late for Master Stone.

A hacking cough shook his body for several minutes before he whispered, "Zel."

I stepped closer.

"No. Stop. Not too close."

I paused. What did he want from me? A horrible, selfish question wormed its way into my mind. When Master Stone died, what would happen to me? Where else could I find shelter?

"I need you …" He broke off as another coughing fit came over him. I stood awkwardly in place, wondering what to do. "I need you to stay here with Ella when I'm gone." He whispered the words in a rush, and my legs went weak with relief. "I know I'm dying, and I don't have much time left. Please, promise me you'll stay here with Ella. Raise your child here with her. Don't leave her alone. Gregor is grieving, and he is too old to care for a small child. She needs you. Promise me, Zel. Promise me."

"I…" Master Stone had sheltered me when I had nowhere else to turn. How could I refuse to shelter his little daughter? And yet, what kind of caretaker would I make? A life of secrets and danger was no life for a child. It was bad enough that my own child would face such a life under my care. What if I ruined Ella's life too?

"Zel, she needs you, and you already care for her. I know you do. You'll do right by her." He coughed again, and the fit went on far too long. What would I do if he stopped breathing altogether? Finally, the coughing fit ended. "That's all a father can ask," he said, his voice paper-thin and achingly weak. "Do right by her. Take care of my girl." Then he was quiet.

I peered through the dim light of his sickroom and realized he had fallen asleep. That was it, then. The conversation was over. How could I deny a man's dying wish? Not even I was so heartless.

"I will," I said to his sleeping face.

I shut the door softly behind me and went to look for dinner. We had no flour to bake with, not after burning it all in the bonfire to purge our home from traces of the plague. I'd have to sneak off to the market and pick up victus for myself and Ella.

~

The Sanitation Ministry workers took Master Stone's body and bedding away late the next morning. I left Ella in Gregor's care while I scrubbed every inch of our living quarters, my back aching and my stomach tightening repeatedly with a strange hardness that spread across my protruding belly and set my back to aching.

When I was done, I washed my body with blistering hot water and soap in the bathroom. I scrubbed until my skin was red and raw. If only I could be certain that would keep the plague away. When I was clean, I went to retrieve Ella.

I darted nervous looks over my shoulder as I walked down the lane to Gregor's shop. When I'd first arrived, there'd been trackers on every major street in the city. It had been a miracle that I had made it all the way to the bakery without getting caught. Since the plague, I hadn't seen nearly as many trackers in the Merchant Quarter, and not a single one near the bakery or at the nearby market where I got victus.

What would I do when the trackers came back? How would I care for myself, Ella, and the baby when I couldn't leave the bakery without fear of getting caught by trackers and being enslaved?

According to the *Herald*, the trackers, guards, and healer mages were the first to encounter new plague victims, and therefore, the first to get sick. Thousands of citizens had fallen sick, and hundreds had died in the first week. No one knew how to stop the plague's horrible spread, but eventually, it had to stop, didn't it? When the city went back to normal, what would I do?

The sky was dark and heavy over our narrow lane. Yet another spring rainstorm. This land saw far more rain than Draicia ever did. Thick, fat drops of rain hit my face as I neared Gregor's house. The wet, ashy remains of our bonfires stained the cobblestones in the street. I stepped around them and knocked lightly on Gregor's door. "Gregor? Ella? It's me."

The door opened a crack. Gregor's lined face was

downcast, his eyes rimmed with red. He didn't speak. He only nodded once and shifted away from the door.

I stepped through, my eyes slowly adjusting to the dim light.

"Zel?" Ella's voice was soft and hesitant. She sat on the floor of the empty shop, surrounded by barren shelves. "You came back for me?"

"Of course, sweetheart. I was just … cleaning things up. I wanted to make sure you didn't get sick."

She nodded solemnly, clambered to her feet, and placed her small hand in mine. Her palm was warm and her skin, soft. She tucked against my side and clung to my hand like it would be a long time before she let go. "Can I come home?"

"Yes, of course." A lump filled my throat. I turned to Gregor. "Thank you."

Gregor didn't respond. He stood by the door, tears coursing down his aged cheeks.

"I'm …" What could I say to man who'd lost his wife, his business, and his best friend in a matter of days? "If you need anything, just … we're here, you know." I stood awkwardly, waiting for him to respond, but he said nothing.

Then Ella let go of my hand and crossed over to Gregor. She wrapped her small arms around his waist as sobs shook his body.

My shoulders crept up, and heat spread across my face. I was a failure at everything—comfort, love, grief. How could Master Stone have expected me to raise his orphaned daughter when I didn't even know how to comfort a grieving neighbor?

I took one hesitant step forward and then another. I raised a hand. What was I doing? Why did I feel so nervous? I thought back to how Darien had rubbed my back so sweetly in the tower when I was too afraid to escape the day of the white, magic storm. If Darien could comfort a monster like me, surely I could comfort a grieving man like Gregor.

I stepped closer, reached out, and patted Gregor's shoulder.

He nodded. "I know, Zel," he whispered hoarsely. "Thank you. And …" He pried his swollen eyes open, meeting my gaze with surprising steadiness.

I nearly yanked my hand away but managed to hold myself still, hoping I didn't look as uncomfortable as I felt.

"Same for you and Ella. If you need anything," he said. Then he shrugged one shoulder, a casual gesture at odds with his next words. "As long as I'm still breathing, I'll be there for both of you. I promise."

Another promise. I nodded awkwardly and pulled my hand away.

He swiped at the tears on his cheeks, squeezed Ella's shoulder, and gave her a gentle shove over to me. As Ella folded herself into my side once again, Gregor said, "She doesn't quite understand yet." His lips lifted in a sad smile. "She's too young. But she will, one day." He nodded, as though reassuring himself. "Off with you both. Leave an old man to his quiet evening, hmm?"

I put a hand on Ella's shoulder. "Let's go, Ella. Dinner's calling our names."

We ate our victus in the kitchen, huddled by the stove out of habit, though it hadn't been used in several days and no longer held any residual warmth from the cinderslick. I could only hope the heavy spring rains let up soon to make way for summer, because without cinderslick, we couldn't bake bread, and without bread, we couldn't afford suffio embers to heat the living quarters upstairs. If things didn't get better by next winter, we'd be frozen in our beds. Surely, the plague wouldn't last that long, would it?

The kitchen was cold and quiet. Ella huddled over her bowl of victus, and though she stirred it several times, she didn't seem to eat much. I supposed she would have to acquire a taste for it after eating fresh food her whole life.

"Don't worry, you'll get used to it eventually," I said, and gave her what I hoped was an encouraging smile.

"What?" Ella's voice was scratchy and nervous, her eyebrows lowered in a frown.

What had I said?

I tapped my spoon on my empty bowl. "You know … the victus. It doesn't taste great, but eventually, you'll get used to it."

"But …" Her beautiful light-green eyes filled with suspicion. "Won't we have real food again once Daddy comes back?"

I chewed on my bottom lip and tapped my spoon on my bowl a few more times. Nothing had ever prepared me for this conversation. "She doesn't understand," Gregor had said. And I was the worst possible person to help her five-year-old mind come to grips with reality. The last thing I wanted was for Ella to be like me, with nothing but a dusty box of dreams in the back of her mind to stop her from losing herself to this new nightmare.

"He's … your daddy is …"

Ella narrowed her eyes. "Why are you crying?"

I dashed the warm, wet tears from my cheeks. I hadn't even realized I'd begun to cry. "Well, it's because …"

Ella got up from her chair and came over to mine, and then she clambered into my lap and wrapped her arms around my neck. I nuzzled her tousled dark hair as she nestled her head against my shoulder. My tears flowed even faster.

"It's going to be fine, Zel," came her muffled voice. "I promise."

Did she know she'd echoed Gregor's words to me?

I wrapped my arms around her thin, warm body and held her tight, rocking back and forth. Why was she comforting me? I should be comforting her! And how did she know everything would be fine? I wasn't sure we stood much chance of lasting very long without her father.

"Your daddy isn't coming back," I said, hating the blunt way the words tripped right off my tongue. Why hadn't I found a way to soften the words? How could I take care of this girl on my own? I couldn't do this. I just couldn't. She'd be better off with Gregor or someone else—another neighbor, perhaps. Not me.

Ella's body tensed. "Not ever?" Her voice was muffled, her face pressed hard against my collarbone now. She held me even tighter than before.

"Not ever, Ella. It's …" I rubbed her back. "It's just you and me now. I'll stay with you. I'll take care of you, just like your daddy did. I promise." Another stricken promise.

Her little arms wrapped around my neck and held me tight, as though she could sense I wanted to flee. Sobs wracked her body, but she made no sound as she cried. I could only feel the wetness from her tears soaking into my shoulder where she kept her face pressed against me.

That night, I held her in the big bed in the upstairs room as the rain beat against the windows outside. It was cold without suffio, but I'd dressed us in warm sweaters over our nightgowns and piled all the spare blankets on top of the bed.

Ella's eyes were red and swollen, and she hadn't spoken since dinner. She'd kept by my side as I'd cleaned up the kitchen and readied the bed, wanting to hold my hand or the folds of my skirt at all times as though she didn't dare let me out of her sight.

Now that we were in bed, though she must have been exhausted from all the crying, she refused to shut her eyes and go to sleep. "Ella, sweetheart, I'm not going anywhere. It's time to sleep."

She only blinked those red-rimmed eyes at me and snuggled closer to my protruding belly. The baby moved rapidly, pressing hard against my belly, and I couldn't help but flinch at the pressure. Ella furrowed her brow.

"It's fine, Ella. The baby inside me is moving, saying hello to you." Ella kept frowning, but nodded slowly. "But now it's time to sleep. Got it?"

She placed one small hand on my belly, and the baby kicked again. "Oh!" Her eyes widened, and then she giggled.

It was the most perfect sound I'd heard in months. "The baby?"

I blinked back another wave of tears. We didn't need any more of those tonight. "Yes. The baby will be coming out soon, I think. And then you'll have a friend to play with. How about that?"

She nodded again, this time more eagerly. And then she frowned again. "You're the baby's mother, Zel?"

"Yes. I'm the … I'm the mother." What a strange and terrifying phrase. It sounded impossibly foreign on my lips, but as it turned out, I should have been more worried about the indignant expression on Ella's young face.

"But … what about me? Who's my mother? Are you my mother now?"

My stomach sank. What could I possibly say in response to that? I couldn't replace her mother, or her father, for that matter. I was just … me. A killer. A creature of the shadows. By my mere presence, I was bringing more danger to her already difficult life.

"No," I said, my voice catching on the word. "But I can be your stepmother."

More indignation. Ella's eyebrows sank lower, and she jutted out her lower lip. For the first time in hours, she looked away from me and kept her eyes on the blanket by her face, twisting it and turning it with her fingers.

Would she cry again? Had I said the wrong thing? But how could I lie to her?

Finally, after several long moments, she spoke again. "But I'll love you like a mother," she whispered. She didn't look at me as she said it. She only stared at the blanket, a fierce and determined look coming over her face.

How could this small girl be so strong? I would be a terrible mother. I'd inevitably fail her by getting caught by the trackers or simply being unable to provide for her. How could I accept such love from a girl who had already lost everything, knowing I had nothing but secrets and danger to give her in return?

She closed her eyes and her breathing slowed as she drifted toward sleep, but I couldn't relax. I held myself still in the bed beside her, worries and fears tormenting me. I'd lost myself in Draicia. Then I'd lost Darien. I'd found shelter here only to see disaster come upon the family who'd sheltered me. And now, I was going to bring a new baby into this nightmare world, all while caring for a small girl who had lost everything, just like me. It was foolish to think I could do this.

But then again, perhaps that was my answer. If Ella could resolve to love me when she had nothing left to give, couldn't I at least try to do the same?

"That's fine, Ella." I whispered the words softly so I wouldn't wake her. "I'll … I'll love you, too."

Chapter 12

"Twins. You're too large to just have one in there, my dear. It must be twins."

"What?" My brain was foggy from exhaustion. I'd been up most of the night with labor pains, and now I lay in the big bed upstairs on a pile of extra linens, gaping like a fool at the midwife Gregor had hired.

"Two babies." She enunciated the words slowly, and I glared at her. I knew what twins meant. I just didn't— I couldn't— How did she expect me to do this?

Then the labor pains made me groan, overtaking me in waves, each one worse than the last. How could I possibly survive this? Twins? How could I deliver one baby, much less two? Or care for them all by myself? She had to be mistaken.

The midwife held my hand. "Breathe," she said again. I wanted to slap her, but I huffed out an annoyed breath. "There you go. That's it. Again. Relax, and breathe. You can't fight this, Zel, is it? You can't fight it. These babies need to come out. So just relax."

Darien. Now he would be a proper target for my anger. How could he have done this to me? He'd promised to be with me. And instead, he'd— He'd—

Another wave of pain overtook me. I didn't know what

infuriated me more. That he'd given me a baby—no, twins!—and then died, leaving me to do this on my own? Or that he'd died for me, for us, in the ultimate act of love, and now we'd have to spend the rest of our lives without him and without his love? How could he? How could he!

It could have been minutes or hours. I thought of nothing but the babies Darien and I had brought in to the world. And then, when I was more exhausted than I'd ever thought possible, the midwife placed a squalling, red-faced baby at my breast. I stared down in surprise. My … my baby.

"They're both girls," said the midwife. "Two strong, healthy girls. Congratulations, honey."

"But … where is the other one?" Panic scrambled through me.

"Oh, she's right here." She gestured to the squirmy bundle in her arms. "It's best you feed them one at a time, at least at first."

Ella's sweet, concerned gaze flitted from me, to one baby, then the other, and back to me, as though she didn't quite know where to settle.

I looked down at the baby girl who nursed earnestly at my breast, her face screwed up in determination, for all the world like she would never let go. How had I gone from being a monster, a killer, locked alone in a tower, to a … a mother? I gripped the baby's warm, tiny body a little tighter. It was too much. Too perfect. I didn't deserve this.

When I'd nursed both babies and learned to wrap them up properly, the midwife set them beside me in two small bassinettes—once again, no doubt, procured by Gregor. The babies slept, their perfect eyes shut in little half-moons, their mouths occasionally making sucking motions even in their sleep. I couldn't bring myself to look away, tired though I was, and neither could Ella. She perched on the bed beside me, staring at the babies with an awestruck look on her face.

The midwife gathered her things. "Before the plague, I'd have to fill out certificates for each baby. But as you know, things are a bit chaotic out there now. I could fill out certificates if I could find the forms, but I wouldn't be able to find anyone to take them." She shrugged. "You can still name your babies now, if you like."

Oh! Names! I hadn't even thought of them yet. I was still shocked I'd made it all the way to this point, with two healthy babies sleeping beside me. "Names? I …"

Ella gaped at me. "They already have names?"

"Well …" I bit my lip and appraised the babies. The baby on the left, the first baby I'd held, had golden skin and hair and delicate pink lips. Her mouth made a fierce sucking motion again in her sleep, and Ella giggled. I thought of the colorful flowers that Belen had said grew wild and stubborn among thickets of thorns in the Badlands in the spring and summer. Perhaps she would be strong, like they were. She would need to be. They both would. "Her name is Briar Rose."

Ella shifted. "That's a weird name."

I laughed, and the midwife smiled at me, her eyes crinkling. "It's a strong name is what it is," said the midwife, nudging Ella. "She's strong enough to grow anywhere. Right, Zel?"

"Right." I stroked the second baby's soft, smooth hair. Her face was utterly peaceful in sleep. Her skin was pale and flawless, her lips rosy red, and her hair dark as night. The black fringe of her long eyelashes stood out on her cheeks, a stark contrast to her light skin.

One evening, when I'd first arrived in Asylia, Ella's father had shared with me his favorite book, a translated encyclopedia of natural wonders written by a Western explorer who had been among the first Westerners to make contact with our isolated walled cities here in Theros. I'd pored over the book by the light of the luminous long after he and Ella had gone to bed that night.

One place had stood out over the rest—a mountain called Alba's Peak, covered with snow year-round, that offered unparalleled views of the rising sun. The peace and perfection of that far-off place had called to me as I'd hunched over the book at the kitchen table, mourning Darien, worrying about the future. I'd fallen asleep that night thinking of dawn sunlight glistening off sparkling snow. And now, looking at my sweet, bright-skinned baby girl, I felt the same peace.

"Alba," I said. "Her name is Alba."

Chapter 13

"The queen passed away." Ella lowered the newspaper she was holding, her beautiful face serious and concerned. We sat together at the kitchen table, sipping lukewarm water and sweating even so early in the morning. Summer in Asylia was a force to be reckoned with. The twins were still sound asleep, thankfully, and Ella and I had stolen downstairs for a quiet morning without them.

"Last night?"

Ella turned the paper toward me, and I craned my head to read it. After three years of plague with no cure, we'd lost a fifth of the city's population, yet still, the deaths kept coming. Queen Cassia had taken ill three days earlier. What would the king do now? His sanity had been in question for years before the plague. My hands shook, and I hid them in my lap.

Asylia's government still existed, but some days, the city seemed to be held together by threads. If they stopped providing victus for food, what would we do? There was no way to sneak in or out of the city. Not for the living, anyway. These days, they only opened the gates to remove the dead.

I leaned back in my chair, took another sip of water from my glass, and set it back on the worn wooden table. Coffee was a distant memory. We were on the verge of running out of victus, but I could not bring myself to leave Ella and the girls alone again.

This morning, there had only been a fine gray powder in the victus canister. I had to go out. I couldn't put it off any longer.

"I better find some mourning garments, then. And go to the market before it gets any later. The line will be down the block already."

Ella nodded solemnly. "Look in my mother's chest. There should be something dark in there."

"Thank you." Ella, my sweet, dedicated, determined helper. I could always count on her to watch the girls for me or to help with the chores—whatever needed doing, she did without complaint. In the past three years, she seemed to have aged ten.

As always, when I thought such things, I couldn't look directly at her. My hot skin grew itchy and I shifted uncomfortably in my seat. We'd survived for three years. That was something, wasn't it? Since her father had passed away, I'd cared for her as if she were one of my own daughters. I taught her to read and write and do sums. We shared countless, companionable meals together. We played together with the twins as they grew from squalling babies into fierce, strong-willed toddlers. Everyone else in the Merchant Quarter survived on victus and water these days, just like us. She would have no easier life with a different family. Would she?

No matter how many times I tried to persuade myself of that fact, I could never quite shake the feeling that I'd stolen Ella's childhood by relying so much on her help.

Ella acknowledged me with a nod and went back to the newspaper. When was the last time she'd smiled or laughed? What kind of child was content to be a helper, a worker, and had no flights of fancy or playful times of her own?

As a child trapped in my tower, I'd reveled in stories of the dreamy, frivolous world of Butterflower and her friends in the seaside city of Lerenia, but Ella had no escape from our prison here. Someday, I vowed to myself, that would have to change.

~

The morning sun beat down on the dirty, garbage-strewn street. I came upon the end of the line for victus three blocks from the nearest market in the Merchant Quarter. Not a good sign.

I bit my lip as I appraised the people waiting in line. Their bodies sagged and they fanned themselves listlessly in the overwhelming heat. From the look of things, they'd already been here for hours. I'd have to try a different market. Perhaps I'd have more luck at a smaller market in the Common Quarter.

I pulled Ella's mother's hat further down over my head to shade my face in the hot sun as I made my way through the Merchant Quarter to the Common Quarter boundary.

At first, I was disoriented. I'd only been to the Common Quarter a few times since coming to Asylia three years ago. Eventually, I realized the streams of people weaving their way through the narrow, crooked streets must be heading to the nearest market, so I simply followed the crowds.

The Common Quarter had more shade than the Merchant Quarter. The buildings were taller, for one thing. I peered up at one cluster of towering stone apartments as I passed. The buildings stretched crookedly up toward the bright, summer sky, as though each subsequent level had been thrown there haphazardly by a mover mage who had gone onto the next task. The Common Quarter was far more crowded than our quarter. They probably needed more housing and were likely happy to take whatever they could get.

I found the end of the victus line. The market entrance was still visible down the street, so the queue had to be shorter than the line at our own market, and it was actually moving. I shrugged and took my place. I had to get victus and get home before the girls woke up. I didn't want Ella to deal with hungry toddlers by herself for too long today.

"Little scamp!"

I jumped guiltily before realizing that the woman in front of me was addressing a child, not me.

She got hold of a small girl, no older than Ella, and proceeded to tickle her until her giggles echoed on the street around us. Then she let the girl go and sent her forward. "Back to your mama, now. Hurry, scamp!" The woman laughed as the girl scurried back to her mother.

"Thank you, Silla!" The girl's mother called out with a wave from where she stood with two other children, several places ahead of us in line.

Silla laughed and patted one of the girls with her on the head. "These little ones! What would they do without us, hmm?" She smiled at me, as though expecting a response.

My mind went blank.

The girl beside her ducked away from her hand. "Aw, Ma …we just wanted to talk. We weren't gonna go play nowhere."

"Anywhere, child. It's play anywhere. And besides, everyone's got to stay with their mama in this line. That's the rule, isn't it?"

The child nodded grudgingly, and her mother ruffled her hair again. They both laughed as she ducked away a second time. "Ma!"

The woman, Silla, laughed and nudged me. "Got to keep them on their toes, don't you think? Get 'em smiling while you can. Before you know it, they'll be gangly youths who'd rather whine than smile, won't they?"

I managed to give her a jerky nod of agreement. What on earth did I know about youths besides the fact that I was one myself, not long ago?

The woman glanced around me and then gave me a knowing smile. "Ah, I see. No littles of your own yet. Just wait, my dear. Your time will come. Then you'll want all the giggles you can get out of them before they get big like this one." She nudged the skinny girl beside her, who gave me a shy grin before turning back to her younger brother.

Big like that one, huh? Ella had to be almost exactly her age, and I'd never seen Ella grin like that, much less break into peals of giggles like the girl further ahead in the line.

I gave the woman another awkward nod. What could I say in response? Actually, I have three little ones at home, and they barely smile, much less giggle or laugh? My eight-year-old would rather read the newspaper than a children's book, and my twin toddlers think a big bowl of victus is a special treat? My face flushed, and I twisted my braid around my fingers.

After a moment of my silence, the woman shrugged and turned back toward the front of the line.

Good. I didn't want to make conversation with someone who was obviously providing a better life for her children, though we lived in the same city with the same dry victus rations every day. I didn't need reminders of how much I'd done wrong.

I got one thing right this morning—I'd failed Ella. I had to change things at home. We couldn't keep living like this. Perhaps, when I got back, I could plan some sort of special game. I couldn't take them on an outing and risk getting caught by trackers. Maybe I could … well, I'd think of something, something that would make Ella laugh.

The line moved again, and I breathed a sigh of relief. Several minutes later, I was beneath the meager shaded canopy of the victus stand where a bored government worker watched me fill my canister with coarse, gray victus powder. I was nearly done filling it when I realized the market had quieted.

I covered the canister, my fingers fumbling with the lid, as three men in black uniforms came through the entrance to the market. Flashes of gold shone on their arms, sparkling in the morning sun.

Tracker mages, here at the market. They must have caught my trace and followed me here.

I clutched the canister of victus to my chest. What would Ella and the girls do without me? I'd never make it home again.

I braced myself for assault, but the trackers hovered at the entrance to the market. Had they lost my trail? Or were they afraid to approach me?

Perhaps they already knew what I was. A sick feeling came over me at the thought, but I shook it off. If they didn't know it was me emitting the absorbent trace, I still had a chance to get away. I owed it to Ella and the twins to try.

I'd read once, in a book from Master Stone's old library, how Western scientists hypothesized that every Therosian mage was constantly either absorbing or expelling trace amounts of magic in the air around them. The change in the magic in the air left a trace everywhere they went that corresponded to their absorbent or expellant capacity, and trackers could discern their path and their mage classification before it faded away.

With an inspiration born of sheer desperation, I inhaled and held my breath, straining with all my might to stop absorbing magic from the air. Would it work? I had no idea. But what else could I do? My lungs burned as I rushed down a narrow gap between the apartment buildings and scaled a ladder to the roof.

By the time I made it to the top, I couldn't hold in my trace any longer. I fell to the roof surface in a heap and gasped for breath, and I could have sworn I felt my body absorb a bit of magic from the air around me. Perhaps the Westerners' theory was right. Too bad it was so difficult.

My straining may have stopped me from using my power to soak up tiny amounts of magic in the air around me and leaving a trail. But I had only been able to do it for a few seconds, no more than a minute. Now I was exhausted. There was no way I could hold in my trace all the way home.

I lay on the roof in the hot morning sun, sweating profusely, the can of victus tucked under my arm. I had to get back soon. My girls had no one but me. I had to get back.

There was a painfully slim chance of that happening. Shouts rang upward from the market below.

I rolled over from where I'd collapsed on the roof and cowered in the narrow strip of shade at the building's edge where a low wall formed a modest barrier between me and the multi-story drop. I didn't dare peek over and risk being seen, but I strained my ears to hear if anyone was coming my way.

The shouts from below grew louder. More trackers must have joined the others. A whistle echoed off the side of the building as the Quarter Guards arrived. They must have figured out exactly what I was. How did they plan to subdue me? Or did they simply plan to kill me?

I shivered despite the heat on the roof. I'd been free for over three years now, and I'd grown complacent, especially with the city in chaos from the plague. I should have known better than to venture out. I should have found another way.

It was too late for regrets now. I'd have to get through this first. Then I'd have the rest of my life to reflect on my failures, however short that life might be.

~

I stayed in the small strip of shade until it dwindled and disappeared in the midday heat. The sun moved directly overhead, scorching my pale skin as the hours passed.

Still, the guards and trackers remained at the market below me. Why wouldn't they give up and leave? As soon as the thought struck, I grimaced at my own foolishness and shook my head. They knew what I was—what a monster I was—which meant they couldn't give up. They couldn't let me roam free in the city. No doubt King Anton himself had already been interrupted in his mourning and informed of my appearance in the Common Quarter market. The guards and trackers wouldn't leave. They couldn't.

That meant it was up to me to leave.

I finally peeled myself off the low wall at the edge of the roof, my sweat-soaked dress sticking to my skin, and scrabbled as quietly as I could across the roof to the other side of the building. No luck. Across the street, black Quarter Guard fomewagons were parked everywhere, and men in various uniforms paced back and forth as though they expected me to walk right down the main street.

I leaned away from the edge. Were the Sentinels among them? If only Darien was here like he'd promised to be. If only I could go down, fling myself into his arms, and trust him to make everything work out. But he wasn't. He was dead. Once again, I'd have to figure this one out on my own.

I stayed low against the roof and half-slid, half-crawled to the next side. This one appeared more promising. The gap between the buildings was narrow, like the one I'd entered on the other side to scale the building. I could most likely make the jump. At least I could have, back when I'd been training my body daily, back before I'd birthed twins and spent three years cooped up in a bakery's upper room, sedentary and useless.

I squeezed the fist of one hand so hard my nails bit into my palm. Why had I allowed myself to grow soft and complacent when I had three little girls depending on me to be strong? I'd been so concerned about staying sane in that upper room that I'd forgotten I had to be ready for anything. Idiot. Fool. Now I'd lose everything for my negligence.

I inhaled again, straining once more to rein in my power and stop it from leaving a trace. Then, before I could give in to fear, I took a running leap and dove across the gap between the buildings. I rolled as I landed, collapsed, and gasped for breath, straining to hear any sign they might have heard or seen my leap. Nothing. The sounds of trackers and guards in the streets hadn't changed at all. I might stand a chance, after all. Now I just had to figure out how to get home.

The sun was close to setting, and the street was shrouded in shade by the time I set eyes on our crooked, dirty lane. My body shook from the effort of simply standing. Each vault from rooftop to rooftop could be a jump to my death instead. I couldn't hold in my trace anymore, not even for the brief seconds it took to cross buildings. I was too exhausted. And I couldn't risk descending to the street. The trackers and guards hadn't followed me to the Merchant Quarter, but I had no doubt they'd be combing the city for me soon. I had to get to the bakery without leaving a trace for them to find, and at least if I stuck to the rooftops, I had a chance.

I lunged across another gap and fell hard on my knees on the next roof. Just three more, and I'd be with my girls again. I had to find the strength.

I dragged myself across the roof, threw myself across the next gap and then the next. I crashed in the middle of the bakery roof, and my head hit the ground hard. I shoved myself up and staggered to the door. I flung it open and rushed down the stairs, feeling drunk on the heat and exhaustion.

Home. I was home. I was already at the bottom of the stairs before I considered what a fright I must look.

Ella was in the room, playing with Bri and Alba. When I descended the stairs, the twins dove at me, wrapping their little arms around my legs and crying, too upset to voice distinct words of complaint. Ella watched me from where she stood, wary and still. Did she know how much I had failed her? How much I would destroy her life? Those green eyes saw too much.

A hoarse tightness closed my throat. I had to do this now. The trackers would be coming to the Merchant Quarter any moment. It was a miracle they weren't on our lane now. If they caught any trace of me in the bakery, it would be over.

"Ella." I pushed the horrible words out even as guilt smothered me and the skittish look in Ella's eyes grew more pronounced. "Downstairs. Now. I want you to clean the whole kitchen and the shop. The stairs to the living quarters, too. Every inch of it, with liquid expurgo and a brush. Scrub it well, do you hear me? And don't come upstairs until you're done."

Could she tell how frightened I was? Could she imagine what danger we faced? Did she know that it was all my fault, that I never should have come into her life, that I should have found a way to survive on my own? It was too late now. We were here, and with trackers hunting for me, we couldn't leave any time soon.

Ella waited another moment, and then she turned and went downstairs. Tears drenched my face as Bri and Alba wailed and yanked at my skirt. Oh, Ella … always helpful and obedient. Always paying the price for my power, for my secret.

I'd make it up to her someday. I had to.

~

"We're out of victus again." Ella's quiet voice floated up the stairs to the bakery's living quarters.

"Completely out?" If there was enough left for the twins and Ella, perhaps I could—

"Completely out."

I paused in the middle of brushing Alba's messy, dark hair. I'd been dreading this moment ever since I'd come back from the market in the Common Quarter two weeks ago. "Well …"

Could I truly send Ella into the city alone to get victus? The very thought made me cringe. Asylia was nowhere as chaotic as Draicia, but how safe could it really be for an innocent girl like Ella?

What choice did I have? Trackers roamed the streets of the Merchant Quarter every day. I observed them from the roof of the bakery, unable to keep myself from staring death in the face. The trackers had already inspected the bakery shop downstairs, but thankfully they had given Ella only a cursory glance and left. I hoped that would be enough, but what if they came back to our lane?

Alba fidgeted, and I forced myself to keep brushing her hair. "Do you know where the nearest market is, El?" I tried to keep my voice calm, as though I didn't much care about the answer.

"Yes … I think so," came her soft reply.

"Please go there now and fill our canister. We need victus for breakfast." I busied my fingers weaving Alba's hair into a short braid and used my shoulder to wipe the single tear that rolled down my cheek. *You're a monster. A thing of pure evil.* I hadn't felt the truth of that woman's words so fully in years. They'd been true in Draicia, and they were true in Asylia.

I might have escaped the Wasp, but I'd never escape myself.

"I will," Ella said. There was a quiet thud as the bakery door shut. She must have already dressed for the market, anticipating what I would require of her.

I told her the truth after the trackers descended on our lane. She took the news in stride, in typical Ella fashion, by simply accepting the truth and asking what I wanted her to do. I'd never forget the sight of her trusting young face watching me, far too serious for her age, utterly resigned to her fate.

At my instruction, she told the trackers that she ran the bakery for her stepmother who was upstairs having a rest. I hid on the roof with the twins and heard their conversation through the bakery door, still open to the street. No doubt the trackers took one look at Ella's thin, hunched shoulders and callused hands and decided her sad tale of neglect was more likely than the truth, that a Draician killer was hiding upstairs. *Monster.*

I finished Alba's hair and squeezed her in a tight hug. "I love you," I whispered.

"Mama!" She wriggled out of my arms and ran across

the room to Bri, who was playing with a tattered rag doll I'd made from their old clothes.

I stood, rubbed my temples, and smoothed the loose tendrils escaping my braid so they were tucked behind my ears. Time to get to work. I lifted one edge of the large table in the center of our room and dragged it with a screech until it was flush against the wall. The girls ignored me, already used to my routine after the past two weeks of training.

I changed from my faded yellow house dress into a pair of hemmed pants and an old shirt from Master Stone's wardrobe. They were loose but easier to move in than my dress.

I launched into my old warm-up routine. My body protested every move. Two weeks of practice had only succeeded in bruising every muscle in my body. When would I ever recover the strength I used to count on? Was it even possible to regain it? If only I hadn't neglected my training the past three years. But I couldn't change the past. All I could do was try to be better now, to be strong enough to protect Ella and the girls, and to keep myself out of the hands of Asylia's trackers.

When I was ready, I began with a new set of exercises, the ones Darien had showed me to increase my strength before he left. My rooftop journey had shown me the painful truth that I was nowhere near strong enough to survive on my own in a city full of trackers. I only hoped his exercises would work.

I did the exercises to strengthen my legs first, holding a pile of books to make them more of a challenge. My legs burned, and I gasped for breath. Then I switched to exercises for my arms which were far harder. I could barely complete the exercises without collapsing, and I didn't even add any weight. As I finished the last exercise, my arms shook and gave out beneath me. I landed on the floor with a thud and groaned before rolling onto my back. Perhaps next week would be better.

I hauled myself off the floor and launched into the

sprinting practice Darien had taught me. My lungs burned. How could I possibly—

"Mine! It's my dolly!" There was a loud smack, and Alba wailed. I stopped running. Bri and Alba tugged on the doll, precariously close to falling off Bri's bed. Alba's face was bright red, and Bri's mouth was set in a determined line.

"Alba—" I panted from the exertion of my sprints. "Go get your own doll, sweetie."

Alba gave me a watery-eyed glare. "No."

Of course, she only wanted her sister's doll. Just how had we survived this long in the bakery's upper room? And what would we do when they got older?

Bri took advantage of Alba's distraction and yanked the doll from her grip, leapt off the bed, and raced to the other side of the room. "It's mine!" She huddled protectively over the doll and sent Alba a fierce scowl.

Stay calm. Stay calm. Stay calm. "Alba, where's your doll, honey? You can play with your own doll. You don't need Bri's."

Instead of answering, she let out a war cry, raced across the room, and tackled Bri to the ground.

I heaved a sigh and pulled the two screaming toddlers apart. Then I sank to the ground and knelt beside them. Tears streamed down Alba's red face, and her chest heaved. Bri clutched the doll to her chest and glared at me, silent and furious. What was I supposed to do with these two angry little girls, trapped in a stifling hot room while trackers roamed the streets not two blocks away?

"How would you like to learn something new?"

Alba narrowed her eyes. Bri's glare softened slightly.

I clapped my hands together and injected as much excitement as I could into my voice. "Want to learn how to do what mommy is doing?"

"Run like mommy?" Bri pursed her little lips. "Yes."

"No." Alba wiped at her snot-covered upper lip, her tantrum forgotten. "No run."

I smiled. "Up to you, dear." If there was one thing I

could count on, it was that Alba always wanted to do what her sister was doing.

"Let's begin, sweet girls. Over here!"

I led them both to the edge of the room, Alba's disagreement already forgotten, and showed them how to run from one side to the other, stopping to pick up or put down a book at each corner. We took turns and cheered each other on, and soon they were both grinning from ear to ear. For each burst across the room that they took, I took four. By the time they lost interest in the activity, I was exhausted but laughing. We'd made it.

Then I heard Ella's voice. "Zel? What's going on?"

I peeked my head through the door. Ella stood halfway up the stairs, holding the canister of victus. "You're back." I smoothed back my hair, still smiling from Alba's and Bri's antics. When I took in the hurt on Ella's face, my smile faded. "Are you well? How was the market?"

"Fine." Her voice was painfully quiet. "I got the victus."

"Thank you, El. I'll be right back." I darted back into the room and grabbed the spare canister of victus we'd reserved for upstairs use. Everything had to be separated now. We couldn't take the risk that my trace would leak onto anything that went downstairs.

I returned to the stairs and descended one step, then held the canister out to Ella. She climbed close enough to pour victus from her canister into mine, her focus on the stairs, the wall … anywhere but my face.

The guilt I'd forgotten during the morning's exercise routine came back a hundred-fold, so heavy it threatened to crush me. "El …"

What could I possibly say to make this better? She'd lost her mother, her father … and now me and the girls. But what could I do? Perhaps Gregor would take her in.

I wracked my brain for other ideas. I'd distracted the twins by involving them in my routine and teaching them something new. Would the same tactic work with Ella? She was smart enough to see through me, but she might not care.

"Did you pick up today's *Herald*?"

Ella nodded, her attention fixed on the lid of the victus canister as she twisted it back on. "Would you like it?"

"I was thinking we could read it together."

She met my eyes at last, shock on her solemn face. "But I thought—"

"I can't come downstairs, but I could sit here, and you could sit there, and we could read it together. Just give me each section when you finish it. We can read while we have our victus."

A slow, bright smile spread across Ella's face as I spoke. "I'll go get it."

For the next hour, I ignored the twins as they ran wild in the upper room. I leaned my back against the wall of the staircase and picked through the *Herald* with Ella.

Her sharp mind never ceased to amaze me. She read the newspaper like a grown adult and knew nearly all the words she encountered. The only things she struggled to understand were the people in the articles and the decisions they made.

Why did the Transportation Ministry change the regulation on trolleys? Why did Asylia have four quarters, and what determined which quarter we lived in?

I answered as best I could. When we finally finished the paper, I was halfway convinced that one day at a time, we'd survive this.

If I could just give Ella and the twins what they needed, if I could just love them enough, if I could just be strong enough, then perhaps we would survive after all.

Chapter 14

"Mama! Bri's doing it again!"

I set down the newspaper. "Doing what?"

"Mama! I *told* you already! She's doing that-that-that thing!" Alba stormed across the room and stood before me with folded arms. Eight years old going on eighteen. Why couldn't they stay small just a little bit longer?

"I'm not doing anything!" Bri stomped over and stood scowling beside Alba. "She's tattling, and I didn't even do anything. She should be in trouble, not me."

I took a deep breath. "Girls. No one is in trouble. Yet. Alba, please tell me—again—what you think Bri is doing."

"I don't think. I *know*. She's doing that thing where she gives me a headache." Alba's nostrils flared. "She is!"

"And how is she giving you a headache?"

Bri rolled her eyes. "I told you, I'm not doing anything."

"Every time she touches me, I get a headache! I'm not lying!"

My stomach sank. So, this was it. They'd lasted longer than I'd expected. I held out my hand to Bri. "Show me, Bri."

Bri rolled her eyes again, but then she grabbed my hand. A headache came over me immediately, and I yawned and leaned back in my chair. She pulled her hand away. "See?

I'm not doing anything."

The headache throbbed. "Not quite." Foreboding soured my stomach, but I addressed Alba anyway. "Alba, did your headache go away already?"

Alba nodded. "Yes. As soon as she let go."

I held out my hand to Alba. "Make my headache go away."

She didn't even argue. She simply pressed her hand into mine, and the headache disappeared. "Oh!" Her eyebrows shot up. "How did I do that? How did I— What did I do, Mama?"

Bri's shoulders hunched up. "I truly gave you a headache, Mama?"

"Oh, girls …" I pulled them into my arms, and they clung to me. "It's—"

"Zel! Alba! Bri! Guess what!" We broke apart as Ella's excited voice drifted up the stairs. "The letter just came in the post. I got it! I got the scholarship! I can't believe it!"

I let out a whoop and rushed down the stairs. "You did it, El! You did it! I knew you would!"

Ella met me on the stairs and threw her arms around my waist. I held her tight and breathed in the scent of cinderslick and winterdrops. It had taken a few years of training, but I'd perfected the art of holding my charge for these brief, comforting touches so I didn't leave any hint of my trace on her skin or clothes. I'd never have to force Ella back to those painful days of isolation again.

"I just— I can't believe it. The Royal Academy." She spoke the words with hushed reverence.

I gave her a squeeze, leaned back, and grinned. "I knew it. You're smarter than any of those Procus students. Much smarter. You'll be working your way to the top of the Commerce Ministry before we know it."

Ella flushed and grinned widely. "The next term starts in a week. I'll need to finish the baking by the first hour after dawn at the latest and arrange to do our deliveries before school in the morning. I'll have to take the trolley all the way to the Procus Quarter. Can you imagine? The *Procus* Quarter?"

Alba leaned around me. "What if you meet a young, handsome Procus lord, and he sweeps you off your feet and—"

"That's enough, Alba. Ella's going to the Royal Academy to study, not to find romance."

Ella nodded solemnly, but I still caught the wink she shot Alba. *Oh, dear.*

"The only thing is, the scholarship paper says it doesn't cover any of the extra costs associated with the school. What do you suppose that means?" Ella's smile faded

I ruffled her hair. It was too soon for that bright smile to disappear already. "Probably uniforms and such. Don't worry, El. We'll figure it out. Just think, in a week's time, you'll be sitting in your very first class at the Royal Academy! You did it, Ella!"

Her smile returned, and we all went downstairs for a midday meal of victus and water.

After a year of searching, the trackers finally left the Merchant Quarter alone. Though the trackers' ranks had been built up since the plague decimated the original number, they didn't seem to be searching for me anymore, and it was rare for any trackers to find their way to our narrow lane in the Merchant Quarter.

The absence of trackers in the Merchant Quarter meant we could all spend time downstairs, which significantly helped my sanity. I did my best to hold in my charge on the lower floor. Hopefully, if a tracker ever happened to enter the kitchen, the hints of my trace would be too light to tell what kind of mage I was. Besides, we would all lose our minds if we had to go back to the austerity of that first horrible year after the market incident.

"Girls, I think it's time for an announcement."

Ella set her spoon in her bowl with a clank, no doubt wary of the hard tone of my voice.

I straightened my spine and attempted a smile. "Alba,

Bri … listen, please."

The twins fell silent, Bri with a guilty look on her face. Perhaps she was still upset about giving us headaches. Well, that was just the beginning.

"This morning …" How could I say this without frightening them? Best to get the words out quickly. "Bri and Alba are mages."

Bri's shoulders hunched up even further, but Alba smiled widely.

"Bri, you're absorbent. I'm no expert, but you're certainly not as absorbent as I am—perhaps in Asylia, some might consider training you to be a tracker or a purifier."

Bri crossed her arms and leaned back. "That's dumb."

I let it slide. "Alba, you're expellant. You healed me quickly this morning, and every time Bri's power gave you a headache, you healed yourself instantly. That means you're expellant enough to be a healer, with the right medical training, of course."

Alba beamed. "What does that mean? Are we supposed to go to learn to be mages now, like Ella is going to the Royal Academy?"

Ella shifted in her chair and flicked a glance at me.

"Not now, no."

"Why not?" Alba leaned forward. "I want to!"

Bri's chair screeched on the floor as she scooted back from the table and stood. "May I be excused?"

"Not yet. Sit down, honey."

Bri flopped back into her chair.

"Alba, you can't go to the Mage Academy because if the trackers ever catch you outside the bakery, they'll want to know who you are and where you've been living. And then they'll find me."

Alba cocked her head. "Mama … honestly, what's so bad about that? I hate having to stay here all the time. Couldn't we just be regular mages and go to school like everyone else?" She shifted in her seat and sneaked a glance at Ella. "Sorry, El. It's not that I don't want to be with you, it's just …"

Ella sent her a half smile. "I understand."

I straightened my spine and tried for a calm smile. "I know, honey. I wish we could all leave too. But … do you remember how I said that I'm more absorbent than Bri?"

Bri straightened in her chair, and Alba nodded slowly.

"We've been staying home in the bakery, not just because I'm a mage, but because of my *kind* of mage. I'm too absorbent. My power is dangerous. If someone else had control of me, they could use me like a weapon. Innocent people might get hurt, and we can't risk that happening." I wiped at a sudden, strange tear that made its way down my cheek. "Not ever."

Bri frowned, and Alba tightened her lips. They both nodded.

"You can go upstairs now, girls. We can discuss this more another time."

They both left in a clatter of dishes and spoons, and soon, only Ella and I remained at the table. Another tear dribbled down my cheek. My poor daughters. Just like Ella, they'd pay the price for my monstrous nature, and now they knew it. I wiped away the tear with my sleeve as Ella's gentle hand settled on my shoulder.

"They'll be fine," Ella said. "We have a good life here. We have the bakery, plenty of victus to eat, and we have each other. And maybe one day, it will get even better. With me going to the Royal Academy, who knows? Anything could happen now!"

Chapter 15

There was a loud thump, like the sound of a book hitting the wall.

"You— You— I hate you! I *hate* you!"

"You hate me? Ha! I hate you! You're the worst sister I could ever—"

"Girls!" They ignored me, so I marched down the stairs from the roof and stepped between them as they screamed at each other. "Alba. Bri. Get yourselves under control. Now!"

They fell silent.

I didn't bother to ask what was going on. It didn't matter. They'd been fighting like this for days. I doubted either of them remembered what the original fight was about anyway. We were only a week into Ella's third year at the Royal Academy, and the girls had unleashed a furious storm upon each other the moment she left for school. Who knew ten-year-old girls could be so vicious? Weren't they still little children?

Then again, they weren't exactly typical children. Bri leaned round me and grabbed Alba's fingers.

Alba ripped them away. "Ouch! Mom, she did it again!"

Bri leaned back on her heels, folded her arms, and smirked. "And she already healed herself, so no harm done."

I took a deep breath. This couldn't continue. We would never survive like this. But what could I possibly do to fix it? "I've had enough, girls. Bri, take your books and your notes and go up on the roof. You may not come down again until bedtime. You've been bullying your sister and using your power to harm her, and I have told you far too many times, that is unacceptable. If you do it one more time, you'll be sleeping on the roof tonight. Understand?"

Bri's face fell. "Sorry, Mom."

"I think you mean, 'Sorry, Alba.'"

Bri scooped up her books from the table and stomped to the stairs. When she was halfway up the stairs, she paused and turned around. "Sorry, Alba," she muttered under her breath.

Alba sniffed and crossed her arms.

When Bri had shut the door to the roof, I said to Alba, "I'm guessing you had something to do with what happened too."

"What? I—" She broke off and sighed without bothering to make up a lie. Alba wasn't the world's best liar, and unlike Bri, she knew when she'd lost.

"Get back to your studies. You'll be reciting the entire first passage of *Altair's History of Mages* at breakfast tomorrow, so you'd better get started memorizing it. And if I catch you antagonizing Bri again, you're both spending the night on the roof." Maybe it wasn't the best idea to lock them away together, but it would hopefully motivate Alba to leave her sister alone.

Alba flounced to the table and sat down in front of her history book with a huff.

When her nose was buried in her book, I went to my vanity and pulled my journal from the drawer. If I didn't find an outlet soon, my frustration was going to erupt through my ears.

I can't do this. I can't! How can I possibly be expected to ...?

This is impossible. It is. No one can do this. Least of all me. Why did I ever ...?

How have we survived so long in this miserable state? Ten years. Ten years! Ten years, and I'm not going to make it a single day more. We can't do this. We can't. It's too...

I just don't understand. I love them. I know they love each other, somewhere deep down. And we have Ella looking out for us. But it's still not enough. They're tearing each other apart.

We can't stay here. We're going mad. We simply can't stay. But what else can we do? As long as I'm with them, they'll always have to worry about getting caught by trackers.

I stopped writing and let out a breath. My fingers traced the words I'd just written, dread seeping into my bones. *As long as I'm with them.* Bri and Alba weren't the problem. I was. They were stuck in this bakery because of me. As long as I was with them, they'd never have a normal life. Not ever.

I'd hoped by this point a new path would have appeared. Where had I gotten such foolish optimism? Darien had appeared at my tower window in Draicia just when I'd needed him the most, but there was no more Darien, no handsome guard coming to help me escape and promising to whisk me off to a better place. It was just me, Ella, and two miserable girls, and as long as they had me, they'd never be safe.

I put my pencil to the page. *I need a new plan. A better plan. Because this one isn't working.* I didn't stop writing until I'd filled the next ten pages, and by then, the light had dimmed so much Alba went to turn up the luminous. I brought a bowl of victus to Bri on the roof, then shared a grim, quiet dinner with Ella and Alba before I went back to my journal. *They have to learn to survive without me. It's the only way they'll have a chance.*

PART III

Chapter 16

The night sky was crisp but dry. A cool wind whistled along the rooftop, and I shivered, pulling my thick sweater tighter around my body. It was cold, but it wasn't raining. That was all that mattered. That was why I'd chosen tonight. I had to remember that instead of agonizing over how I'd sent two helpless, naïve, eleven-year-old girls out in the cold city streets all alone.

The air smelled of dirt and old garbage. A loose cobblestone clattered somewhere in the street below me, and I jumped. I strained my eyes, but there was no sign of Bri or Alba on any of the surrounding rooftops. It wouldn't be long before dawn. Had I made a horrible mistake?

A dark shape moved on the roof of the next building over. Was it—

"Mom!" Bri whispered, but in the quiet night, I could hear her loud and clear.

I rushed to the edge of the roof and peered into the night. Bri huddled on the other side of the narrow gap between our building and our next-door neighbor's carpentry shop.

"Alba's gone. I lost her. I thought she was right behind me, and then I couldn't … she was just … she's gone!" Bri's voice crept up an octave.

"Come over here." I stepped to the side to make more room for her landing. "Now, Bri." She was growing hysterical. I had to stay calm. We'd find Alba if I had to hunt through the city myself.

Bri hurtled her body across the gap and landed gracefully beside me. Unlike Alba, she'd taken to the rooftops with the grace of the big, wild cats that stalked the Badlands. Some nights, she seemed to enjoy the freedom of the city's rooftops a little too much. How much longer would I be able to hold her to the bakery? It wouldn't be long before we'd have to put my plan into action—no more practice runs.

There was a thud, and Bri and I whirled around. Alba crashed to her knees on the other side of the roof and knocked over a rusty chair when she attempted to stabilize her landing. The loud clank made us tense, and I crossed the roof to her as silently as possible. I placed a hand on her shoulder. In the dim light, with no luminous streetlamps on our lane, I couldn't make out her face. "Are you well?" I breathed.

She nodded.

Bri appeared at my side. "Why did you leave me? Alba, I thought— I was so worried."

Alba stood and wiped the dirt from her knees. "I just got turned around, Bri. It's fine. Don't worry about me."

I hustled them downstairs. "Get cleaned up. Quietly, now. Don't you dare wake Ella. Then I'll receive your reports."

Alba yawned and rubbed her eyes. "Mom, can't we just do that in the morning?"

"No. If you can't handle missing a few hours of sleep …"

"Then how can we be expected to survive on our own?" Alba finished my sentence with an annoyed whisper. "I know, I know. Fine."

When the girls were in their nightgowns and ready for bed, I called them to the large table we used for meals and schoolwork upstairs. "Bri first."

Bri held up a tattered canvas bag, then poured its contents unceremoniously onto the table. "*The Well-Trained Tracker*, from the Mage Academy Library. Goldblossom cutting from the Falconus family garden. And a discarded polishing rag from the Argentarius compound fomecoach garage." She waved her hand over each object with a flourish.

"I didn't tell you to take that goldblossom cutting, Bri. Those are expensive. That's stealing."

Bri jutted out her chin. "Well, I wanted proof."

"You didn't need it. Oh, forget it. Just make sure you return *The Well-Trained Tracker* to the library on your next outing. And … you did well, honey."

Bri nodded, and the corner of her mouth twisted up. She had precious little to be proud of. I had to give her something.

"Alba? Your turn."

Alba fidgeted before dumping her suspiciously limp canvas bag on the table. "I couldn't find anything. I got lost, like I said, and I was all by myself without Bri …" Her bottom lip quivered.

"Oh, sweetheart. It's fine. Next time, you'll do better." I'd pushed them too hard with this one, and she was overly tired, but I stood by my plan. If Alba couldn't handle a night alone on the city's rooftops, how would she ever be able to survive by herself once I turned myself in? Bri couldn't do everything for her.

Alba wouldn't meet my eyes. I hugged her shoulders and gave her a little shove toward her bed. "Go to sleep, and in the morning, you'll practice your scripts."

"Can't we sleep in?" Alba paused halfway to her bed and pouted.

"No. You'll be up for breakfast with Ella as usual, and I don't want to hear about it again."

I lay in my bed as the soft light of the moon filtered through the window. Bri and Alba snored softly from the opposite side of the room, tucked into their narrow beds, the thin curtains that bought them privacy doing little to muffle the sounds of sleep. I rolled to my side and faced the window. Now, it was my turn to train.

I thought back to the last time I'd been under the Wasp Queen's control—the helplessness as she'd forced me to confess about Darien. I remembered walking into the Tiger compound for the last time with her threat of death hanging over my head and the way my True Name squeezed me until no drop of willpower remained.

I imagined straining to keep my willpower, to keep my own control, even as my True Name tried to force itself on me. I envisioned the tight leash of my True Name stretching and growing brittle as my will strengthened and shoved against it, growing larger and stronger. Would my True Name snap, when I finally bucked it completely? Or would it lessen gradually and then fizzle away? What would I do if it snapped right back as soon as I let my guard down?

One thing I knew—the more I considered what the Wasp Queen had done to me, the more certain I became that no one should ever hold another's True Name.

I stretched out in my bed and snuggled deeper beneath my blanket. *Darien's warm, large body curved protectively around me, his hand resting on my arm, his lips pressed against my hair.* I tried to resist the memory, but as usual, I was too weak. I failed and gave in.

I drifted off to sleep, half convinced I was still in his arms, but then I woke while it was still dark, my pillow wet with tears. He was gone, and he wasn't coming back. Why did I insist on torturing myself with memories every night?

The next morning, we ate in the kitchen, huddled beside the oven for heat as rain pelted the small kitchen window.

Ella didn't comment on Bri's and Alba's bloodshot eyes and wide yawns during breakfast. Why would she? Ella had to be just as tired as they were. She'd no doubt gotten up to do the baking not long after they'd gone to bed.

Not much longer, Ella. Just hold on a little bit longer. As soon as the twins were ready, I'd turn myself into the Asylian authorities and trust that my nightly training would prevent them from using my True Name to control me again. Then the twins would approach the Mage Division as new mages who'd just discovered their powers and had no relation to me. Ella would be free of us. She could sell the bakery and live a happy life, and she'd never have to touch cinderslick or knead dough ever again.

I gave her a smile as she handed me the next section of the *Herald*. "Thank you."

She mustered an answering smile. "The new flour is good. Way better than the old stuff."

"The new flour?"

"You know … that Lerenian imported flour. From Gregor."

Ah. That flour. I'd been so wrapped up in preparing the twins for life outside the bakery, I'd forgotten all about the new imports that had started pouring in once the city gates opened. "Glad to hear it."

Ella buried her head in the newspaper again, and I turned to the new section. *The Rise and Fall of a Draician Killer: Drusilla, Lady of the Wasps*. I sucked in a breath and gripped the paper so hard it crumpled in my hand.

"Zel? What's wrong?" Ella's worried face came into view.

"I-I don't … I'll be upstairs. Please, enjoy breakfast." I held the newspaper section to my chest and rushed to the upstairs room. Then I grabbed my thickest sweater and headed to the roof. The small overhang by the door to the roof provided just enough shelter from the rain.

I sat on the stoop and read.

The gates are open, and news from Draicia, that shattered jewel of Theros, seeps in through the Badlands. Two-thirds of the Draician population perished due to the plague; those who remain are besotted by the addictive aurae essence and helpless against its influence. And, most fascinatingly, survivors whisper stories of an unprecedented shake-up among the ruling clans of the city. In this special investigative report, learn the dramatic story of a Draician lady's violent, bloodthirsty rise—and her sudden fall.

I skimmed through the article as fast as I could, my fist pressed against my mouth to silence the wail of fear that wanted to come out.

The story documented the Wasp clan's rise, the mysterious white dust storm that hit the Wasp territory in the middle of a clan battle, and Lady Drusilla's unlikely resurrection of an old Draician government position—the city praetor. She'd claimed the position for herself in a matter of months through a series of brutal murders. Me. Because of me, she'd risen to the top of the city's clans. And then …

The article told how after becoming praetor, she'd attempted another murder, and for the first time, she'd been stopped. She'd barely escaped with her life, making it to the edge of the city along with her maid. No one had seen or heard from either of them since. The Wolf clan leader had taken the role of Draicia's praetor for himself as soon as she disappeared.

Her name. I fixed my mind on that one, small piece. Now I knew her name. Lady Drusilla of the Wasps—Darien's murderer, my captor, and the woman who'd deliberately turned me into a monster. She was still out there.

~

"I'm but a poor orphan from the broken city of Draicia!" Alba spread her hands out dramatically and fluttered her eyelashes, her cheeks dimpling. "But I possess a healing touch. Perhaps I might be of use in your fine city?"

"You sound ridiculous." Bri slouched in her chair at the table.

"Bri! Enough commentary. But Alba … please stick to the script. Stop adding words and changing things. It sounds a bit overdramatic."

Alba pouted and held up her script. "I've just come from Draicia. I lost both of my parents in the plague, and I have no family—it's just me. I've heard that mages in Asylia are given an opportunity to serve in the government. Please, sir, give me a chance to train with the mages here." She dove to her knees and held up her hands in a pleading gesture. "Please! I beg of you!"

"Fine, fine, enough." I couldn't help but smile, but I sure hoped she wouldn't do that when the time came. For the thousandth time, I wondered if I was making a horrible mistake, entrusting something so big to girls so young. But what choice did I have?

"Do what you like until dinner. And well done, both of you. You're getting better." They were still nowhere near ready, but they were indeed better. That was something.

I went up to the roof and pulled the morning's newspaper clipping from my dress pocket. Cool wind whipped across the rooftop, sending sheets of icy rain prickling against my face, but I barely felt the cold.

I flipped to the second page of the article, which I'd missed that morning. There, buried among the small, dense paragraphs of ink-smeared text, was an etching of the Wasp's face—Lady Drusilla's face. She smirked at me from the newspaper, her lips pursed in a thin, mocking smile, her eyes sharp enough to see through me as I huddled on the roof.

She'd flicked her fingers at the thought of my baby, as though killing my child would be as easy as brushing a bit of dust off her garment. What would she do now if she knew I'd carried twin babes in my womb when I'd destroyed her ambitions?

There could be no doubt that it was me who'd caused her fall from power. I'd left her screaming on the streets of Draicia eleven years ago. According to the article, she'd fled Draicia that same year. I had enabled her reign, but at least I'd also been the one to end it.

One thing was certain—I couldn't take the twins out

into the Badlands if the Wasp was out there. We'd have to follow through with my plan to shelter the twins in Asylia's Mage Division.

A feminine screech split the air, and I swung the door open. "What is it?"

Alba's red, tear-stained face appeared at the bottom of the stairs. She inhaled sharp, hysterical breaths. "I … I … I hate her!"

Not again. I descended the stairs and fixed a patient expression onto my face as I shoved the clipping back in my pocket. "What happened this time?"

"Mom, I just told her the truth. That's all. I don't see why she's being so *overdramatic.*" Bri stuck her tongue out at her sister. Use my words against her own sister, would she? We'd just see about that.

"What did you say?"

"She … she … she said that—" Alba broke into another wail. It certainly didn't look like she was acting this time.

Alba rushed into my embrace, burying her head on my chest. "She said I'm ugly." The fabric of my dress muffled her words, but the pain in her anguished voice was undeniable. "She said I look Kireth because of my skin. And that means I'll always be ugly, and Prince Estevan will never fall in love with me."

I addressed Bri over Alba's head. "Is that true? You said that to your sister?"

Bri bit her lip as her golden cheeks flushed pink. "I just meant … Well, it's the same for me too, so I wasn't being mean! She kept going on and on about Prince Estevan, and I just told her the truth. He would never marry her. Or me, for that matter. We both know it's true! I don't know why she's crying. I've got blonde, Kireth hair, and she's got pale, Kireth skin. The prince would only marry a beautiful, Procus lady with Fenra coloring—dark skin and dark hair. And we're none of those things." She crossed her arms. "Why should I get in trouble for telling the truth? She should get in trouble for acting like a baby."

Bri stood confidently, her back straight and legs splayed as though ready for a fight, but her eyes had dark circles beneath them. She was tired. They both were.

I pulled Alba over to my bed and helped her sit down, then beckoned Bri over. Bri hesitated for a moment before she sat beside me, sagging against me and resting her head on my shoulder. Two tired, unhappy, beautiful girls. They might not fit the Fenra mold of beauty, but they were both fierce and lovely. Any man would count himself lucky to know them when they were grown, if I could ever get them out of the bakery safely. All they knew of the world was what the *Herald* told them, and it had given them a confusing, skewed image of Asylia. Most often, the society pages of the paper contained stories about the narrow-minded, Procus elite, not commoners or mages.

From my observations at the beginning of the plague, when I'd been able to go out freely in Asylia, no one but the Procus elite cared whether a person looked true Fenra.

True Fenra? I held back a snort. *Please.* A pretty girl was a pretty girl, to most men at least. I'd certainly drawn plenty of admiring looks whenever I'd ventured out of the bakery in those early years, though I'd been too heartbroken and worried about trackers to appreciate them. And Ella, despite the light-green Kireth eyes that caused her so much insecurity, had been drawing the attention of interested young men for years—not that she ever noticed.

The Procus families claimed superior bloodlines because their dark hair and skin hinted at little or no Kireth mage blood in their family line. What nonsense. Our two peoples had intermingled in Theros for a millennium, so by now, there was no telling who was a mage and who wasn't. Plenty of people who looked pure Fenra still carried Kireth blood in their veins, and vice versa.

I wanted to reassure the twins about their beauty, but I held back my words. That might have worked a few years ago, but they were getting older. This wouldn't be the first time they'd ask this question. I had to give them something stronger, an answer they could hold onto after I was gone.

"No one is in trouble. Not this time." Alba gave a soft whimper, but didn't protest any further. I squeezed each girl around the shoulders, kissing one head and then the other. I nudged Alba. "What shade is my skin? Is it pale?"

Alba placed her finger against my hand where it rested on her arm. "Yes. But not as pale as mine," she whimpered.

"And Bri, what shade is my hair?"

Bri sighed against my shoulder. "Gold. Like mine."

"Perhaps a Procus lord—or a prince—would not find me beautiful. But you know who did? Your father." I shut my eyes against the excruciating pain the words evoked. I didn't want to break down in the middle of this story. I cleared my throat and forced myself to continue. "He was strong and smart and capable. But he was also kind. He saw the way I was treated in Draicia, and he hated it. He told me he didn't want to see me trapped, and he promised to free me. But then, he fell in love with me."

Alba sighed and snuggled closer.

"He called me beautiful, and he meant it. He loved everything about me, even the things I hated. The things I was ashamed of. He didn't care whether I looked Fenra or Kireth, about the shade of my skin and hair. He loved me. Just … me. And he was beautiful to me, too."

Alba gave a snorting giggle and peeked up at me. "You mean handsome, mom."

"Well, fine. Handsome, then. But listen to my story, would you?"

Alba nodded against my shoulder.

"He risked a great deal because he loved me. He risked his life to care for me when I was hurt, and to find food for me when I had none of my own. And one day, he … he gave everything for me. He gave his very life." I paused and clenched my jaw, willing the tears not to fall. Why did his death still hurt so much, eleven years later? Would my heart never heal? "He fought my captor so I would have a chance to get away, and she—she killed him while I escaped. He loved me, and he gave his life for me. That's what it means to be beautiful, Alba. Not a certain shade of skin or hair. Not a Procus title. To love someone so much you would give your life for them—that's beautiful. And that's something that anyone can do, no matter what they look like on the outside."

Alba chewed on her lip but didn't answer.

Bri lifted her head from my shoulder. "Like Ella. Right, Mom?"

"What do you mean?"

"Ella's beautiful like that. Because she loves us, and she would do anything for us."

Guilt formed a lump in my throat. "Like Ella," I echoed, my voice hoarse. "Just like her."

That night I went back up to the roof and opened the newspaper clipping again. Lady Drusilla smirked at me from the paper. I ripped it in half, taking a perverse satisfaction in the tearing sound as her lovely, delicate face split in two. Then I ripped it again. And again. And again. She would never get the chance to come after my girls the way she'd killed Darien. I'd get them safely ensconced in the Mage Division soon, and no one would ever know they were my daughters. After that, we'd just have to see.

I'll always find you, she'd said.

Well, I'd be ready.

Chapter 17

I knelt beside our rooftop vegetable bed and placed my hand on a budding lemonburst plant. The pre-dawn sky had lightened just enough for me to see the plant's dark green leaves flutter against my hand in the spring breeze. I inhaled, and the tart, citrusy scent of the lemonburst plant seeped into my bones. I placed my other hand on the small brambleweed plant growing beside it. Time to try again.

My power awakened, pulsing with hunger to absorb the living magic in the air and plants around me. I focused on the small, delicate lemonburst plant and let my power taste the tiniest hint of its life. The plant listed slightly to the side in response as my power strained for more.

Ready—now! I unleashed my ravenous power, and at the last moment redirected it through my other hand to the weed. I gave it just long enough to gulp up the weed's imbued magic, then cut it off. I blinked. The weed was gone, leaving nothing but a cloud of dust that blew away in the light wind.

I exhaled. The lemonburst plant was fine. The plant retained its healthy green color. I'd done it.

I rocked back on my heels and allowed myself a smile. I'd never controlled my power at such a minute level before. If only I could be certain that, when the time came, I'd be able to buck my True Name's control too. I wouldn't know until it happened. Until then, I'd continue my exercises as frequently as I could.

It was time to admit the truth—we were ready.

"Mom?"

I whirled around. Bri stood behind me, pulling a dark hood off her head.

"You're back late. Any problems?"

She fiddled with the strap of the bag on her shoulder and didn't meet my eyes. "No …"

Alba thumped onto the roof beside Bri and smiled brightly. "We're back!"

"Quiet! Downstairs. Let's go. I want to know what took you so long. But don't make so much noise." I hustled downstairs to our apartment, and we gathered at the table. It was after dawn, and I put the luminous on the dimmest setting. On the ground floor, Ella clattered around the kitchen, no doubt finishing the day's baking so she could get back to studying for her final exam. I only hoped she was too caught up in her own work to wonder what we'd been up to.

"Well?"

Bri set her bag on the table without bothering to open it. "Got everything."

"And what did you observe about the River Quarter?"

"That I don't want to go there again."

"And I don't want to send you back there. But if you're going to convince the Mage Division authorities that you've been living there for nearly thirteen years, you have to have firsthand experience."

"Fine. But I don't see why Alba gets to skate by on your stories of Draicia, and I have to go research the River Quarter in real life."

I opened my mouth to continue my lecture, but she rushed forward and cut me off.

"Fine. Here's what I observed. Everyone in the River Quarter lives in these little shacks made of old junk. At first,

I thought they were all the same, because from a distance, they are all the same shape. But when I arrived, I realized each shack uses a different material. I think they scavenge from the old warehouses to build their homes. But there are some people who live in the tenements by the main River Quarter market. The tenements are really tall. Way higher than any buildings in the other quarters. I didn't go inside because there were so many people about, even in the middle of the night. I think it would be easier to just say I lived in a shack."

I pursed my lips. "Perhaps. But if living conditions are better in the tenements, that might explain any ways in which you seem different from others who grew up in the River Quarter. You'll have to investigate the inside. See if you can get a glimpse inside the door of someone's personal living quarters in a tenement building. Tomorrow night, sweetheart. We can't waste any more time. And if there are lots of people, at least they'll be less likely to realize you don't belong."

Bri sighed and scooped her bag off the table. "Fine."

"Alba? What did you learn?"

Her eyes darted to the side, and she busied herself opening the enclosure of her bag. "Well, first I found—"

"Hold on. I didn't ask what you found. I asked what you learned. What did you observe of the Mage Division?"

"It's … it's … very large and … very grand. I think it will be a wonderful place to live!" Her voice crept up an octave, and she smiled brightly.

"Alba…" What was going on? Why would neither girl meet my eyes this morning? They'd been doing so well for the past few months, each girl returning with a bag full of every assignment on my list. They were both ready. I'd be turning myself in any day now, and then they would be going to the Mage Division with their scripted stories after that. First, Bri would go, and then Alba would show up a few weeks later. At least, that was the plan. So why did I get the feeling they were lying to me?

Alba's face flushed. Bri shifted on her feet. Lying. Definitely, lying.

"Tell me what you're hiding. Sit down and tell me now, or I'll—" I didn't finish, because I didn't know what I would do if they were lying. There was no other option. They had to be ready now.

Alba gave in first. She sank into a chair, and after a long pause, Bri followed suit.

I stood before them and crossed my arms. I had to stay calm. "Well?"

"I didn't go to the Mage Division tonight." Alba's voice was small. She picked at the peeling wood on the table.

I'd gathered as much. "And where did you go instead?"

"Th-the rooftop next door."

I stilled. "What?"

"I took a nap on the roof of the building next door. Bri went to the Mage Division and completed my assignments."

I gritted my teeth. "Bri, is this true?"

She nodded, her attention devoted to a thread coming loose from the wrist of her sweater.

Then another thought hit me. "Is this the first time?"

Bri gave just the slightest shake of her head, as though her own body objected to telling me the truth.

Alba's cheeks turned bright red. "She's been getting my assignments for the past few months."

The past few months? They'd been cheating ever since I'd begun to think they were ready to survive in the city without me. How could I have been so blind?

I took a deep breath and exhaled, fighting desperately to keep my panic under wraps. "Why? Why would you do such a thing?"

Bri sat up a little straighter in her chair. "Alba can't go out in the city on her own, Mom. She's too scared. But I can do it for her. She doesn't need to do it alone. And once she's in the Mage Division, it won't matter, will it? She can move about freely and—"

"That's not the point!" I put my hands on my hips. "If

you two don't learn about life outside the bakery, no one will ever believe that you've been living a normal life up until now. They'll realize you've been in hiding, and they'll figure out that you've been with me all this time. No one can know that you're my daughters, or you'll never be safe!"

Alba's lip quivered, and Bri leaned back, her face pale.

I sighed, and my shoulders slumped as I dropped my hands at my sides. "Get some sleep. I'll see you at breakfast."

I wrapped my sweater tighter around my torso and went back to the roof. I stood at the edge of the roof as dawn turned the sky a gentle wash of pink and blue. The herby, musky scent of the garden wrapped itself around me, and I shut my eyes against the bright sky and rising sun. Exhaustion tugged at me, but there was no way I could sleep now, not after finding out they'd been lying to my face for months.

Alba was scared of the city? She was so full of laughter, warmth, and daydreams. She talked of nothing but falling in love with a handsome mage or a rich Procus lord as soon as she was at the Mage Division, although she was careful to keep her wording vague when Ella was around. Yet she was too scared to go about in the city alone? How could we possibly do this?

Perhaps I could keep the twins together. They could both claim to be from the River Quarter. They could be orphaned friends, not sisters—for they looked nothing alike—who had just discovered their mage powers recently. Bri could look out for Alba, and Alba wouldn't have to lie convincingly about Draicia after all. Was the risk too great? What if—

I shook my head at the thought. Everything was a risk. Hadn't we learned that the hard way? If they were together, Alba stood a better chance of surviving. And Bri … well, she'd brought this on herself by doing her sister's assignments for her. She'd take care of her sister.

I would turn myself in to the Asylian authorities and

claim I'd been hiding in the Badlands ever since that incident in the Common Quarter market, and when the furor died down, Bri and Alba would seek shelter at the Mage Division like new mages who had nothing to do with me. When they inevitably put me under the control of my True Name, at least I would know that my girls were safe on their own. Hopefully, after all this preparation, I would be able to retain some part of my own will this time. I had to believe it was possible.

Everything would work out. Everyone would survive. But what would I do about Ella?

"Zel? What are you doing up here already?" Ella elbowed the door to downstairs shut, her hands full with a tray of breakfast, coffee, and a small crystal vase.

I forced my lips into a smile. "Just enjoying the view this morning. Breakfast time already?"

Ella set the tray down on the rusty little table at the center of the roof. "I thought I'd make up the table with something special this morning, since it's my final exam day and all. Almost done with school! Commerce Ministry, here I come."

She grinned, but her smile looked as forced as mine felt. Dark circles surrounded her tired, bloodshot eyes, and the golden sheen of residual cinderslick coated her hands and cheeks. She had to be exhausted. *Soon, Ella. Just hold on a little longer.*

"A lovely idea." I pulled the tattered white tablecloth off the tray and spread it over the table when she lifted the tray. "I'll find a few flowers."

We filled the vase with a mix of yellow butterflowers, white rosedrops, and an array of feathery greens. Ella set out plates and pulled the checked blue and white cloth off a basket of honey-scented, golden scones. Then she pulled a folded copy of the *Herald* from her apron pocket and set it on the table.

The sight of so much familiar comfort in one place made my stomach hurt. One of these breakfasts would be our last one together. How could I possibly leave Ella here alone? On the other hand, how could I stay and let three innocent girls keep paying for my secret?

The morning sun warmed my shoulders as I sat beside Ella at the table. She poured us each a cup of coffee, and we sat in companionable silence, perusing the newspaper as we waited for the girls to come up to the roof.

Ella nudged me with her forearm as she gripped the Commerce section. "We've come a long way since those cold bowls of victus, haven't we?"

"We sure have. Thanks to you, El."

Ella dodged my praise, like always. Her cheeks flushed as she simply shook her head and lifted the newspaper again. There was a long, quiet pause, and then she lowered the newspaper and met my eyes. "I don't know what I would have done without you."

The sincerity in her beautiful green eyes made my stomach drop.

"If you hadn't come, I would have been all alone when Father died. I never would have been able to keep the bakery. And I certainly never would have applied for that Royal Academy scholarship if you hadn't spent so much time teaching me and encouraging me to apply." Ella lifted one shoulder and her mouth tilted into a small smile. "Anything I've done for our family, I did because I wanted to, for you and the girls. You don't have to thank me."

A lump formed in my throat. I didn't trust myself to speak, so I reached out and squeezed her hand. When I let go, she set aside the newspaper and flipped through her notes for the exam, and I leaned back in my chair, my hands shaking too much to grip my coffee cup.

She would be crushed when we left. I'd been dreading that conversation for two years, and now it was almost time to have it. I wanted her to understand that as long as I was with her, she'd continue to pay for my secret. I had to leave, and so did the girls. No one could ever find out that Ella had knowingly sheltered three unregistered mages for all those years. I had to leave because I loved her too much to make her suffer for my presence.

I had a feeling she wouldn't see it that way.

Bri and Alba joined us a few minutes later, still bleary-eyed from sleep, their hair mussed and their morning dresses buttoned haphazardly. When they saw the scones, they fell upon them like wolves in the Badlands. Ella laughed and teased them, putting a smile back on Alba's face. Bri stayed quiet, still looking guilty about her role in their deception.

I glanced across the alley to where Alba had supposedly spent last night napping on the roof. She'd lied to my face for months, and she was scared of the city. I still couldn't quite believe it, but I had my solution. I'd keep her and Bri together, and I'd turn myself in as soon as Bri had a chance to flesh out the details of their fabricated life in the River Quarter slums. Then they would leave too, and Ella would finally be free to sell the bakery and pursue her dreams without worrying about protecting us.

Only one problem remained unsolved. Whatever would I do about Ella, and her tender, vulnerable heart? I couldn't leave without hurting her, but I couldn't stay without hurting her even more. Impossible.

I spent the rest of breakfast staring blankly at a long article about the Crimson Blight—something about the group's mysterious appearance in Asylia five years earlier. I tried to follow the journalist's various theories on the origins of that violent, red-masked group of men, but all I could think about was Ella. She was about to graduate from the Royal Academy, and she deserved to be free of us, didn't she? Then why did the thought of leaving her make my stomach twist so sourly?

Alba prattled on about Prince Estevan's selection ball, and then Ella went downstairs to get ready and Bri cleared the table. I left her and Alba to clean up and went to the edge of the roof again. I imagined my will coming under the leash of my True Name, then straining and growing and stretching my True Name until it snapped, never to be forced on me again. I would be strong enough. I had to be.

Darien had believed I could one day be physically strong enough to resist the Wasp Queen's magic. After years of consistent meals and physical training, my muscles were very strong now—perhaps strong enough to do just that. My will was even stronger. I'd survived thirteen years in hiding, caring for three little girls by myself. I'd kept us all safe, alive, and mostly happy. If I could do that, couldn't I resist my True Name's control?

I watched people come and go along our lane as the girls went downstairs, staring without seeing until one young man caught my eye. He was tall and broad-shouldered, with golden hair, tan skin, and fine clothing—far too fine for a commoner. He had to be a mage.

He wore no gold service armband. That and his downcast face told me everything I needed to know. He must be an outcast like the ones Ella's father and Belen had told me about—a mage too weak to be of use to the city government. He stopped in front of the bakery and squared his shoulders, as though mustering the will to enter.

A cast out mage, seeking shelter at the bakery? If so, he would be the first since the plague. I shoved my hands in my dress pockets and chewed on my lower lip. Perhaps there was a way I could ensure Ella was taken care of even after I left. I'd have to tell him everything—my secret, the whole plan to turn myself in.

What if he turned me in before I was ready, hoping for a reward? Then again, if he knew I was about to turn myself in anyway, he wouldn't have anything to gain by telling on me. Besides, I doubted a blacklisted mage had any loyalty to the Mage Division or the city government after getting cast out.

The young man ran a hand through his blond hair and then walked out of my sight, into the bakery's front shop.

He was young and too handsome, but there was nothing we could do about that. He looked strong enough to protect

Ella from the riffraff who were always leaving threatening notes at the bakery, and to help her with whatever chores she needed done. And if he was here, he was desperate. He would owe me.

Perfect.

Chapter 18

The mage raised a well-groomed eyebrow as I strode forward to meet him inside the bakery shop.

"I'm looking for Master Stone—is he in?" He held himself like he was seconds from stepping back out the door and walking away.

I fought to keep my delighted smile under control. "Master Stone passed away in the plague. I am his—well, I am in charge here. What do you need?"

The young mage shut the door behind him and looked around the bakery's bare, dim shop with obvious distaste. "Master Stone and his wife … I had heard—"

"Say no more, mage." I folded my hands together primly and tried to look harmless. "You're in need of shelter, are you not?"

His shoulders sagged. "I've been cast out. Blacklisted. They sent me away with nothing but the clothes on my back. My mother said I should come here."

I patted him on the shoulder. "You've come to the right place. There will only be a short interview."

"Interview? But I thought—"

"Oh, dear. Well, we don't shelter just any mage, you know. And there are certain responsibilities that will come along with seeking shelter at the Golden Loaf."

He straightened his spine. "I assure you, I am able to meet whatever requirements you set before me."

"Very good. Now, tell me why you were blacklisted from the Mage Division."

He blanched, but after a moment of hesitant silence, he forced the terse words out. "I had an affair with my patron's granddaughter." Red tinged his cheeks and ears, and he hunched his shoulders almost imperceptibly, but he didn't look away. "I'm a weak expellant mage, specializing in appearance. They said my magic wasn't worth the trouble I caused, and when they discovered the affair, they cast me out."

My smile faded into a scowl. I'd hoped perhaps he'd designed an unflattering dress and been cast out by his patron in a fit of vanity. An affair, at his age? He couldn't be much older than Ella. How could I trust him to be here with her? With her green eyes, strong will, and wild, dark hair, she was far lovelier than any Procus lady.

It wasn't as though I had any other ideas, and it was past time for me and the girls to leave her in peace. I'd have to make this work. Perhaps once he knew what kind of mage I was, he would be intimidated enough to leave Ella alone.

"I see. And can you be discrete?"

He met my eyes. "I can."

"I have your word?"

His gaze didn't waver. "Yes. You have my word."

I took comfort in the certainty I found in his expression. Beyond his clear desire to survive, there was a steady beat of sincerity, the potential for loyalty. He might have been blacklisted, but he hadn't yet been broken.

"If you accept our offer of shelter here, you'll pay your way with labor in the bakery and help with whatever else our family needs."

He nodded. "I understand."

"You'll be required to keep silent about whatever you learn here."

He squared his jaw and nodded again. "Won't be a

problem."

"Then your interview is complete. You will have shelter here as long as you keep up your side of the bargain."

His shoulders sagged, and then he frowned. "My side?"

I searched the room for inspiration, then grabbed a small clipping of fresh mint Ella had left on the bakery counter. It was now or never.

I held up the bright green clipping and let the cool scent fill my senses. The mage shifted on his feet, clearly confused. Then I unleashed my hungry power, and a moment later, the plant was nothing but a thin layer of dust on the bakery floor. I wiped my hand on my dress.

He took a step back, his eyes wide. "You can't be— That's impossible. You can't have the—"

"The Touch. I can, and I do."

Panic scrambled across his face, but he didn't move. Was he sufficiently frightened? It seemed so.

"Don't worry, mage. The time has come for me to turn myself in to the Asylian authorities." I kept my voice low and willed Ella to stay in the kitchen for a few minutes longer. "My family can bear the weight of this secret no longer."

His face softened.

Was that sympathy? I crossed my arms and continued, "When I leave, I'll need someone trustworthy to stay here and help my stepdaughter with whatever she needs to survive … to help her move on. She doesn't know that I'm leaving, and she won't take it well. You'll remain here to keep her safe and out of trouble and assist her in everything until she is able to survive on her own. When that time comes, you will leave. Go to the Badlands, or wherever else you might find a way to survive."

I didn't miss the way his face soured at the mention of the Badlands. This mage would not have an easy time of things if he still hoped to be welcomed back at the Mage Division.

He shoved his hands in his pockets. "Keep your

stepdaughter out of trouble. Got it. I can do that."

"You will put her needs first and take care of her no matter what? I have your word?"

He frowned, but nodded slowly. "You have my word."

"And what is your name?"

"Weslan. Weslan Fortis."

I held out my hand. "Zel. It's nice to meet you, Weslan."

He stared at my hand for a long moment before reaching out to shake it. When I let go, he exhaled.

"Welcome to the Golden Loaf."

There was a sharp gasp, and Ella came rushing over from the kitchen door. "Stepmother, Alba has been asking for you upstairs." Her soft voice shook. Poor Ella probably thought I'd been discovered by a tracker in disguise. "Please allow me to help this gentleman with whatever he may need."

I bit my lip. It was time. I only hoped she'd cooperate. "Ella, I'd like you to meet someone."

Ella and Weslan faced each other. Ella frowned, and Weslan smiled slowly, looking her up and down with obvious interest. My stomach curdled at the sight, but it was too late to back out now. "Weslan, this is my stepdaughter, Ariella Stone. Ella, this is Weslan Fortis." I plastered an enthusiastic smile onto my face. "He's going to be staying here and helping you with the bakery now."

Ella's glare whipped to my face. "I don't need any help."

"You're about to graduate from the academy, and who knows what your apprenticeship will be like? Don't you think it will be nice to have someone to help with the baking and deliveries so you don't have to do it all yourself?"

Her eyes nearly bugged out of her head. "But that's beside the point, Zel! Do you really think that someone like … him … should be here with us?"

Oh, Ella. Always protecting me. Now let me protect you. I gave her a smile and placed a hand on her arm in an attempt to calm her down. Weslan flinched. "Weslan is exactly the right person to be here with us. He knows."

Ella swayed like she might fall over. It wasn't fair for me to dump this on her so quickly, but I had to seize the opportunities that came along, didn't I?

"Weslan's mother knew that your father sometimes used the bakery to shelter mages who found themselves in need, just like I did so many years ago. Weslan has found himself in a difficult position, so his mother sent him here until things … get sorted out. And I've told him he can stay."

Ella shook her head. "I've got to get to school." She spun and glared at Weslan. "If you're going to be helping, I guess you could start by sanding down the front door. Someone left me a little note this morning."

Another Cinderella note? When would those idiots leave her alone? Before I could stop her, she was gone.

Weslan watched her through the bakery front windows as she stormed down the street. "So that's your stepdaughter, huh? Ariella. Ella." Hushed reverence coated his deep voice as he spoke her name.

"Don't even think it."

He crossed his arms. "Think what?"

"You know exactly what I mean. And I'm telling you, if you want to stay here, you won't even think of her like that. She is my stepdaughter, and she is very precious to me. If you hurt her in any way, things will not go well for you. Understand?"

Anger sizzled all the way to my fingertips. At this point, I wasn't even sure if I was bluffing or not. I only knew I didn't want to see that hungry, lovesick expression directed toward Ella ever again. Darien had broken my monstrous heart thirteen years ago, and it still wasn't healed. I couldn't imagine what heartbreak would do to sweet, innocent Ella.

He was silent, his jaw working as he looked out the window after Ella.

"Weslan …"

"Fine."

"Then get to work sanding down the door. You'll find whatever supplies you need in the kitchen."

He nodded curtly and strode to the kitchen, and I marched up the stairs and straight to the roof. I shut the door behind me, and leaned against it, inhaling the calming scent of the garden plants.

I'd done the right thing. Ella wouldn't be alone. I'd be abandoning her, but Weslan would help her survive—as long as he kept his affections to himself. It was all I could offer. I only hoped it was better than nothing.

~

A loud pounding noise startled me awake. I shoved my loose hair away from my face and staggered unsteadily to my feet. I was still on the roof, and my neck ached from the odd position I'd fallen asleep in, leaning against the door to the stairs. The sun was not yet at its zenith, so I couldn't have been up here long, though I hadn't intended to fall asleep. Perhaps I'd missed too much sleep lately.

The pounding came again, and I realized it was the door that led from the back alley into the kitchen. Only Gregor came to that entrance. What could it be?

The pounding stopped, and muffled male voices floated up to me, too distant to hear. I stood and stretched. Perhaps I shouldn't have left Weslan downstairs by himself, but I'd been too upset to think clearly after seeing him with Ella. Time to go see how he was doing.

I lingered on the stairs first, until I was certain it was Gregor's voice in the kitchen. Then I entered the room and stopped short at the sight of Gregor's grieving face. "Gregor? What is it?"

"You haven't heard." He stepped toward me and then stopped to hold out his hands. "Zel, I'm so sorry."

"Sorry for what? What haven't I heard?"

The twins were studying in the upper room. What could possibly have happened? Unless Ella—

"There was an attack at Ella's school. The market was all abuzz with the news. The Crimson Blight set off a suffio bomb in a Royal Academy classroom just after school began this morning. I came to see if Ella had come home, but Weslan here says he hasn't heard from her."

I swayed. If Ella's school had been attacked, she would have come home immediately. That meant—

My knees buckled, and I collapsed to the floor. I was dimly aware of Weslan and Gregor helping me into a chair, and loud sobs coming from my own mouth. "She can't be. She can't be." It was several minutes before I realized I was speaking the words over and over, not thinking them. *Get yourself together.* I choked back the next sob and searched the room until I found Weslan.

He stood beside me, his body stiff and a dark expression on his face.

"Weslan, you gave me your word. Now go and find her." He nodded curtly and left the kitchen with a resolute stride.

"Can I do anything, Zel?" Gregor wrung his hands.

I shook my head mutely. "Weslan will find out where she is and what has happened. And until then… I'll just wait."

Gregor nodded. "Then I'll wait too."

I didn't have the energy to send him away, so I sat numbly while he made a pot of coffee and poured me a mug.

When Weslan didn't return within an hour, I took that as a good sign. Surely, she was still alive, or he would have come sooner. Unless her body was unrecognizable, like some of the Blight's victims. I shuddered and sipped my cold coffee.

"You don't have to stay, Gregor." My voice was toneless and numb. "I'll send for you when we have word."

His chair screeched as he stood up. "I'll be on my way, then." He didn't sound much better. "Whatever happens, I'll do what I can to help out."

I nodded. "Thank you." I grimaced as Gregor left and shut the door behind him. It was a nice sentiment, but I knew we couldn't accept too much help from Gregor. He was old and all alone, and I'd inflicted enough pain on Ella with my secrets. I couldn't bring another innocent person into our mess.

Like Weslan? A guilty voice reminded me.

Weslan was different. He was a mage like me and the twins, and he had nothing left to lose.

Eventually, the twins came downstairs, looking for a midday meal, and I had to tell them what had happened. I couldn't hide it, not once they saw my face.

"But she's fine. Right?" Alba's face was white. Bri braced her body like she was ready to go fight the Crimson Blight herself.

"Right. I-I'm sure she's fine. We're just waiting to get the official word. I've hired someone to help at the bakery, and he will bring back a message any minute now."

Alba nodded, and she and Bri ate a quiet lunch of day-old bread and cold victus before heading back upstairs.

The minutes turned into hours, and I sat at the kitchen table, stewing in my worry until I was sick. Where was Weslan? Had he abandoned us after all? What had I been thinking, entrusting my family to him? What if Ella was dead, and he'd turned me in? I'd have to send the twins out to the Mage Division first, before I was brought in. Maybe even tonight. Weslan didn't know about them yet, so they would still have a chance. If I turned myself in peacefully, even after Weslan had reported me, perhaps the authorities would still be lenient.

The front door opened and shut. I leapt to my feet and rushed to the front shop, stopping when I encountered Weslan on his way in. "Well? What did you find out? Is she … Is she—" I couldn't bring myself to say the word aloud.

"She's alive."

I nearly collapsed with relief. "What happened? Where is she? What took you so long?"

"She's alive, but she was hurt. Badly. She was close to the bomb when it went off, they said. It was right there in her classroom."

What had my stepdaughter ever done to the Blight? Why

would they do such a thing to innocent students?

"Many in her classroom were injured, but they're all from Procus families. They have their own healers at their compounds." Weslan's expression soured. "It took me hours to find out which hospital they took Ella to after the attack. It's in the River Quarter."

I pressed my lips together. At least she was alive. Better to be alive in the slums than die among the Procus set.

"Why didn't she come home with you?"

Weslan ran a hand through his formerly neat blonde hair. "She's still unconscious. She nearly died from a head wound. They saved her life, but they're keeping her under with sopor because she's not completely healed."

From the way his lip curled, I knew what he was thinking. I was thinking the same thing. A Procus family's healer would have healed the wound completely right away, and induced sleep only to aid recovery. The fact that they'd left her unconscious and unhealed meant that they'd deliberately used less magic on her. No doubt the River Quarter hospital healers didn't bother to waste too much magic on commoners.

"There's something else." His face darkened. "They healed the inner damage—the injury to her brain and skull. But they stopped short of healing her face. They said it's too expensive, and they can't heal the rest until we've paid for the healing they've already done."

"How much do we owe them? And how much to heal her face?"

"Eight hundred marks," he said.

My stomach dropped. "Total?"

"No. That's how much is owed so far. Another thousand marks to heal her face."

I hissed. I'd go down to that hospital and show those stingy healers just what—

"Zel, I'm sorry, but they said if we don't pay today, they can't promise she'll continue to have a bed in the hospital. It might hurt her more if she wakes up too soon, but they don't care. They said the hospital is already too crowded."

My nostrils flared. Unbelievable. "Fine. We'll pay. Give me a moment."

I stormed upstairs.

Alba and Bri looked up, startled at my sudden entrance.

"She's alive, girls. Just unconscious at the hospital. I need to pay the healers."

Alba clapped her hands. "I wish we could go see her!"

"You'll see her soon enough, honey." I went to my wardrobe and dug through the folded winter clothes until I'd uncovered the old hollowed-out book. I flipped it open and removed the envelope of marks I'd been saving to pay our merchant tax this year. My hands shook with fury. How could they? This city had done nothing but bully my stepdaughter since she won the scholarship, and now the Blight had nearly taken her life. And here I was, trapped in this forsaken bakery, helpless to protect her.

I hurried downstairs and shoved the envelope into Weslan's hands. He took it, his eyebrows raised. "It's all we have." My voice was hard. "And it's not enough. Take our cinderslick rations cards and sell next week's rations at the nearest market. It's not strictly legal, but Ella's done it plenty of times. The cinderslick vendors at the market will know what to do." I hunted through the cupboards until I found the ration cards. "Together, this should be enough to pay the hospital but not enough to heal her face. We'll just have to hope that her body can heal on its own."

Weslan nodded. "I'll go now."

He paused when he was nearly at the door. "Ella truly is important to you, isn't she?"

I frowned, surprised at the question. "Of course she is."

"I'm sorry for what happened," he said grimly. "And I'll bring her home. I swear it."

He left as twilight fell over the city. I collapsed back into my seat at the table. I'd been right to hire Weslan. That much was certain. At least one good thing had come of today.

~

"But I thought you said I was supposed to see inside a tenement first, before we decided." Bri had already dressed in her dark clothes and hooded sweater for the night.

I put an arm around her shoulders, walked her away from the stairs, and pushed her gently into a chair at the table. "That was before. After what happened to Ella, we can't risk it." Ella had been in the hospital for three days now. According to Weslan, she was doing well, but the healers thought she should be left unconscious for at least two more weeks because the wound on her face was bound to be painful.

"But you said Ella was going to be fine." Bri pursed her lips.

"And she is fine. I mean, she will be fine. But …" How could I explain that I couldn't bear to send away my two daughters when I had nearly lost my stepdaughter only days earlier? "You're not going anywhere until Ella is safely back home—not to the River Quarter, not to the Mage Division, and not to a single rooftop other than our own. And I don't want to hear any more arguing."

Alba leaned her hip against the table. "Well, I don't mind staying here." She grinned. "Bri, do you want to listen to those fabulator crystals Weslan gave us?"

Bri's scowl softened and she nodded. "Sure. Those are nice."

Bri and Alba huddled on Alba's bed to listen to the dramatic tale unfolding from the fabulator crystals, and I sat down at my vanity with my journal. Weslan was with Ella. The twins were home safe with me. For the moment, I could relax. I should relax. But instead, I was wound tight.

My entire plan depended on Ella being strong enough to live on her own, without us. Weslan might be able to help her with the bakery and keep her safe, but he couldn't heal her wounds—or her heart—once we left. It didn't help that the merchant tax notice had been slipped under our front door that morning. If I could get myself and the girls away soon, Ella could sell the bakery, and we wouldn't have to worry about the tax.

But what if Ella needed more time to recover? How much longer could we put the payment off? And where would we ever get the money to pay for it?

I shook my head and put my pencil to the paper. There had to be more we could sell. We couldn't leave until Ella had healed from the attack. We owed Ella everything, even our very lives. We couldn't abandon her now.

~

"They're home!" Bri rushed down the stairs from the roof. "I just saw them in the front. Weslan's carrying Ella."

Alba let out a shriek, and they both hurried down to the bakery.

I got up from where I'd been going over the bakery's books at the table. Why was she home so early? Hadn't Weslan said she needed at least another week under sedation?

My legs shook as I stumbled down the stairs to greet her. Ella stood just inside the front door of the bakery, her arms wrapped tightly around Bri and Alba, her face pressed against Alba's tousled dark hair. Weslan hovered beside her like a mother hen.

She lifted her head and sent me a lopsided smile when she caught sight of me. The side of her face was wrapped in a clean white bandage. Traces of dark blue-green bruising showed from under its edges. The rest of her face was swollen and sickly looking.

"Ella …" My voice was barely above a whisper. Somehow, I made it the rest of the way down the stairs, and when the twins stepped back, I pulled Ella into my arms. My poor, sweet girl. What had they done to her? My face grew wet, and it was several moments before I realized I was the one crying, not her. I pulled back and led her to the kitchen. I helped her into a chair.

"Zel," she said, "What happened?" Her voice was slurred and thick, like she couldn't quite form the words properly. She swayed in her chair.

I placed a gentle hand on hers. What had the Blight done to her? And those healers—they should be cast out for sending her home in such a state. "Let's talk about that later. Right now, I just want to be happy that you're home."

She pulled her hand back. "Please. I need to know what happened."

I tried to keep a calm expression on my face. "Your school was attacked. Trackers found the remains of a suffio bomb afterward, and it wasn't far from where you were sitting. They said you're lucky to be alive today."

A strange, panicky look came over Ella, and her eyes flicked around the room, as though she expected another attack to happen at any moment. "Attacked? By whom?"

I didn't want to talk about this, but at the sight of her swollen, bruised face and bloodshot eyes, I couldn't deny her anything.

I told her what I'd learned about the attack—what Gregor and Weslan had found out through various channels—all the while silently willing her not to bring up the subject that Weslan had informed me of this morning.

"When do I have to retake my final exam?"

No luck. How could I break this to her? She'd be devastated. She'd worked for so long, and those Procus rats had slammed the door in her face when she'd done nothing wrong.

Weslan stepped closer and spoke up when I couldn't find the words. "The term is over. They … ah … won't be offering another chance to retake the exam. All the other students retook it last week, while you were in the hospital."

Ella collapsed in her chair. "I'll just have to retake the year then. That's fine. My apprenticeship can wait another year."

I opened my mouth, but the right words wouldn't come

out. "Honey, I'm so sorry," was all I could think to say. "So very sorry."

"What are you talking about?" She turned to Weslan. "What is she saying? Why is she sorry?"

He told her what he'd told me that morning. "I've been to every higher academy in the city. There are no more scholarship places left. There's no place for you to retake the term."

"You're wrong." Ella swayed in her chair, but there was no mistaking the hardness in her voice. She was furious.

"No, Ella. I spoke to every government official and school administrator I could find. All the scholarship spots for the final grade have been filled by upcoming students from the lower grades."

She stood quickly and immediately tipped over to one side. I held her up. "Sit down, sweetheart. You need to rest."

"But ... I've worked so hard ... I don't understand! How could they just shut me out?"

"The fact remains that they have." How would she ever recover from this? And if she couldn't recover, we couldn't leave, and she'd never know an ounce of peace and safety. How I despised the Crimson Blight. The sheer impossibility of our predicament infuriated me, and my voice turned harder than it should have. "And you need to lie down and rest. You've been asleep for a week, Ella. You can deal with this later."

"So that's it? I'm just not going to graduate? This is ridiculous!" Ella's normally soft, gentle voice was sharp enough to slice through skin. "This isn't happening. I was so close to graduating. What am I going to do? I'll never be able to get a government job. I'll never get any kind of job at all. I'll never be able to leave this stricken bakery!"

Bri and Alba gasped. For all their admiration of Ella's love and service to us, it had probably never occurred to them that she resented her work at the bakery. She was just a girl like them, like I had been when I came to the bakery. My poor, hurt girl. She had to recover soon. I couldn't keep doing this to her—depending on her, letting her sacrifice her dreams and her happiness to keep us safe in the bakery. I just couldn't. But I couldn't leave her now, either. The plan would have to wait, no matter how much it hurt. There wasn't much I could do for her now.

I let Weslan carry her to her bedroom while I took the twins upstairs.

"Why did she say that, Mama?" Alba scooted her chair closer to me as I passed out the borrowed library books that served as their school textbooks. "She doesn't like it here?"

Bri frowned at Alba. "You don't like it here either, so what do you care? You're the one who never stops talking about moving to the Mage Division."

Alba stuck her tongue out. "I was just asking."

"Well, I think … I think Ella is just like us, honey. She knows we can't keep living like this. And she thought that if she got a government job, she'd be able to make more money, and maybe move us somewhere more comfortable."

"But she doesn't know that we're leaving." Alba chewed on her lower lip.

"That's right. And you can't tell her now. She wouldn't understand, and it would be too much for her, especially now that she has been injured and needs time to heal."

Reluctantly, they set about their usual studies. The twins studied quietly for over an hour before Alba broke the silence. "But when will she be ready? When will she be able to understand?"

"I don't know."

~

As the days went on and spring shifted into full-fledged, sweat-soaked summer, I became even less sure of the answer.

Ella's wound healed, and the scar faded significantly. But everything else got worse. She was frightened by the smallest things—the red cover on Alba's history book, harmless ribbons, the sound of pots clattering in the kitchen. She barely slept. She nagged Weslan, criticized his every move, and burst into tears the moment he returned the favor. When we were all ready to throw up our hands, she would cry out at night in her sleep, pitifully fearful cries that drifted upstairs through the open windows. On top of it all, the past-due merchant tax loomed over the bakery like an ominous dark cloud, threatening us with disaster any day.

I often caught her rubbing against her temple and grimacing as though in pain, but when I pressed, she would shrug her shoulders and insist she was fine.

Ella had been home from the hospital for two weeks when I heard a pained cry from the kitchen. I hurried downstairs and rushed to her side, only to knock over a stack of pans on the counter and frighten her even further. I fought to keep calm and comfort her even as my power raged against the Blight. If I could get my hands on those cowards, the things I would do—

The bright red bloodstains on Ella's apron and dishtowel interrupted the dark turn of my thoughts. "What happened to your hand? You're bleeding everywhere." I snagged a clean linen cloth and pressed it to her bleeding hand.

"The cloth will be ruined."

As if I cared about a clean cloth at a time like this. "Doesn't matter. All that matters to me is that you're safe." I took a deep breath as I bandaged her cut, attempting to inject as much assurance into my expression as I could. "Don't worry, I really believe we will find the money to pay for—" Wait, what was I doing? Ella had no need to worry about the tax. "We will find the money, and things will get better. One way or another. I promise."

"Money to pay for what? Cinderslick?"

Why had I attempted to reassure her? Now I'd only make things worse. I couldn't lie to her about this on top of everything else I was hiding. "You know it's almost summer. Inspector Cyrus has been by to ask for our tax." Weslan had met him at the door earlier that day.

Ella cringed. "And you used money set aside for the tax to pay for my healing."

"Yes." I wished I hadn't brought this up.

Ella swayed and grabbed the counter behind her. Why had I told her? Now she would faint, and surely it wasn't good for her injured head to be in a state of such stress.

"Why did you do that? What were you thinking? You're going to lose everything. After all that I've done to keep you safe, how could you risk it all for me?" The raw pain and confusion in Ella's voice made my heart ache.

I grabbed her by the shoulders and resisted the urge to give her a shake. Why did she always doubt her importance to our family? "You matter to us. You matter. We couldn't have let you die, not when the healers had the power to save your life and we had the money to pay for it." I pried my fingers off her shoulders and folded them at my waist. It wouldn't do to cause her any more stress, but I had to make her listen to me. "I have no regrets. And neither do the girls. It was the right decision. And I know you would've done the same for any of us."

Ella was silent for a long moment, and then squared her shoulders. "Well, we'll just have to get the money somehow."

I smiled and took her hands. It was just like Ella to leap past my declaration and jump right into problem-solving mode. "We'll be fine, Ella. We're going to find the money, and I don't want you to worry about it. We'll have more bakery orders with the prince's selection ball in a couple of weeks. So just hold on until then. Everything is going to work out." One way or another, I would make sure that Ella survived, even if it meant selling the bakery and building a life for herself without us.

The corners of her mouth lifted into a forced smile. "Fine, Zel. You win. I'll hope for the best."

What else could I ask of her? I'd already asked far too much. As soon as she was better and able to survive on her own—with Weslan's help—we'd be gone. Forget Inspector Cyrus and his inconvenient, impossibly high merchant tax. We couldn't do this to her any longer.

~

Early the next morning, I sent Ella to the market to sell some fresh herbs from the rooftop garden. Many merchants in the quarter tended a rooftop garden to supplement their family's diet and their shop's income, but Ella and I had made a careful study of the market before planting ours. All the herbs we grew were very expensive to import from Lerenia, where a vast army of grower mages helped produce their fabled high-quality crops. We didn't produce much in our garden, but what we did grow sold for a healthy stack of quarter marks. It would be enough to stock up on cinderslick, at least.

I puttered around the kitchen while the sun rose. Then the bakery door slammed, and Ella rushed into the kitchen. The next thing I knew, she was holding me around the neck and sobbing. What could possibly be wrong? She'd been gone less than an hour.

"What's happened? Please, talk to me!"

It was only between her sobs and sniffles that I finally discerned what had taken place—Inspector Cyrus had attempted to blackmail her because of our tax, and he somehow knew that we were hiding something at the bakery. A wave of cold anger rushed through me. If he knew what we were really hiding, what I really was, he wouldn't be so quick to threaten Ella. He certainly would not dare threaten me.

His ignorance would keep both him and us safe. "It's fine. Everything will work out."

"You don't understand." Ella dashed at the streams of tears running down her cheeks. She twisted around to look in the direction of the front door. "He threatened me too."

"He did what?" The cold wave of anger engulfed me

again. "What did he do?"

"He grabbed me. He pulled me close … and touched me. He told me that if I offered him something now, he wouldn't contact the trackers yet."

I heard her words from a distance, my powers raging and swelling in response. I'd kill him. I'd destroy him, and he'd never hurt her again.

Somewhere, in real life, my sweet stepdaughter needed comfort and a gentle embrace, but I was too far away to respond. I managed to find my self-control long enough to form words. "What happened next?"

Ella exhaled a shaky breath. "I ran away."

Innocent, self-sacrificing Ella had survived an attack from the Blight. Then, she'd been denied the dream of graduating. And now, the local inspector dared to assault her? I'd end him. I had to. My power strained hungrily. Once again, my mouth formed the right words. "Did the inspector follow you?" I desperately hoped so.

"I don't know."

The bleak, despairing expression on Ella's face brought me closer to reality. I did my best to focus on her words and ignore the ravenous pulsing of my power in the back of my mind.

"I didn't hear any footsteps behind me," she said. "I suppose if he were planning to come here, I would have been arrested by now."

If he hadn't come here, I'd have to go to him. I glanced at Weslan, who had entered the room just after Ella's return. He gave me an almost imperceptible nod. Good. He understood. I'd do what was necessary, and he'd handle things here if I was caught.

Don't leave the girls like this, a voice whispered. I was too enraged to follow the thought through.

"I'll go to him. I'll speak to him, and he'll see that we have nothing to hide." And if that greasy coward collapsed in a lifeless pile of drained, dusty flesh after our conversation, all the better.

"What? No, Zel! You can't leave here. What if he's already contacted trackers?"

I'd be putting my plan in to action early, that was all. I fumbled for a reasonable-sounding explanation. "He hasn't. It's too early, and I know men like him. He's lazy. He only cornered you because he thought you were easy prey. Because everyone thinks you're easy prey. Because of the rumors we've intentionally circulated about your status in this home." As I spoke, my power quieted slightly. I sighed at the stricken, tortured look on Ella's tear-stained face. If only she could accept her true value to us. "Those rumors used to protect us, and I'm grateful for all the sacrifices you've made to keep us safe. But if those rumors are endangering you, we must put them to rest. We must make it clear that no one may threaten you and get away with it. It's the only way."

Panic flickered in Ella's red-rimmed eyes. "What if you're caught?"

"If I'm caught, they'll know that I have the Touch, and we will deal with whatever results."

Ella flinched.

My power ached, drawing me away to the front door. I held on against the pull as long as I could. What could I possibly say to make it all better? How could I continue to be the gentle stepmother she loved when anger raged like a storm inside me?

"I'm grateful for all that you've given up for us, to hide us, to protect us," I said. "Your father would be proud of you. I will always consider you as dear to me as my own daughters. But now you need to let me protect you."

If the worst happened, perhaps she would remember that I'd loved her and wanted to protect her, and not the fact that I'd abandoned her.

Chapter 19

The sun rose outside the bakery. The summer heat shimmered around me, and the warm, pungent scent of old garbage made my eyes water. I held my charge in as long as I could, making it several blocks before I was finally forced to release my trace. At least this way, any trackers who found me wouldn't know I'd been staying at the bakery. I walked the route I remembered taking to our nearest market, my feet carrying me via a nearly-forgotten memory.

I hadn't set foot on the city streets in years. Since that close encounter with the trackers in the Common Quarter, I'd stuck to the rooftops. The rage propelling me forward didn't care about trackers. It just wanted me to find him as quickly as possible.

The precinct inspector's lodging and office were on the lane next to the market. I remembered that much. When I finally saw the small, battered sign on the door, my power surged excitedly. I reined it in, marched up onto the stoop, and flung the door open.

The dark foyer was cool compared to the hot, dusty street outside. I curled my lip at the sight of rat droppings, weathered papers, and shards of broken glass littering the floor. I followed the strong, sour smell of spilled beer down the hallway and into a study, where a large, greasy-haired man slept with his shirt half open and his feet propped up on a paper-strewn desk.

My power quaked with excitement. One touch. Just one touch. He would never even get the chance to scream. How many other young women like Ella had he threatened? How many had been intimidated into paying for his silence with their bodies? Ella would be the last. I had a feeling none of the other girls had a stepmother like me.

I stepped closer, anger sizzling in my veins. A beer bottle had overturned on his desk, and the whole thing was a sticky, stinky mess. Sunlight streaming in from the single window flickered on a piece of broken glass by his head, and I bent closer. An etching of a woman and a child, both unsmiling, stood out beneath a smashed glass picture frame.

Now that I thought of it, perhaps I remembered seeing Inspector Cyrus's wife many years ago, at one of the only precinct meetings I'd ever attended. More victims of the plague, perhaps. Pity trickled through me, weakening my rage, but I snarled it away. Grief was no excuse to use his power against others, no excuse for threatening our family or my stepdaughter.

He mumbled in his sleep, stirring slightly, and I edged closer. Now was my chance. I could do the job and be gone, back to my tower with no one the wiser. And the only person who suspected our secret, the only threat to our family, would be gone.

Wait … my tower?

My rage evaporated like the night's dew in the heat of the summer sun. My tower. At the first sign of a real threat, I'd let my power take over. For the first time, I'd been about to use my power deliberately, of my own will, not in response to my True Name's control and not in the heat of self-defense. I'd been ready to kill in cold blood to protect my secret.

And to protect Ella, a voice in the back of my mind whispered. Ella had been threatened. Surely, he deserved death and much more …

I shook off the voice. No. I couldn't lie to myself. Ella didn't need a murderer on her side. She needed a stepmother who would be there for her. I'd nearly thrown away our last days together—thrown away the chance to explain my decision before I left, thrown away my chance to say good-bye. A chill came over me as I realized I'd nearly lost my last good-bye to the twins. If I got caught this morning, I'd never see any of my girls again.

I stepped back. My hands shook as I pressed my ice-cold fingers against my burning hot face. What had I done? All this time, I thought I'd left the old Zel—the monster, the killer—back in Draicia with the Wasp, but the monster had been with me all along. What if she wasn't the old Zel? What if she was the *real* Zel? What if it was better for everyone if I remained under my True Name's control?

I took another step back, knocking back a chair that fell with a crash in the process.

Inspector Cyrus jolted awake and peered up at me with heavy-lidded eyes. A flash of recognition darted across his face, and he sat up straight, removing his feet from his desk. "You."

I hid my trembling hands in my skirt pockets. "Inspector Cyrus."

"What are you doing here? Got your tax money at last?"

I lifted my chin and tried to project confidence. "We will be paying our tax in three weeks' time. And, of course, the sum will include an extra administrative fee to compensate for any inconvenience brought on by our late payment."

He grunted, looking me up and down in an oily way that made my power crackle with hunger again. If he tried something with me like he had with Ella—

"Fine. See yourself out. And don't be late again."

I nodded and left, my back stiff. Either Weslan would help Ella sell the bakery in three weeks, after we'd left, or we'd get the extra money another way. But I wouldn't give Inspector Cyrus any more leverage over our family.

I rushed the whole way back to the bakery, holding in

my trace the last few blocks, and I nearly collapsed when I made it inside the front door.

The scent of bacon and eggs wafted toward me from the kitchen. Ella and Weslan must have cooked breakfast while I was out. I approached the kitchen. I had to face her. I had to look her in the eye, knowing what I'd almost done … I swallowed another sob.

At least I would get to say good-bye. I had to hold onto that thought. It was the only thing that distracted me from the truly terrifying question still lurking in the back of my mind—which mage was the real Zel? The old Zel, or the new one?

~

Weslan slumped across the table from me, his blond hair hanging in sweaty clumps over his forehead. We were both baking in the sweltering upstairs room. I'd sent the twins downstairs to help Ella with the bakery while Weslan and I ostensibly had a chat about his employment. In reality, we were working on the plan to get the twins safely settled in the Mage Division after I turned myself in. It was also a chance to gain new, insider information about the Mage Division. I couldn't pass up the opportunity to improve my plan.

I traced my finger on the rivulets of water condensing on the outside of my glass. Weslan had been silent long enough. "Well? The Mage Division. What is the process for bringing in new mages?"

He shifted restlessly. "I don't know. Trust me, I want to help. I do. I just never paid attention to those things before." He drummed his fingers on the table. "Every mage starts at the Mage Academy when their powers first exhibit. For some, that's six or seven. I was five. For others, it's eight or nine, but no older than ten. But Alba and Bri are almost thirteen, right?"

I nodded.

He stretched his neck and rolled his shoulders, pausing for another moment of thought. "Still, the fact that everyone comes at a different age means they must have some way to evaluate the mages first. And not everyone's power is easy to classify. It also depends on their mental aptitude for the field of study. A strong expellant mage might make a poor grower but a powerful mover, for example. Someone in authority on the Mage Division must make the decision about which classification they'll train in, which means they must evaluate the childrens' powers and aptitude firsthand."

I leaned forward. "So the twins need to prove their powers, but in a way, that confirms they didn't realize they had them until now. We'll need to make sure they can show potential without demonstrating familiarity with it. Or they'll fall under suspicion."

Weslan frowned, but he nodded. "You're probably right. Mages as old as the twins almost never come to the campus for the first time. They'll already be suspicious. And I know you don't want to hear this, but it doesn't look good for two 'friends' to discover their powers at the same mature age. I don't know much about anything on the authority side of things, but even I would be suspicious."

I shook my head and went back to tracing droplets of water on my glass. "There's no help for it. Alba can't go into the city alone. She will be so anxious when she reaches the Mage Division that I fear she'll give herself away. I want to believe they won't punish my children for keeping my secret, but . . ." I fell silent.

Weslan wiped his forehead with his sleeve. "I know. I know. They have to go together. We'll think of something."

A series of stomping footsteps pounded up the staircase. A moment later, Ella flung the door open. She stopped in the doorway and leveled a fierce glare at Weslan. "What are you doing? I told you I needed help with the kneading."

"The twins can—"

"Well, I told *you* to do it. And just why are you lounging

upstairs and letting children do your work for you?"

I stood up. "Ella …"

She kept her glare fixed on Weslan, but her pink cheeks indicated she knew she was out of line. My victory in getting Inspector Cyrus to agree to a late payment last week hadn't improved her anger and bitterness. If anything, she was more anxious than before. No matter how many times I assured her that everything would work out, she couldn't relax, and she was taking her nerves out on Weslan.

"Fine. I'm coming." Weslan stood up and shouldered his way past Ella. She scowled and followed him, slamming the door shut behind her.

I slumped back at the table and sighed. Ella was exhausted, and she was hurting. I understood that. She was so lost in her despair and frustration that she couldn't see what was so obvious to the rest of us—Weslan was hurting too.

He'd been humiliated by his Procus patron, cast out by the only community he'd ever known, and lost access to his family and friends. He was penniless and dependent on a family of commoners for his daily room and board. Unless the Mage Division rescinded his expulsion, his best bet for survival in the long term lay in the Badlands, a fate I wouldn't wish on anyone.

Ella simply couldn't see past her own pain. What would he do when she finally pushed him too far? She didn't realize how much we needed him, much less how much *she* needed him. How could I make her understand?

Later that night, the twins were asleep, and I was just getting ready for bed when the kitchen door slammed. Weslan had come home late.

A rumble of angry voices reached me through the open window below mine. Ella's voice was shrill and furious, Weslan's low and slurred. I wrapped my robe around my body and flicked my long braid over my shoulder. Should I intervene or wait? I paused, straining to hear their words, but it was too hard to make out the conversation. Then

Weslan gave a roar of rage. Not good at all.

I rushed down the stairs and entered the kitchen. Ella cowered against the far counter while Weslan stood on the other side of the kitchen, his chest heaving, his jacket on the floor beside him. What had happened? What had he done? Why did she look so frightened? If he'd hurt her—

"Weslan." I let the threat in my voice fill the room.

His shoulders sagged, shame and guilt weighing down his normally proud face.

I rushed to Ella and stood in front of her, facing Weslan and using my body to shield Ella. I'd been ready to depend on Weslan, but if Ella couldn't trust him, all our planning would be in vain. He'd never be able to help her. He'd promised me he would put her needs first, and now he'd gone back on his word. From the despairing look in his eyes, he knew it.

He left in silence, shutting the door quietly on his way out.

~

For three days, we heard nothing from Weslan. Ella was killing herself trying to run the bakery without his help. How would I ever be able to leave her in such a state? Why had she antagonized him so much? If only I'd stepped in sooner, instead of letting it get to such a point.

I considered sending Bri out to see if she could sense any hint of his trail, but on the fourth day, I caught sight of Weslan walking down the alley behind the bakery at twilight.

He was thinner and dirtier, his hair matted against his head, his clothing filthy. When he'd first come to the bakery, he'd used his magic to keep his appearance immaculate most of the time, even when he was in the middle of kneading dough. Gradually, he'd given up the practice, and now it looked as though he hadn't even found a way to wash. At least he was still alive—that was something. From the raw, desperate look on his face, he was here to beg forgiveness.

Would Ella forgive him?

I hovered at the edge of the roof as he knocked on the door. Should I go downstairs to make sure everything went smoothly? I twisted the folds of my dress and paced on the roof as he entered the kitchen, and I lost sight of him.

No, Ella needed to handle this by herself. She wasn't in any danger from him. I'd known it the moment he left, and I'd regretted frightening him away. He was her best chance for survival. He was loyal and trustworthy. He would help her, if for no other reason than to honor his promise to me. But if she wouldn't accept him or if she refused to trust him, then it would never work out.

I forced myself to stay on the roof and finish harvesting the last of our cucumbers and green beans. Several minutes passed, and the kitchen was too quiet for me to hear what they were saying. I took my time arranging the small cucumbers in their basket, and then I couldn't take it any longer. I stripped off my dirty gloves, tossed them on top of the cucumbers, and went downstairs.

From the base of the stairs, I caught a glimpse of Ella and Weslan sitting face to face, on opposite sides of the kitchen table. No tears or shouting yet. That had to be a good sign.

I entered the kitchen just as Ella uttered a soft, foreign word, her face awed and eyes wide. Weslan tensed at the sound, and it took me a moment to recognize the power in the word. His True Name. She'd spoken his True Name. No, no, no! She couldn't! He couldn't. His True Name?

"Oh, Ella, Weslan … what have you done?"

I nearly retched on the floor in front of them. As one, they faced me. Weslan grimaced, but Ella's face reflected confusion. *Keep it together.* "Go to bed. I'll speak with each of you in the morning." I couldn't bear to look at them any longer. I went back up the stairs, fighting to keep my dinner down. How could she?

That night, I barely slept. It was my fault. I'd never told her about True Names. I didn't want to speak of them, didn't want to ruin her innocence any more than I already had, and I didn't want her to worry more about my secret. If she'd known how completely the Wasp Queen could control me, she would have had nightmares for months.

I'd told the girls about their True Names so they would know what to expect. They had nothing to fear from giving up their True Name. The conversation made my stomach hurt, but it was true. They would be safe. They might be controlled in service to the city, but at least they would be provided for. And they wouldn't be forced to kill anyone. It was better than the fate that awaited me.

Should I have told Ella after all? I hadn't wanted to frighten her, but keeping her ignorant had backfired. Perhaps she wasn't frightened enough of getting involved in mage business. Whatever had Weslan been thinking?

I rolled to my side and squeezed my blanket in my fists. I had to calm down by morning. I couldn't let her know how close I was to losing my mind and falling apart completely. For Ella, I had to stay strong.

~

The next morning, I lectured Ella and Weslan separately. I reminded Weslan of his promise not to pursue Ella, and he agreed readily enough. I still couldn't shake the feeling that he wasn't very concerned about keeping the promise. Was he counting on Ella to make the first move? She wouldn't do that. She hated him … didn't she?

Regardless, things between them changed. Ella welcomed him back. He helped with the bakery, and she didn't rip him apart every chance she got. The rest of the day passed in harmony and goodwill. The next day, Ella and Weslan surprised the twins with a birthday cake, and the easy camaraderie between them was a dramatic change from the antagonism she'd shown since he arrived.

I could no longer deny the truth. Ella was ready. It was time. I had to tell her we were leaving. I went to bed and promised myself I'd find the words before I slept.

The next morning, the words still hadn't come. I hastily ate a small breakfast alone at my vanity before retreating to the roof to pace in the morning sun. I pulled my braid over my shoulder and twisted it with one hand, breathing in the scent of dirt and tomatoes.

I had to find the words … the right words, the perfect words. *Ella, thank you for all that you've done for us. We love you dearly. But it's time for us to—*

We have to—

We can't risk staying here anymore, letting you do all the work to provide for us.

No, that would make her think we were leaving because of her. She'd be even more devastated. *The twins are too old to stay—*

I strangled a groan and flung open the door to downstairs. I had to get this over with. The words would be the wrong ones, but perhaps she'd see on my face that I loved her. Hopefully, she would understand I wasn't abandoning her because I wanted to but because it was the right thing to do. And it was.

When I entered the kitchen, Ella greeted me with a brilliant smile lighting her face. "You're never going to believe this."

I'd hear her story, and then I'd tell her. I breathed a sigh of relief at the short reprieve. "Morning, dear. Believe what?"

She dropped a heavy pouch onto the table. The dull clank of coins caught my attention.

I glanced inside. What was she talking about? "What is this? Where did you get this?"

"You know how, last night, Weslan said my cake was so good that we could sell it?"

Nervous butterflies danced in my stomach. I listened with half an ear, mentally preparing my speech at the same time. *We love you, but it's time for the twins to* … No, that didn't sound right. "It was good. You're a talented cook."

"Well, this morning, I made another cake. Actually, I made a whole bunch of small cakes with Weslan's help. And then I sold them in the street before anyone was even down for breakfast. All the students and workers on their way out of the quarter snatched them up. I sold out before a half hour had passed! Can you believe it?"

She was halfway through her story before her words sunk in. Wait—she'd sold mage-craft cakes out in the open? "They bought them all?" All thoughts of revealing my decision to leave fled my mind.

Ella frowned. "Yes. I charged low prices, so I guess it was an easy sell. But we made more than enough money to cover the cost of the ingredients, and Weslan used some of the profit to buy more ingredients for breakfast today. And the best part is—"

"Hold on. You sold them in front of the bakery?" She could have drawn trackers right to our door, and I never would have gotten the chance to say good-bye! "What were you thinking?"

"What are you talking about? I thought you would be happy! We finally made money."

"I told you not to worry about it, Ella! I had it covered." My cheeks flared with heat, and I pulled at the end of my braid, twisting it around my fingers. "Money is fine, sure. But not at the risk of giving away our safety here. You could've led any tracker to our door with the kind of attention you must've drawn."

Ella flinched as though I'd slapped her, and I cringed inwardly.

I'd almost lost her. And now I'd lost the nerve to tell her the truth. Furious and ashamed, I spun on my heel and fled.

Chapter 20

Ella and Alba lay side by side on Alba's bed, flipping through the pages of the *Herald* and dissecting Ella's latest dress at the market. "Was it more like this one?" Alba asked, "or this one?" They lay on their stomachs, huddled over the newspaper, their feet swinging in unison as though they'd coordinated their movements. Weslan had been using his power as an appearance mage to transform her ragged clothes into beautiful ballgowns at the market every day, and Alba couldn't stop asking about them.

Weslan's dramatic magical displays each morning had drawn masses of customers to their stand at the market, and they'd made up the initial investment with surprising speed. I'd realized from the first day how wrong I'd been about Ella's plan. It was risky, but it was working. It would change everything for her.

I fixed my attention back on the bakery's books. Ella had meticulously recorded her daily expenses and sales at the market stall, and even when I deducted money to set aside for our meals, water, luminous, and other necessities, we were swimming in marks. Thanks to her bakery stall, we would be able to pay off Cyrus, including the generous late fee I'd promised, within the next two days.

I heaved a sigh. Still, she would never be safe as long as

I lived in the bakery. Whether she kept the bakery or not, the twins and I had to leave.

Ella and Alba were lost in their conversation about dresses. How many more moments would they have as sisters? I couldn't watch any longer.

I got up and went downstairs to the kitchen. Weslan slumped at the table, devouring yet another bowl of victus. He exhausted himself every day helping Ella with the stand. I didn't dare confront him. He was only doing what I'd hoped he would do when I hired him—putting her needs first and helping her survive.

Even better, their new stall at the market had given her a fresh interest in life. She'd lost her future in government work, but with Weslan's help, she'd gained a new dream for the bakery. She was far happier now than she'd ever been at the Royal Academy. At least when we paid the fine, she'd have a choice about whether to continue here or not.

Weslan truly had helped her heal from the attack. Ella's scar still ran angrily down the side of her face, a stark, jagged line from temple to jaw, but the lightness in her step and the persistent, genuine smile on her face made her lovelier than ever. No doubt Weslan had noticed too. I just hoped he'd remember his promise and keep his hands to himself.

"Weslan."

He straightened slightly. "Yes?"

I searched his face. Why had I come downstairs? Perhaps I simply couldn't bear to observe Ella and Alba in what could be one of their last sisterly moments.

"Nothing. I just …" I trailed off and joined him at the kitchen table. "Soon. Ella is better, thanks to you. We'll be able to pay off Cyrus in a day or two. I'm going to leave as soon as we do. You can send the twins out, once the furor of my surrender dies down. Hopefully, no more than a week or two later. If the authorities don't believe the twins' story of hiding in the Badlands and they send trackers to search the city for my trace, I don't want the twins or Ella here when they come to the bakery."

He nodded solemnly. "Does Ella know?"

I folded my fingers together. Then, I unfolded them. I'd wanted to tell her, I just …

He sighed. "Zel …"

"I know, I know." I leaned back in my chair and tilted my head toward the ceiling. "I just can't do it."

"She'll be upset no matter what, but she'll be devastated if you don't tell her yourself."

"But can't you explain once I—"

"No! Zel, don't ask me to do that."

I shifted in my chair, my skin tightening uncomfortably as guilt pricked at me.

"She's finally trusting me," he said. "She's been hurt so much already. Please, don't make me hurt her like that. Didn't you say she needed to trust me once you left? Well, if she finds out that I knew you were leaving and didn't tell her, all that trust we've built will be lost."

I heaved a sigh. I wanted to plant my forehead on the table, but I held myself upright. "Fine. I'll … I'll try. I'll do it. Not today, but soon."

~

The next day I paid the tax. When Cyrus saw the thickness of the envelope, he yanked it from my hands and licked his lips like a starving man as he thumbed through to count the marks. It was all I could do to hold myself still in his dark, dirty office and wait for his confirmation.

"Where'd you get this money?" He peered at me over the thick envelope, watching me with a new fascination.

I hovered between fight and flight instincts, my power teetering on the brink of wildness once again. I took a deep breath and tried to calm myself. "Ella has a new stall at the Theros Street Market. It's quite successful."

He raised his eyebrows and watched me as though waiting for more information, but I couldn't speak any more. At the sight of his hungry gaze, my mouth went dry.

"I see." He stuffed the envelope into his pocket and leaned back on his heels, a satisfied grin easing across his face. "Be on your way then, *Mrs. Stone.*"

I stiffened. He'd emphasized my name like he knew it was a façade. He was rubbing in the fact that he knew I had never been with Ella's father, and that Ella and I had been hiding something all this time.

I left, not trusting myself to stay another moment longer. In the bright light of the morning street outside Cyrus's office, I felt like a fool. I had to get back to the bakery before I was caught. At least this time I hadn't rushed off impulsively, and I'd managed to hold in my trace in the blocks closest to the bakery. Still, in the back of my mind, the idea of getting taken without having to explain myself to Ella had its appeal.

I was a coward. That was my problem. I was terrified of confronting my problems head on. I needed to take a cue from Weslan and Ella and be brave, didn't I? If they had found a way to thrive when they'd both lost everything, I could do the right thing, tell Ella my plan, and set her free from me.

Tomorrow. I'd tell her tomorrow.

The next day, I kept watch on the streets around us from the roof, pacing and practicing my speech to Ella in my head. Well past noon, I spied Gregor hurrying down the alley toward the bakery, his face weathered by worry and fear. *No. Not again.*

I rushed downstairs and met him at the back door of the bakery. "Gregor? Is it—"

He nodded helplessly. "Another attack at the Theros Street Market. The Blight … they came in with knives and went after commoners shopping at the market. That's all I know."

His words echoed in my ears, quiet and dim compared to the strange roaring sound that accompanied them. I nearly rushed past him out of the bakery to the market but held myself back. The last time I'd gone off impetuously, I'd almost blown my chance to say good-bye to Ella and the twins. I wouldn't be so reckless this time. "When?"

"Mid-morning … that's what I heard. I tried to go there, but the streets around the market are all gated off by the Quarter Guard."

I fought the rush of panic threatening to pull me under again. In the back of my mind, my power rumbled, hungry to take control again and end the Blight myself. I'd find them. I'd find where they were hiding, and I'd—

Gregor placed a hand on my elbow and ushered me to a chair. "I'm sure she'll be home soon. I'll go to the Quarter Guard station now and see if there is any word of who—" He broke off mid-sentence. "Of survivors."

I nodded numbly. "Thank you."

Gregor must have left at some point. but I didn't know when. I sat at the kitchen table, my fingers twined in the folds of my dress as I strained to control my breathing. The Blight was ruining Ella's life.

If she still lived, she had no doubt been hurt, or she would have come straight home. She'd lose the progress she'd made. She'd go back to the nightmares, the starts of fear in the middle of the day, and the search for nonexistent threats. And if she were dead?

My power heaved and strained at the thought. If she were dead, I'd destroy the Blight before they even had a chance to beg for mercy. They'd never see me coming. I sat in my chair and squeezed my eyes shut. *Stay under control. You can do this.*

The wildness of my power eased slightly, and I opened my eyes. A worn, old book sat on the table beside me, along with a thin stack of papers covered in neatly slanted notes. Ella must have left them on the kitchen table that morning. I craned my neck to read the title—*A Theory of Common Commerce.* She must have been searching through her old Royal Academy textbooks to find ideas for the market stall's operation.

The sight of her innocent attempt at research was simply

too much. My self-control snapped like a weakened thread, and I shot to my feet. My sweet, hardworking stepdaughter had never hurt anyone, yet the Blight had tried to steal her future again. I would end them.

I strode to the door and slipped outside. I'd start with the market, and if any of the Blight dared to linger there, I'd—

"Zel?" Weslan sent me a worried glance. He and Ella stood before me beside their beat-up handcart with a sad collection of smashed bakery trays piled inside. They were both dusty, disheveled, and—Weslan, especially—covered in dried blood, but they were alive.

~

They went back to the Theros Street Market the very day it re-opened. I couldn't believe my ears when Ella herself insisted on being part of the opening. She knew it was their stall the Crimson Blight had been targeting, and yet, out of some misplaced loyalty to the city that had been nothing but cruel to her, she wanted to give the market another chance.

Ella, the girl who had been crying out from nightmares and starting with fright at the glimpse of anything red for weeks now! What was happening to my sweet girl?

Then the Quarter Guard had piled on so many fines because of the "unapproved use of magic," the bakery stand had been crushed anyway. And she still wouldn't give up. Now she was trying to persuade me to go along with her wildest scheme yet—an experiment in using magic to help the other shops on our lane, in order to persuade the Asylian government to change their regulations on mage employment.

I blamed Weslan for this strong, brave, new Ella. Weslan and his flirtatious smile and his frustratingly loyal support of her schemes. The boy needed to stop thinking with his heart and use his head. Hadn't I hired him to keep her *out* of trouble?

Ella leaned forward and clasped her hands as she rested them on the dinner table. "If we can just convince the government to change the regulation on mages, everything will be different! Imagine, Zel. Yes, Weslan and I could operate the bakery without those extra fines for unapproved use of magic. We'd be profitable again. But it would be so much bigger than just us." She smiled and shot a sideways glance at Weslan. "Imagine what all those mages could do for the city's merchants and commoners if they were free to use their powers for profit, instead of living as—well, as little more than slaves for the government and the Procus families."

Weslan was watching Ella with completely undisguised longing. I kicked his knee under the table. He squared his jaw and shifted closer to Ella. *Weslan …*

Ella continued without noticing our exchange, her words jumbling together as she rushed through her explanation. "All we have to do is get the initial numbers. I know it's risky. I'll admit that. But if we can get numbers to prove that mages working with merchants will help the city's economy recover from the plague, that should be enough to convince the prince to consider the change." She stopped at last and drew in a deep breath. "What do you think?"

I leaned back and raised my face to the cloudy night sky. The twins had taken the dinner dishes down from the roof, but a small luminous lantern remained on the bare table, offering a bit of light against the heavy darkness. I breathed in the familiar scents of the garden—dirt, vegetables, and herbs. "Fine." I exhaled in a long sigh. "I don't know what else to say, El. Just promise me you'll be careful."

"I will! Of course I will. And … well, if this works, and they change the regulations on mages, maybe you and the girls could be free too."

Oh, Ella. The Asylian government would never let me go free, and if they knew Ella and the girls had helped keep my secret, they'd punish them too. "Perhaps."

"Whatever happens, at least we can say that we tried,

right?" Weslan leaned closer to Ella as he spoke. "I don't—I won't—"

I silenced him with a glare, and he broke off mid-sentence.

He met my gaze, and this time, he didn't look away. The sheer defiance in his eyes startled me. I'd hired him so he would owe me, and his sense of obligation would drive him to take care of Ella for me when I left. He'd done his job too well, and now, he was loyal to Ella first. It would only be a matter of time before she discovered his feelings. And though she tried to hide it, I suspected she felt the same way about Weslan.

I wanted to grab Ella and pull her away from him. How could I in good conscience seek to protect her from every other threat and do nothing about the danger Weslan posed to her heart? One way or another, Weslan would eventually break her heart, just like Darien's death had destroyed mine.

I clenched my fists in my lap and bit my tongue to keep from speaking. Ella was a grown woman now, a nervous, innocent student no longer. She'd survived two attacks by the Blight and been bankrupted by government regulations, but instead of breaking her will, each obstacle had made her stronger, more determined. If I kept trying to protect her from pain and failure, I'd no doubt end up driving her even further away.

I stood and settled for glaring at Weslan. "It's on you, then, Ella." She was probably confused, but I was past caring. I hoped Weslan knew that I'd blame him if anything happened to her because of this. "I won't stop you. But know this is on you."

Chapter 21

Five days later, I banished the twins to the roof for extra script practice before bed, and I paced back and forth in the kitchen. My daughters were ready. I was the one who wasn't ready.

Ella was fine. She was falling in love with Weslan. She was getting ready to attend Prince Estevan's selection ball tonight, masquerading as a Procus lady. She was risking her life in a wild attempt to change hundreds of years of mage regulations. Why wouldn't she be fine? A hysterical laugh bubbled out of my throat.

No, everyone was fine but me.

I couldn't bring myself to leave or send Bri and Alba away. Each day, I pushed them to practice a little more, to get their script down a little smoother. I simply couldn't work up the courage to tell Ella the truth. She'd gone forward with her experiment, and somehow, the Crimson Blight had gotten word. They'd destroyed the shops that had made use of Weslan's magical tools, and the blast had taken poor Gregor's life. I'd held her that night as she sobbed and wailed and came apart at the seams. She was only a child, and she'd been forced to bear far too much grief in her short life. I'd been certain this would finally be the end of it.

But the next morning, she'd woken up even more determined to go through with her plan. Now she was marching into the belly of the beast, armed only with a fanciful dream to change things for the mages in the city, and I didn't even have the guts to tell her I was turning myself in tonight. Every time I imagined saying good-bye, I thought of her narrow shoulders shaking as she cried in my arms the night Gregor died. I might be a monster, but even I wasn't sure I could leave her like this.

I scowled at the ceiling as though I could see through it to where Weslan and Ella were ensconced in my living quarters, making use of my full-length mirror. Weslan was using his powers to prepare Ella for the ball. They'd taken long enough. Just what did he need to do that required so much time?

What if Weslan had finally declared his intentions?

I sped up the stairs to the living quarters and stopped short in my tracks.

Weslan and Ella stood face to face, a mere hand's breadth apart, with matching expressions of longing on their faces. Ella wore a glowing, pale blue ball gown that spilled off her shoulders and wrapped around her body in an artful way only mage-craft could accomplish. Her dark hair flowed down in perfect, tousled tendrils from the voluminous pile atop her head, caressing her shoulders and framing her face. And her skin glowed like a fine luminous lamp, not from the mage-craft makeup but from the obvious adoration directed toward Weslan.

Should I step in?

Ella leaned closer to Weslan, and he mirrored her movement. Weslan wore a common laborer's brown work pants and white, buttoned shirt, loosely tucked in with the sleeves rolled up to his elbows. Yet the two of them looked perfect together, as though the rest of the city had simply faded away and left them alone in their own glowing, magical bubble.

Weslan's blond hair fell into his eyes. "Ella … I need

to—"

I couldn't take it anymore. "Ready?" My voice sounded sharp even to me.

Ella and Weslan jumped guiltily.

I narrowed my eyes at Weslan. "Ella, I thought you were planning to be somewhere tonight."

Ella flushed and ducked her head. "I was about to leave."

I regretted my harsh interruption immediately, but she was already striding downstairs. Weslan avoided my gaze as he helped her down the steps.

Say something. Apologize. Say good-bye, in case this is the last time …

But it was too late. Ella sped off to the ball in a gleaming white and silver fomecoach as Weslan collapsed against the side of the bakery in the alley.

I pressed a hand to my stomach. The sight of Ella's extravagant dress and the fomecoach had nauseated me. She'd looked just like the old me, the way I used to look when the Wasp sent me on an outing from my tower. But Ella wasn't going off to murder some poor fool who'd crossed the wrong Draician clan leader. She wasn't being compelled by her True Name to use her power for evil. No, she didn't even have a mage's power or a True Name. She was doing this on her own.

Ella was free, yet she was laying down her freedom for the Asylian people who didn't deserve her sacrifice one bit. She was dressing up like a Procus beauty and throwing herself into harm's way, not to advance her own interests, but to help the city that had always hated her, to free mages who would never give her the time of day. How could one girl be so strong? And why was I so weak?

I helped Weslan inside and shut the door. He collapsed into a chair in the kitchen, and I poured him a glass of water. He took it but didn't drink.

"Weslan," I said, my voice quiet as a whisper, "I'm sorry …"

He shook his head, and I trailed off.

The accusation on his face made my insides twist into knots. "I won't hurt her. I promised I wouldn't. But you will."

I shrank back and crossed my arms. "No, I—"

"You will. There are many ways to hurt someone. Ella wants nothing more than to be trusted, to be wanted. And if you leave tonight, you'll destroy her. It would be the worst thing you could do."

"Fine. Then I won't."

He rapped the table with his knuckles. "And you need to tell her. If you don't tell her tomorrow, I will. I'm serious. This has gone on long enough."

I glared at him, but he straightened in his chair and glared right back at me.

"I know you think I forced her to form a bond with me when I gave her my True Name, but she's a grown woman. She forgave me of her own volition, and she's the one who chose to accept my name. She's not a child. I've done nothing to pressure her or push her to be with me. I'll give her time and space to make her own free choice, and if she rejects my suit, I'll leave her be. I'll never take her choices from her, Zel. I swear it."

My face burned, and my pulse raced. Just what was he saying?

"But you … you've never once given her a choice. You decided you had to leave, and you never even discussed it with her. You told me that the evil of using a True Name is to have your choices taken away. But isn't that what you've done to Ella?"

"How dare you?" I clenched my fists and took a step toward Weslan.

He stood up and shoved his chair back. "You just don't want to hear it because you know it's true. You don't need Ella's True Name to take her choices away because you've never given her any in the first place."

My power sizzled with rage. I inhaled sharply, straining

with all my might to keep it under wraps.

If Weslan noticed my struggle, his face didn't give it away.

"I've given her everything I could," I hissed. "Everything!" I stomped out of the kitchen and up the stairs.

I paced in our living quarters, flipped aimlessly through the faded pages of my journal, and stared at one page of a novel without seeing any of the words on it. Then I gave up and called the twins down from the roof and told them to get ready for bed.

"Did you see her, Mom?" Alba twirled and flung the skirt of her dress out around her. "She looked like a princess … a fairytale princess. I've never seen anyone so beautiful."

"I saw her. She was quite beautiful." Guilt and anger still battered me from the inside, so I didn't continue the discussion. "Get ready for bed."

They washed up and put on their nightgowns, then lay down in bed. Would this be our last night? I sat on my bed, numb and drained.

"Mom?" Bri's voice was unusually soft and hesitant. "Are you leaving soon?"

"Yes." I could barely force the word out past the lump in my throat.

"You'll tell us before you leave, right?"

"Yes," I whispered. "I will."

The twins fell into a deep sleep, but I just sat there. Weslan was right. I needed to get it together. I needed to be stronger for the twins, for Ella. Why couldn't I be better? Kinder? Braver? It had been over thirteen years since I left Draicia, and yet I was still the same frightened girl, cowering in her tower, too scared to stay and too scared to flee.

Much later, the unfamiliar sound of a fomecoach in the alley startled me out of my guilt-ridden daze. I straightened and peered out the window, but all I could see was the building across the alley. The kitchen door slammed, and soft voices reached me from the kitchen. Ella was back.

Then new sounds interrupted the night—a series of fomecoaches rolling down the narrow cobblestone lane in front of the bakery, unfamiliar voices, and lots of footsteps. I turned my luminous dial all the way down and peered down at the street.

They'd found me. The fomecoaches's doors bore the unmistakable flashing gold of the trackers' insignia. I stood as though in a trance. I had to leave. If they found the girls here, they'd never admit them to the Mage Academy. The twins would be arrested and sent straight to the dungeon. I hurried down the stairs before he could wake the twins. If I surrendered to the trackers before they had the chance to come inside, perhaps—

"FEMALE CITIZENS. ASSEMBLE." The tracker's amplified voice was painfully loud in the quiet of the night.

What?

"CITIZENS," the voice said, "You are harboring a fugitive suspected of attempting to assassinate the crown prince. Assemble in the street now. All female citizens aged thirteen to twenty-one will be taken in for questioning now."

Ella and Weslan were already in the bakery's shop when I joined them.

"Assassinate?" Ella looked like she was about to faint. "I don't understand—"

"CITIZENS. All female citizens aged thirteen to twenty-one, assemble now, or we will enter and bring you out."

They weren't here for me. Relief rocked me, and then the tracker's words finally hit me. They weren't here for me. Even worse—they were here for Ella.

"Mom?" Bri rubbed her eyes sleepily. Alba huddled at her side. "What's going on?"

I opened my mouth, but no words came out. In all the good-byes I'd ever imagined, I'd never thought of seeing Ella led off to her execution.

"Zel, I'm so sorry." Ella's voice was raw and broken. "I never thought this would … I don't know why they're doing this. I'll go out, tell them it was me, and get them to leave."

No! It was supposed to be me. I grabbed her arm and held tight. "Ella, if you go out now, they'll execute you. If you're even just suspected of this crime, you'll be executed without trial."

"I-I-I don't know what to say. I'm just so sorry."

Ella pulled away. but Bri stepped in front of her. "Stay in here, Ella."

I gaped at Bri. What was she doing? In a heartbeat, Bri whisked outside and into the street. And Alba followed her sister.

Ella rushed after them, but Weslan held her back from the door. "Ella, wait. Think! They're obviously too young to have infiltrated the ball and gotten anywhere near the prince. The guards will take them in for questioning, bring them home, and keep looking for the real culprit. This way, no one will come looking inside our house. That's all that matters. Keep the trackers out. The girls will be home as soon as anyone gets a clear look at them."

Somehow, his logic finally reached me. He was right. Unlike me or Ella, the twins would be safe with the Quarter Guard. I stepped in front of Ella.

She wriggled in Weslan's grip. "You can't know that! It's too big of a risk!"

"You're a fine one to talk about risk." Hadn't she been telling me all this time that the risks we'd taken were worth it? "Would you rather risk your execution, or risk that the twins will be held in the Quarter Guard station for the night?" Ella sagged as the fight drained out of her. Weslan let her go as I pushed her toward the kitchen. "Go to your room and shut the door. If they decide to search the bakery for more girls who fit the description, there's a better chance they won't see you."

I waited until the twins entered a fomecoach and the line of coaches left the street. My power was quiet. All I felt was a thick fog of grief and helplessness—unbearable, smothering, and tearing my heart in two.

"I'm so sorry." Ella came out of her room. Her voice was hollow.

"It's not your fault." It wasn't. It was no one's. After all my plans to leave Ella, after resolving to let Ella make her own choices and take her own risks, I had never foreseen something like this. I collapsed into a chair at the kitchen table. "I thought …"

Fresh tears fell. Perhaps it was indeed my fault. I'd told them about Darien, hadn't I? What had I said? *To love someone so much you would give your life for them—that's beautiful.* They'd taken me at my word and offered themselves up in Ella's place. I hunched my shoulders and tried to breathe.

"I told them about their father. How he sacrificed his life for me so I could get away, so I could leave Draicia." I choked out the words like someone had a death-grip on my throat. "I thought if they knew of his love, it would be a comfort. But I should have known Bri would want to be just like her father."

I stared at the table, replaying that conversation with Bri and Alba in my head. Had I been wrong to tell them about him? Had I been wrong about love, about beauty, all along? He'd loved me, but he'd left me. What was the point of love that sacrificed itself? Then there was none of it left for comfort, for help. And yet, what was the point of love that was unwilling to make a sacrifice? Was that truly love?

A knock sounded at the front door.

Weslan stood and placed a hand on my shoulder. "Don't worry, Zel. That must be them now." He left the room.

I held my breath. Back so soon? I strained to hear the rumble of male voices at the front door, but I stayed where I was.

Suddenly, Weslan shouted, his voice sharp and angry. "What's the meaning of this?"

The door slammed, and Weslan entered the kitchen, cradling a dusty box in his arms like a baby. He held the box out to me, his face heavy with sorrow. What was he doing?

I took the box and lifted the lid. All the air whooshed

out of my lungs. It couldn't be. How? Why? What were my daughters doing out there without their shoes? A small scrap of red paper peeked out of one shoe. Reality stretched, then snapped.

The Blight. They'd taken my precious girls. An image of slender bare feet slipped into my mind, and then an image of the ruthless men who'd taken them. I'd kill the Blight for this. I'd kill them all.

I was dimly aware of Ella speaking and Weslan standing at my side. There would be no more fighting the rage. No more holding back my power. I let the waves of hunger crash over me as my power strained to absorb every last drop of Crimson Blight and the trackers who'd obviously helped them.

"Weslan, you'll come with me." My voice was hollow and distant. "We will get them home safely, whatever it takes." And when the girls were safe, I'd unleash my power on the enemy who'd been tormenting my family for months. There would be nothing left of them by the time I was through.

My power strained again, but I kept it under control long enough to meet Ella's eyes. I couldn't leave her like this. I had to give her something to hold onto. "Stay here and stay safe, Ella. I-I forgive you. And I love you like a daughter, no matter what. Never forget that." The truth of those words sent pain spiking through my chest, but I smothered it.

I had to act. The time for cowering in the bakery was over. I let my power sweep me away again, and I left her in the bakery alone.

~

Weslan led me through the dark, city streets. "The old warehouse at Merchant and Silvus streets. In the River Quarter. That's where he said to get them."

I let my power's hunger carry me along. I didn't know how long we walked, and I barely felt the ache of my feet when we finally entered the dusty, dirty River Quarter. I only knew I had to find my daughters and kill their captors.

After several more blocks, Weslan stopped and pointed. "There it is. Silvus Lane."

A faded old street sign was nailed to the building on the corner where we stood. We were close.

I pressed my fingers to my temples. Now that I'd surrendered to my power, its hunger was only growing. A vicious headache stabbed at my temples. It had to be at least two hours past midnight by now. We had to get this over with. "When we arrive, stay out of sight. I'll stay at the entrance, and only go in if they let the girls out first. Then you take the girls and run."

He nodded. "Agreed. But what about you?"

What about me? I simply shook my head to dismiss his foolish question. What did it matter what happened to me? Once inside, I'd kill them all or die trying. There was nothing left for me to worry about.

When we reached the warehouse. I signaled for Weslan to stay back. He melted into the shadows across the street. Then I approached the door. *Soon*, I whispered to my power. As soon as the girls were safe, I'd let it loose.

The door opened before I raised my hand to knock. A tall, blond man answered the door with a smile, and light spilled out of the warehouse, illuminating the shadowy street. His face was finely structured, and his body was long and narrow. His appearance was Kireth in every way—golden, pale, and terrifying. Just like me.

My power wanted to rush at him, but I held it back. "Send them out." My voice was cold and empty. "Send them out now, and I'll come inside with you."

"Of course," he said, his smile widening. "Wait but a moment."

I held myself still, though I ached to wrap my hands around his throat. Then two men appeared behind him, with Bri and Alba gripped tightly in front of them like shields. My daughters were bound and gagged, clad in their soft, white nightgowns, and wearing a single shoe each. They were silent. They weren't even crying. They only watched me from over the strips of dirty rags binding their mouths, their eyes wide and faces pale.

At the sight of their helpless, terrified faces, my power strained even harder. "Send them out," I repeated. "Now." I stretched out my hand to the blond man to let him know what would happen if he didn't.

Instead of rearing back in fear, he inched closer, watching me with unwavering attention, his lips parted as though with anticipation.

Then he broke into laughter.

I tensed. Could I kill him and his men before either of his men had a chance to hurt my girls? I'd been fast before, but I hadn't been tested in thirteen years. Perhaps I still had my old speed.

A cry of pain came from the street behind me. I whirled around, my stomach sinking.

Weslan fell to his knees several steps away from me as two large, muscular men shoved him down. A third man—thin and pale, with stringy black hair—stood over him, his face twisted in horrifying excitement. He grabbed Weslan's hair, pulled out a long, wicked knife, and held it to Weslan's throat.

I started toward the man with the knife, but then he jabbed the tip into Weslan's throat, drawing blood as Weslan let out a hoarse gasp. The man with black hair smiled.

I turned back to see the blond man in the doorway had stepped closer to me. He drew closer still, until our bodies were mere inches apart.

My power raged with hunger at his nearness. With one touch, his life would be mine.

"Your True Name, my dear. Or all these precious young mages will die."

The two men holding Bri and Alba drew long knives like the one at Weslan's throat. Alba let out a high, fearful noise.

Bri leaned away from the man's knife, but he responded by pulling her closer to it. She shut her eyes.

Fury ripped through me like lightning in a summer storm. I was fast, but not that fast. I'd have to choose—save one of them. An impossible choice.

I looked over my shoulder at Weslan. "Don't do it," he managed, before the knife was pressed against his throat again.

I took a deep breath. I'd trained for this, hadn't I? I'd prepared myself to be under my True Name's control again. I could do this. For my daughters. For Weslan. For Ella. I could be strong.

"Rapunzel," I breathed as the man leaned closer. My voice was soft and light as a feather, but the power in my name filled the air.

The blond man sighed, a rapt expression coming over his face. "Rapunzel," he repeated.

I tensed. Now was my chance. I'd find out if my training had any affect.

"Rapunzel, don't move a muscle unless I tell you to."

I straightened my spine as the leash of my True Name circled around my will. I'd fight it. I'd kill him, and then …

The leash tightened, and my will disappeared. My arms fell slack at my sides. I stared straight ahead, my face relaxing into a blank, neutral expression. I was his.

~

The Blight's leader, Flavian, kept us in the hot, stifling warehouse for hours. I had no idea how much time had passed, but from the occasional glimpse of outside light, it had to be midday or later. That meant we'd been here for at least twelve hours. I could swear I'd been enduring his constant torment and humiliation for weeks. I followed dutifully on Flavian's heels, stopping only when he came to a halt in the warehouse's old loading bay. The air smelled of dust and rat droppings. I wanted to sneeze, but I couldn't.

Don't move a muscle. My eyes watered as my thoughts screamed.

Flavian took a step to the side. I followed, compelled by his command, stopping when I was mere inches away from his side. He sighed gleefully. "I'll never get tired of this. Never."

He placed a hand on my back, then dragged it to my waist. I longed to move away, but no matter how I pulled at my True Name, the leash held.

He winked. Then he pinched me, twisting the thin skin at my waist until I wanted to cry. Still, I didn't move. He winked again and dropped his hand at last.

The men around him waited silently, their expressions covered by close-fitting red masks. Finally done playing with me for the moment, Flavian addressed them. "We'll take the Mage Division first. Argentarius and Falconus will take care of each other while we do so. Rapunzel here will eliminate the other top-ranked authorities, but I'll require the rest of you to handle those lower in rank. Give every mage a choice—join us or die."

A man with a gravelly voice spoke. "What about humans?"

"No choice. Just kill them."

The masked man nodded. His tight-fitting red mask twitched. I had a feeling he was smiling.

"Wait! Zel! Wait, it's me!" Ella's voice rang out, echoing in the large empty bay.

No. Impossible. How had she found us? What was she doing here?

"Zel, I brought help," Ella said as she came to a stop in front of us. Her wobbly voice was nearly swallowed up by the ominous silence in the air around us. "Prince Estevan's men are here." She gulped. "I mean, they'll be here soon."

Get out, Ella! Run! My screams never reached my mouth. I only stood silently, watching my worst nightmare unfold.

The man with the gravelly voice grabbed Ella by the arm as Flavian laughed again. "Cinderella, Cinderella. Here you are. After all our little shared moments, I'd started to miss you."

He knew her? How could he possibly know her?

"Call me Flavian. It's so nice to meet formally, isn't it? I chose you the day you won the scholarship, and I bided my time. Who knew I had selected such a prize? You led me to your stepmother. I couldn't have asked for more."

He continued to taunt her as she sobbed hysterically, and as I listened, the pieces of a horrible puzzle clicked into place. Ella's nightmares, her constant fear and paranoia, the attack on her school, the market, the bakery's street—none of them had been a coincidence. He'd been stalking her deliberately, tormenting her under my very nose, and I'd never suspected it. What kind of stepmother was I? All I'd ever wanted was to protect her, and I'd utterly failed.

I blocked out his voice and strained with all my might at my True Name, unleashing my rage against it. My power pulsed with hunger for his life, but as I fought my Name, my body grew even more taut and still. His command held. My Name would not falter. There was nothing I could do.

Then my Name rang out from his mouth once again. "Rapunzel, my dear, kill her."

No, no, no! I'd always known that my power would ruin Ella's life, but not like this. Please, not like this.

My feet stepped toward Ella, closer and closer. She moved desperately in the bruising grip of the guard who held her. He was too strong, and she was too small. She couldn't escape.

I raised my hand toward her throat just as she collapsed and stopped fighting. This was it. After all my plans and prepared speeches, I was finally saying good-bye in the worst possible way, just like the monster I was.

Chapter 22

Ella met and held my gaze. The strength in her eyes was like a knife in my heart. Why was she so strong after everything she'd been through? And why was I so weak? I couldn't even buck my True Name, and that was the one thing I'd been training myself to do for years. It was the one thing that mattered.

Then she spoke, and her voice was small but firm and certain, no longer wobbling in fear. "Zel, I forgive you."

What was she doing? My hand drew closer. *Monster, monster, monster …*

"I love you like my own mother. No matter what. Never, never forget that."

I'd spoken the same words to her last night. How could she forgive me? How could she love me? I'd ruined her life. I was worthless. No, I was worse than worthless—I was evil. A nightmare personified, dropped into Ella's life when she had no choice in the matter.

The soft feel of my bed's coverlet. Cold spring rain hitting the window beside our heads. My belly swollen and straining, the twins moving restlessly in my womb as little Ella lay beside me, twisting the folds of the blanket with her fingers.

My hand moved closer.

Ella's soft, determined voice. "But I'll love you like a mother."

Time slowed down. My hand inched ever closer.

"That's fine, Ella. I'll—I'll love you too."

Her gaze was fixed stubbornly on mine. She wouldn't look away or close her eyes. My hand moved to her throat. One inch, and her innocent life would be gone—lost to my power, like so many other lives. *Monster. Nightmare.*

She'd chosen me that rainy night, so many years ago. I'd chosen her too, but at some point, I'd given up choosing her. I'd decided she was better off without me.

I drew in a breath. The familiar scent of Ella—coffee, sugar, and winterdrops—filled my nose. My girl. My Ella.

She knew who she was. She was my daughter. But who was I? A monster, or a woman? A nightmare, or a mother?

I strained against my True Name's leash once again. It didn't budge. What if I'd been wrong all along? What if it wasn't supposed to?

The new thought seemed to unlock something strange inside me. I froze, and my hand stopped its terrible progress. It should have been impossible. I was dimly aware of Flavian speaking, but I was too locked in my own struggle to listen to his words.

What if my True Name wasn't meant to disappear? What if it wasn't a leash, the way I'd envisioned it, ever since the Wasp Queen had taken my Name from me as a child? What if it was simply … me?

For the first time, I imagined my True Name and my will as a unified, powerful body, erupting from the ground like a massive snow-capped mountain, like Alba's Peak. Flavian's superimposed will encircled my enormous mountain like a thin, weak rope. The mountain grew and grew as I strained harder, stretching up to the sky, and the rope of his will snapped.

I was free.

I whirled away from Ella. My body obeyed with speed and precision, like nothing I'd ever felt on one of the Wasp's outings. A moment later, Flavian was gone. Then I took out the man holding Ella, and one by one, I took the life of every other red-masked monster in the shipping bay. My body moved fluidly through each darting movement—controlled, deadly, and mine. *Mine.* My body was mine to control and no one else's. My power didn't rule me. My rage didn't control me, and neither did Flavian.

When the masked men were all gone, I stood in the middle of the carnage, my power sated, my heart racing from the thrill of victory. Bri, Alba, Ella, and Weslan were safe. I'd done it.

A woman's voice called out, echoing in the silent loading bay. "Zel Stone, by order of the crown prince, you're under arrest. Come peacefully, or die now."

The words sank in slowly as I came back to reality. I followed the sound of her voice to the door Ella had entered through. A small group of black-clad men followed a woman with a gold armband, swords at the ready and crossbows trained on me.

Under arrest? Ridiculous. How did they expect to take me?

And yet, wasn't this what I'd wanted all along? I had planned to turn myself in, to stop hiding at last. I faced the woman who'd spoken and held up my hands in surrender, sinking to my knees.

The group approached slowly. A tall, broad man with wild, brown hair and a scruffy beard drew ahead of them. My heart skipped a beat when he met my eyes without smiling. His face was a mask of stone. "I've got her," he said to the soldiers at his side.

I couldn't breathe. I couldn't move. Darien? Alive? All this time? That was impossible.

He stopped in front of me and held out his hand. "Come with me, Zel." His voice was gruff, his expression indecipherable.

The room spun. I couldn't breathe. Darien. He was here. He was alive.

Chapter 23

Darien extended his hand to me, and he pulled me gently to my feet. The other black-clad men drew closer, weapons trained on me.

Darien pushed me behind him, using his body as a shield between me and their weapons. His shoulders were taut. "I said I've got her." There was no mistaking the hard threat in his voice.

I held my breath.

One by one, they lowered their weapons. Darien shifted his body toward me again and placed a firm hand on my lower back. "Just stay with me."

I followed wordlessly, in too much of a daze to think straight, much less question him. Less than an hour later, he led me into a small room in the Sentinels' basement headquarters at the palace.

The room was dim and musty. Dust covered most of the surfaces and a single small luminous lit the room from the ceiling. Darien waited warily at the door. He glanced over his shoulder. "Stand guard. Don't leave. I'll question her first."

"Hey, are you sure—"

Darien stepped into the room and shut the door, cutting off the man's objection.

My heart pounded. It was him. Alive, whole, and here. "How?" Had he abandoned me, after all? "Why?" My voice was barely more than a hoarse whisper.

He flinched at my words but stepped closer, his face twisted as though in physical pain. "The Wasp left me for dead that night. I nearly bled to death in the street, but I managed to crawl to safety. King Anton had sent a team of Sentinels after me, and they found me and saved my life. I'd gone rogue to come get you, and they brought me back to Asylia. But when I got back, the king detained me as punishment for going out on my own." His shoulders hunched as he spoke. "For three years, I was locked in the dungeons. It wasn't until the king passed responsibility for the Sentinels to Prince Estevan that I got another chance to search for you."

The roaring in my ears made it difficult to listen. I stumbled to a chair at the room's small table and stared down at my hands. Why were my hands blurry? I blinked rapidly, and a spattering of tears dripped onto my palms.

Darien knelt before me and looked at me intently. "It was you, wasn't it?" His voice was rough. "At that market in the Common Quarter after the queen died?"

I simply nodded. I couldn't speak.

He shook his head. "I thought you'd fled to the Badlands from the market. We searched the city for months. No one found any trace of you. I led teams to the Badlands whenever Prince Estevan allowed it, Zel. For years on end. I never gave up looking for you. I swear it. I was just looking in the wrong striking place." Self-loathing coated his voice.

My fingers twitched to reach out to him, to show him the comfort he would have shown me had our roles been reversed. I kept my hands in my lap instead. I didn't know what I was feeling. I wanted to slap him, kiss him, or scream at him. I held myself still and focused on not falling apart completely.

"I failed you, Zel. You and our—" His voice broke.

"Our daughters," I finished. My voice was numb, empty.

"Our girls."

His face crumpled. "All this time, I never imagined. I was such a stupid, striking fool! To get you with child and then just leave you there, to put my trust in the king and the Sentinels. I can never—" He gritted his teeth and cut himself off. "I'm so striking sorry. It's not enough. But I am."

I stroked the warm skin of his cheek. He shut his eyes and pressed his face into my hand. He was so familiar and yet so strange. I'd longed for him and dreamed of him for over thirteen years, and here he was—alive but broken, kneeling before me, unwilling to meet my eyes.

I traced the harsh lines on his face with the tips of my fingers. I'd mourned him all this time, believing he'd died for me, but he'd known I was alive. He'd been tortured with that knowledge, year after year, unable to find me.

I slid onto the floor so that I was on my knees, level with him.

His eyes remained shut, his body impossibly still.

I put one hand on his chest, feeling the steady beat of his heart. My heart had broken from grief, but his had broken too. How could two broken hearts continue to beat for so long?

Tears streamed down my face as I lifted my lips to his. I kissed him hesitantly, the saltiness of my tears mingling with the foreign taste of his lips. Then the desire I'd thought had died with him flared to life. I pressed my lips harder against his, and he groaned, wrapping his arms around me and pressing me closer.

"Zel," he breathed against my lips, "I love you."

I couldn't speak. I could only cry, my tears drenching his face as I met kiss after hungry kiss.

~

"Be ready." Darien eyed the closed door. "They'll be here to question you any moment. We won't have much time to get the girls."

"I'm ready."

He gripped my hand. "I won't leave you again. Not ever."

I nodded without speaking. He planned to break us out so we could flee to the Badlands. We'd take our chances there, together, as a family. But after everything that had happened, how could I leave Ella?

Footsteps thumped unevenly in the hallway outside the door. Darien tensed. Voices muttered just on the other side of the door, and then the door swung open. Darien leapt to his feet.

Prince Estevan limped inside, his mouth twisted in a wry grin. He shut the door behind him. "Stop plotting your breakout. We've a few matters to discuss."

Darien's shoulders sagged, and he sank to the floor, kneeling with his head bowed before the prince. I followed suit.

The prince ignored us. He staggered over to the table and collapsed into a chair. Darien rose and pulled me with him, gripping my hand tightly as we faced the prince. From the corner of my eye, I peeked at Darien. His posture was stiff, his shoulders high and tense. He held my hand like it was a lifeline. What would he do if Prince Estevan ordered us to stay in Asylia?

I squeezed Darien's hand once. "What matters do we need to discuss, Your Highness?" My voice was scratchy but level.

The prince leaned heavily against the back of his chair, but his slight smile remained. "It's nice to meet you, Zel. I've been hearing about you for years." The prince watched me with a strange expression, as though I were a bug he'd like to dissect. "I'm not one for love, but I have to admit that if there's anyone who knows what true love is, it's this man right here. He never gave up, you know. He knew you'd survived. He knew you were out there, somewhere. He never stopped searching for you."

Darien shifted on his feet and pulled me closer to him so that we stood with shoulders touching. He gave me a rueful half smile. "They thought I'd gone mad."

The prince let out a short laugh. "That we did." He crossed his arms and addressed me. "Here's the problem. They told me what you did at the warehouse."

Bucking my True Name. Killing the man who should have been able to control me. How could they allow me to live if they couldn't control me? Sickness seeped into my stomach, but I squared my shoulders and straightened my spine. I would never be controlled again. I'd never be anyone else's weapon. And I'd pay the price for that, whatever it was. Even if it meant death or imprisonment.

"You'd be safer in the Badlands. You and Darien and your children. I'd understand if you decided to leave. And if you do, you'll be free to go—all of you."

I exhaled slowly and felt Darien relax beside me. That was the last thing I had expected.

"But I'm here to ask a favor of you both." Prince Estevan leaned forward in his chair and winced. Then he rested his forearms on the table and settled his weight on them. "Don't go. Stay here, and help me."

I raised my eyebrows. Help him?

"The True Name system was already unsustainable. I've known it for years. We can't rebuild a city when a good portion of our population is controlled and resentful, rightfully so. Now we know for sure that True Names can be resisted, or broken, or whatever it is that you did. Word will spread. Mages will rebel, and the city will panic. The mage authority structure will crumble, and we will need to be ready with an alternative when it does." He tapped his fingers restlessly on the table and met my eyes. "I'm hoping you'll agree to help me find that alternative. If the most powerful mage in the city can resist her True Name but still chooses to stay and seek the good of the city, it will help restore confidence."

Beside me, Darien grew stiff again. He didn't want us to

stay. I pressed my shoulder gently against his, hoping my presence would keep him calm long enough to hear the prince out.

"There's another reason I need you. If we want to end the True Name system, every single mage in the city will need to be able to resist their True Name. Otherwise, we'll have an army of mages in Asylia that our enemies might be able to control. I've never heard of anyone doing what you did. That means you're our best chance of teaching our mages how to resist their True Name."

I nodded slowly. His logic made sense. And staying in the city would allow me to stay closer to Ella, and the twins could live a normal life.

"If we stay," Darien said, "we'll need assurances, Your Highness."

The prince tipped his head back. "Yes?"

"Secure housing for our family. Zel and our daughters will be targets when the city learns what happened. They'll be feared, probably threatened." He darted a glance at me. "They'll need to be protected."

The prince nodded. "You'll have it. What else?"

Darien squeezed my hand.

I spoke up. "The girls need a normal life, as much as possible. The Mage Academy. Training, and all that. They've been in hiding with me for thirteen years. I don't want them to pay for my Touch anymore. I want them to be free."

Darien tucked me under his arm and held me at his side. I felt his lips touch the top of my head in a quick, gentle kiss.

Prince Estevan's eyes flicked from Darien to me, his expression indecipherable. "Of course. They'll be treated as normal mages. As much as is possible, given that we don't yet know what threats will come against you. But if you want real security, you'll have to stay in the Mage Division at all times. Either that or in the palace. But the Mage Division offers more freedom. That's the best I can offer."

I supposed that was all I could hope for.

"One more thing." I lifted my chin. "Ella Stone must be

allowed to visit us whenever she wants."

~

The prince agreed to our requests and left us in the room. Minutes later, the door opened again, and a guard ushered Bri and Alba into the room. They dove at me, and I wrapped my arms around them, rocking back and forth as though they were little babies again. "Oh, girls … I'm so sorry …"

Bri shook her head vehemently, and then pressed it back against my shoulder again. "What else could you have done, Mom? They were evil. And you beat them. I wish I was as strong as you."

"I love you both so much." I pressed a kiss onto each precious head. "Everything is going to be fine now. We'll be free. Free!"

Alba tilted her head up, lips trembling. "You mean we can stay together?"

"We can."

She let out a pitiful sob and buried her head on my shoulder again. "Good," she mumbled through her tears.

How had I ever thought I could send them away? Why hadn't I seen that it was far too much to ask of her? *Monster.*

I silenced the spiteful voice in my head. I'd made a plan that would help them survive. I'd done my best with what I had. I wasn't perfect, but I'd kept them alive and as happy as possible for thirteen years. No, I wouldn't be listening to that voice anymore.

When Alba's sobs had quieted, I leaned back slightly. "Girls, there's someone I'd like you to meet."

Bri tensed.

Alba rubbed her eyes. "Who?"

I peeled myself away from the girls and went to stand by Darien, who was watching them silently with an expression of awe on his face. "This is Darien, your father," I said softly. "He didn't die in Draicia, the way I thought he did.

He's been looking for us all this time."

Alba blanched and took a step back.

Bri narrowed her eyes at him but addressed me. "He was here all along? Why didn't he find us sooner?"

I slid my hand into Darien's. What would it be like, to be meeting your daughters for the very first time? The girls he should have held as babies were young women already.

"We were very careful about not leaving traces in the city. You know that. But it turns out we were too careful. He thought we were hiding in the Badlands. He was searching the Badlands for us, never knowing that we were hiding at the bakery inside the city all along."

Bri nodded slowly. She fixed her gaze on Darien. "You wanted us. You just couldn't find us. But you … you *did* want us?"

Darien held out one hand to her, meeting her gaze unwaveringly. "I did. I do. I swear it. My daughters …"

Bri threw herself into his arms and wrapped him in a tight hug. "Daddy," she whispered against his shirt. A quiet, steady stream of tears escaped her eyes and flowed down her cheeks.

My throat tightened. It was the first time I'd seen Bri cry since she was a child.

Alba stood at the edge of the room with her arms wrapped protectively around her torso, watching Bri and Darien with furrowed brows. She caught my eye and shook her head. I went to her and put my arm around her.

"It's fine, sweetheart," I whispered. "When you're ready."

She leaned into me but didn't answer.

Chapter 24

I walked alone through the crowded, clean-swept streets of the Mage Division while Bri and Alba napped in our temporary housing in the mage barracks. I could not stay in the oppressively hot building a moment longer.

The warmth of the cobblestones seeped through my thin shoes as I watched the mages pass me on the footpath. Some even brushed against me as they hurried to class or work. None of them knew who I was. That would change soon enough, as Prince Estevan planned to announce my role in the upcoming reformations on mage controls.

I was free. After a lifetime of worry, I didn't have to hide anymore. Prince Estevan wouldn't force me to work for his government. Even if he changed his mind, he wouldn't be *able* to force me.

I stopped in the middle of the footpath and tilted my face toward the sky. The setting sun painted a soft mixture of pink, orange, and gray on the clouds over Asylia. The gorgeous sky seemed to reach for me, and I wanted to lift my hands and dance in a circle like a carefree little girl. I kept my body still, but I couldn't hide the smile that spread across my face as the joyful thought repeated in my head. *I'm free.* This was my home now—it was truly my home.

Someone bumped against me in the street, and I

apologized reflexively. The woman was bone-thin and clad in dusty rags, and she sped past me without acknowledging my apology. Curiosity nudged me to follow her, and I increased my pace. Why was she so thin? Was she from the River Quarter? They had victus there too, didn't they? An acrid smell tickled my nose. Wood smoke? I hadn't smelled the distinct scent of wood smoke since my time in Draicia and the Badlands.

Then the woman paused and looked over her shoulder at me, her lips curved up in a smug smile.

I stopped in my tracks. "Helis?" I whispered.

She nodded and ducked into a narrow side street.

I rushed forward. Had she escaped the Wasp? What was she doing in Asylia? Did she need help? She must have just come from the Badlands.

When I rounded the corner into the alley, I skidded to a halt. My stomach twisted. Helis wasn't alone.

"Hello, Rapunzel." The Wasp Queen—no, Lady Drusilla—stepped forward. Her narrow face was painfully thin, her cheekbones jutting out, her lips thin and dry. Her formerly glossy, dark hair hung in ragged, gray-black clumps around her heavily lined face, but her eyes were unmistakably familiar—sharp, mocking, and all-seeing. "I told you I'd always find you, didn't I?"

I inhaled sharply as the alley seemed to spin around me. "Where have you been?"

Drusilla only smirked. "Rapunzel, follow me and speak to no one," she said smugly. "And Rapunzel—do no harm."

Her will settled over me, but I flexed my True Name and shattered her commands before I took my next breath. "No." I stretched my hand toward her. She flinched, and Helis took several nervous steps backward. "That won't work anymore, Drusilla. And I'm not your slave."

Her nostrils flared. "Fine. I don't need your True Name anymore. My masters are too powerful for such child's play." She put her hand in her ragged cloak and drew out a small crystal vial, a glassy look coming over her eyes.

Her masters? What was she talking about? She opened the vial and flung the contents at me. I shot backward to get out of reach, but it was too late. A wave of tingling magic rushed at me, stinging my skin like sand whipped up by heavy winds. The magic faded, and a strange, crushing weight settled over me.

"You'll come with me now, Rapunzel." Her voice was distant and difficult to hear. "They want to meet you."

~

We were nearly to the city's south gate when I realized I'd been following her without protest. What had she done to me?

I opened my mouth to speak, but that painful, tingling magic sizzled around me again, forcing my mouth shut. I tried to slow my footsteps, but the sharp tingles increased their pressure and shoved me forward.

My head spun. The Wasp was controlling me, not with my True Name or her own will, but with some new, strange magic that had nothing to do with either. I'd sworn I'd never be controlled again, yet here I was, helpless and desperate.

We approached the gate too quickly. Would the guards recognize me and stop us from leaving the city? What if the same controlling power forced me to kill them too? Terror washed through me, setting my nerves on end.

A familiar man stepped out of the guardhouse by the gate, and I didn't know whether to be thrilled or horrified. Darien was here. He must have been working with the gate guards as part of the Sentinels' efforts to round up the last of the Blight.

He strode toward us, his crossbow raised, a look of utter fury on his face. "Get back, Wasp." His voice was hard as steel.

But she kept walking, and my body forced me forward, the painful tingles growing more biting the more I fought it.

"I said get back!" He fired on her, but she sent a blast of

magic to knock the arrow out of its path. Then she sent a gust of magic toward Darien. It shoved him violently backward, and he crashed on the ground by the gate.

Soldiers came running as he scrambled to his feet. He waved them back and ran at Drusilla again. What was he doing? Fear for him twisted my stomach into knots.

This time, when she blasted him with her magic, he dodged it by diving to the side. He corrected course and tackled her to the ground before she could gather another blast. She shrieked and pummeled him with a third blast of magic, but he held on, his arms in a vice-like grip around her neck.

A horrible screeching echoed in the street. A driverless fomewagon barreled toward Drusilla and Darien. Drusilla ignored Darien's grip on her neck and watched the fomewagon with a wild, excited look in her eyes. Was she using her power to force it to hit them? She would be willing to die just to kill Darien?

I opened my mouth to warn Darien, but the magic forced it closed. No! Not when I had just found him!

Darien released the Wasp at the last moment and dove out of its path, but the Wasp kept her glassy gaze fixed on the fomewagon as it sped toward her. Helis shrieked and lurched into the path of the fomewagon, the same dazed look in her eyes. Two, wet thumps followed.

The fomewagon stopped, a bloody mess on the ground beneath it. My stomach churned.

Darien dragged himself off the ground and raced toward me, but when he came close enough to embrace me, he hesitated. "Zel? Are you well?"

I couldn't answer him. The tingles had sealed my mouth shut. I sent him a panicked look and hoped he could tell from my expression that I was absolutely not well. My feet resumed shuffling toward the gate. Why hadn't the control ended when Drusilla was killed?

Darien's face mirrored my horror. What kind of new magic was this? And if he tried to stop me, what would the magic force me to do?

Darien looked from me to Drusilla's corpse on the ground, indecision and worry twisting his face. "Zel …"

I shambled forward, holding my hands at my sides and hoping he would be fast enough to get away if the magic pushed me to touch him.

"Purifier!" he shouted, "Get over here!"

A young woman in a gate guard's uniform rushed to him. "Sir?"

"I need you to remove whatever magic is controlling her."

The purifier's eyes widened. "But doesn't she have the—"

"She has the Touch. I know." Darien shook his head helplessly. "But if you don't do it, what will the magic force her to do?"

The young purifier's face blanched, but she squared her shoulders and nodded. "Yes, sir."

I held my breath as she walked bravely toward me, my tottering gait closing the gap between us all too quickly. Was she walking to her own death?

"Get it out as quickly as you can, then let go," Darien said, his voice tortured.

"I will." She grabbed my hand and shut her eyes. The tingles urged my power to come to life and stop her, but in the next instant, the heaviness and tingles left me. The purifier mage dropped her hand and stepped back, but she kept her eyes shut. After a long, quiet pause, she looked at me. "I did it. Dismantled it. The magic is gone."

I collapsed into Darien's arms, drained and exhausted. "What *was* that?"

He held me tight. "I don't know. But we'll find out."

Chapter 25

Sunlight streamed through the villa's generous windows, filling the kitchen with warmth despite the early hour. I rinsed a bowl of brambleberries, set it on the table, and sliced the fresh honeybread Ella had brought that morning.

Ella nudged me. "Coffee?"

I nudged her back. "Do you even have to ask?"

She giggled and spun to the other side of the kitchen, her blue skirt twirling around her. Grabbing the coffee pot with graceful fingers, she poured me a cup. "Then it's yours."

A knock sounded at the front door.

"Oh! That must be Wes." Pink flooded Ella's tan cheeks. She straightened her shoulders and smoothed her long, wavy hair until it flowed smoothly down either side of her face. She caught me watching and winked.

I couldn't help but laugh. "Go get him, then!"

"I'm going. I'm going." She practically skipped to the front door.

The twins and I had moved into a vacant professor's villa in the Mage Division two weeks earlier. After the chaos around the Blight's takedown had settled and the guards around our villa had worked out a routine for visitors, Ella had finally been allowed to see us, bringing a freshly sparkling smile, blushing cheeks, and a story about

Weslan—*Wes*—that had her and Alba squealing and giggling the whole morning.

I still struggled with the desire to protect Ella from whatever heartbreak the future might hold for them. If Darien and I could still love each other after over thirteen years of grief and pain, couldn't I believe in a future for Ella and Weslan?

I did my best, at any rate.

Today, Ella and Weslan had a break from the committee on mage regulations, and I had a break from meeting with the professor I'd be working with at the Mage Academy. We'd all be having breakfast together—a family, of sorts.

A rough beard nuzzled the skin on my bare neck and was followed by a sigh-inducing series of kisses. "Good morning," Darien whispered.

I leaned back against him as his arms came around me. "Good morning. I missed you." I peeked up at him over my shoulder. "I'm not sure how much longer I can take this."

He laughed, but the humor in his eyes was quickly replaced by desire. "Soon." He grinned and released me as Ella returned to the kitchen.

For the past two weeks, Darien had lived in the Sentinels' barracks. We wanted Alba to have more time to get used to him before he moved into the villa. He came to visit frequently, slipping in via the back door to help us get settled in the villa, helping us learn our way around the Mage Division and the Royal Palace. Even so, the distance was taking its toll on both of us.

Ella cleared her throat from the entrance to the kitchen. "Zel … it wasn't Weslan."

"Who was it?" Darien angled his body slightly in front of me.

"She says she's from the *Herald*."

I pressed a hand to my stomach. *Not yet. I'm not ready.* "She can come in. I knew this was coming. Prince Estevan told me last week. I just—" I broke off as goosebumps stood up on my arms.

Darien frowned. "What is it?"

"She's writing an article about me for the *Herald.* To tell the city my side of the story, I suppose. What it was like, to be enslaved in Draicia, to hide in Asylia for so long. To tell them what I plan to do now."

Darien rested a comforting hand on my back. "That's good, then. Isn't it?"

It was. At least, I hoped it would be. Either that, or the Asylians would be horrified that a murderer was free to walk their streets. One or the other. We'd find out soon enough which it was.

The woman who entered the kitchen was young, not much older than Ella. She smiled as she entered. "Zel? I'm Ruby Contos, from the *Herald.*"

Her voice was quiet and unassuming, at odds with the wild, bright red-orange curls that flowed nearly to her waist. Her skin was pale and creamy, but studded with countless orange freckles. A Westerner, working for the *Herald*? Her voice held no trace of an accent, but her coloring was undeniable. No one else had such odd hair and skin. I'd never seen a Westerner in person, and from the looks on their faces, neither had Darien or Ella.

She twisted a strand of red-orange hair around her fingers when none of us spoke. "I'm here for your interview."

I nodded slowly. "Please have a seat, then."

Darien pulled a chair out for her at the kitchen table.

"We were just sitting down to breakfast. Would you like to join us before the interview?"

"That's very generous. Thank you." She smoothed down her faded green dress as she sat and folded her hands in her lap.

We'd just joined her at the table when the twins' latest squabble over their fabulator crystals reached my ears.

"It's my turn!"

"Um, liar! You had your turn last night." Bri entered the kitchen scowling, then stopped short.

Alba followed and jabbed Bri in the side. She flushed bright red when she caught sight of our visitor.

I sighed. "Girls …"

Darien leaned back in his chair. "Breakfast first. And you can meet our visitor. Then we'll go together to buy another set of crystals. How about that?"

I pressed my lips together to hide a smile. He'd been planning this treat for a week but hadn't told them yet. Stepping in to save the day was a smart move.

Bri nodded eagerly. "Thanks, Dad."

Even Alba smiled wide enough to show her dimples. "A second set? Yes please!"

Darien was no doubt shouting for joy in his head, but he managed to keep his answering smile relatively staid.

I waved them over. "Come have a seat, girls. This is Ruby, from the *Herald*. She's doing an article on me. Ruby, these are my—our daughters, Alba and Bri, and you already met my other daughter, Ella."

Alba and Bri murmured greetings as they sat. Alba chewed on her bottom lip and appraised Ruby. "Is she interviewing us too?"

I didn't want any information about them spread through the city, but I couldn't exactly control what Ruby wrote about us.

Ruby shook her head, answering my unspoken question. "Not unless you want me to, Zel. I plan to focus on your time in Draicia and your work at the Mage Academy right now. I want to show the cost of the True Name system and share your experience as someone who has been … well, affected by it, for lack of a better term."

Affected? The old anger stirred within me, but I quieted it and focused on chewing a bite of honeybread. I swallowed, the normally delicious bread dry and tasteless in my mouth. "Then let's leave everyone else out of the article, please."

Bri sat back in her chair and sighed with obvious relief, but Alba pouted.

"That's fine." Ruby took a sip of her coffee before smiling at the twins. "You know, if you're planning to get a new set of fabulator crystals, I've heard they're releasing a new story tomorrow. If you bring your old crystals to the Falconus public studio, they might let you exchange them for the new ones and let you buy the new story early. Just tell them I sent you."

"Really?" Alba's pout morphed into wide-eyed excitement in the space of a heartbeat. "How do you know?"

Ruby's lips twitched. "Let's just say I have my sources."

Weslan joined us for the rest of breakfast, and after breakfast, Ruby and I took our coffees to the small sitting room at the front of the house. She sat in one of the soft, blue-cushioned chairs that had come with the villa, and I took the other.

Ruby pulled a thick notebook from her satchel, set it on her lap, and flipped it open to a fresh page. She pulled out a pencil and tapped it on the page for a long, quiet moment.

The silence in the sitting room set my nerves on edge. What if I said the wrong thing? Or what if I was honest, as Prince Estevan had instructed me to be, and I only made everything worse? What if, when the public knew my real story, they hated and feared me all the more?

She finally spoke. "Let's begin with your childhood in Draicia. Where did you grow up? What was it like?" Ruby's voice was gentle and encouraging, her expression confident.

Would she be so gentle and confident once she knew what I was and what I had done?

I took a deep breath. "I was born in the Draician slums, in a shack at the edge of Wasp clan territory."

I spoke until my mouth was dry and my coffee was lukewarm and sour. The sun shifted through the sky, warming the sitting room until sweat covered my back despite the soft breeze from the open windows.

Ruby wrote and wrote, nodding occasionally. No matter what I said, she never even flinched. Who was this strange, calm Western girl, so fearless and unaffected by stories of evil?

Finally, we got to the end of my story—how I'd learned to resist my True Name, prevented a bloody mage rebellion, and stopped the Crimson Blight. I told her how I was working for the Mage Academy now, and how Prince Estevan wanted me to help other mages learn to resist their True Name so they couldn't be used as weapons as I had been.

Finally, my words ran dry. I set my tepid coffee down with shaking hands. My fingers ached from gripping the cup so tightly. I stretched them out as subtly as I could.

Ruby wrote several more things in her notebook. When she stopped and looked up, her expression was sober. "Many in the city will fear the news that a mage with the Touch is living free and uncontrolled in Asylia—a mage who has used her power to kill in the past. Are they right to be afraid? What would you say to them?"

I bit my lip, suddenly terrified. What *would* I say? After a lifetime of being hidden away from the world, I finally had the chance to speak my piece. Was I too much of a coward to say it?

Ruby held my gaze unflinchingly. "What would you say, Zel?" She asked again.

"I-I would say that … I would say …" I folded my shaking hands in my lap and squeezed them together. For Bri and Alba and for every young mage like them, I had to force the words out.

"I would say that I never asked to be born with the Touch. I've never—not once—used my power of *my* volition to harm an innocent person. But because of my Touch, I've been imprisoned, controlled, and forced to hide since I was six years old." My voice grew firmer. "If I intentionally use my power to hurt or kill an innocent, I should face the requirements of the law and be dealt justice like anyone else. But I haven't ever used my power that way. So why have I been paying my whole life for something I've never done?"

A short while later, I saw Ruby to the door. "You should see the article in about a week," she said as she stepped onto the front stoop.

"That's fine." I didn't know if I'd be able to bring myself to read it when the time came.

She smiled knowingly. "You're a brave woman, Zel. It was an honor to meet you."

Really? "Um … that's— Well, thank you."

She waved good-bye, and I shut the door as she walked away. I turned and rested my back against the closed door, letting the cool, polished wood of the door sooth my overheated skin through my dress.

My words at the end of the interview echoed in my mind. It hadn't been until I'd spoken them aloud that I'd realized how true they were. I'd been tempted to use my power against others, especially Cyrus, but I hadn't done it. Being tempted wasn't the same thing as committing the crime, was it? It couldn't be. By that logic, they'd have to lock up the entire city.

I'd lived my whole life believing I was a monster, and every time I was tempted to use my power on my own, it felt like confirmation of the truth. But maybe it just made me human.

So much had happened in the past two weeks, I could barely keep up. Now that we were out of the bakery, in the real Asylia, I'd learned that the city didn't slow down for anyone. In less than a month, I'd start teaching classes at the Mage Academy where Bri and Alba would be students. Around that time, Ella would be wrapping up the first set of changes to mage regulations. I had a feeling Weslan would soon be giving her the same traditional words of love and promise Darien had given me in the tower years ago.

Ella, engaged to be married? It was too much. I couldn't help but let out a quiet laugh under my breath. Why did life's moments always slow down when I wanted them to hurry, and speed up when I wanted them to last?

Darien and the Sentinels still hadn't discovered anything about the strange magic Drusilla had used on me before she and Helis were killed. They had searched the Badlands outside Asylia and found no trace of where she had stayed or who her masters had been.

At Prince Estevan's insistence, we had kept the incident quiet. No one knew except the guards who had been there. The public would be frightened enough when they learned that mages would no longer be under True Name control. We couldn't risk introducing knowledge of a new threat now.

It had been over thirteen years since Darien had appeared in my tower, offering hope to a hopeless young woman. I had spent those years hiding, worrying, grieving, and barely surviving. But that time had also been spent loving my three daughters and working for each of them to have a future. They'd been years of laughing, hoping, learning, quiet breakfasts, and long nights. Years full of heartache, but of sweet, cherished memories too.

I returned to the kitchen and smiled as I gathered the breakfast dishes and put them in the sink. How many times in our final few months at the bakery had I worried that we were eating our last breakfast together as a family? And now, our family had expanded to include Darien and Weslan.

Ella and Weslan had left before the interview, and Darien and the twins were out on their shopping trip. It was time for a fresh cup of coffee and a quiet moment with my journal.

Who knew how long this moment would last? I planned to make the most of it.

AFTERWORD

Thank you for taking the time to read Zel's retelling of the Rapunzel story. I hope you enjoyed this story as much as I enjoyed writing it. If so, please make my day and leave a quick review! Reviews are often the best way to get the word out about indie books like this one.

In the original Grimm version of Rapunzel, she marries her prince while still trapped in her tower. When the enchantress discovers Rapunzel's betrayal, she casts Rapunzel out to the desert, where Rapunzel raises her twin children "in wretchedness." Years later, the heartbroken, blinded prince stumbles across Rapunzel in the desert. Her tears heal his blindness and they *finally* live happily ever after.

When I first read that story, I thought, "No wonder you don't see many Rapunzel retellings." But isn't Rapunzel's fairy tale ending a bit closer to real life than we'd care to admit? Just because we fall in love and get married doesn't mean heartbreak and hardship are over.

Here's to everyone who is still waiting for happily ever after to show up. Keep loving, keep hoping, and don't forget who you are. Who knows? Maybe the hard times will end up holding sweet memories too.

Craving more of Zel and her family? Sign up for my new release email list at http://smarturl.it/torn-freebie and get the free prequel novelette *Torn*, a short story set two years before the *Destined* series begins.

ACKNOWLEDGEMENTS

Special thanks to my editor Kathrese, whose hard work and invaluable advice made this book what it is.

Thanks to my mom, for being the very first reader of this book and loving it, for caring deeply about the characters in the *Destined* world, and for helping make this book better with countless spreadsheets and notes.

And thanks to my dad, for teaching me that princesses should have "skills." (You meant assassin skills, right, Dad?)

Thanks to my husband, for being utterly determined to love me, no matter what.

Finally, thanks to God, for showing me that the even the irredeemable can be redeemed.

ABOUT THE AUTHOR

Kaylin Lee is an Army wife, mama, and white cheddar popcorn devotee. She lives in the Pacific Northwest with her real-life hero husband and sweet toddler girl. After a lifetime of staying up too late reading stories, she now wakes up too early writing them. It was probably inevitable.

88348286R00137

Made in the USA
Columbia, SC
31 January 2018